TWIST OF FATE

"You live here? Do you mean to say you *own* this house?" Her brows were furrowed and her expression was downright adorable. She still couldn't quite believe that her former head groom lived in a house grander than her own.

"I do."

"You're C. A. Kitchen Tools?"

"I am."

"And you . . ." She couldn't complete the sentence, so he did it for her.

". . . enjoy the opera."

Her face turned the brightest red he'd ever seen on another human. She appeared both horrified and outraged, and he threw back his head and laughed.

"You are my new neighbor. My awful new neighbor," she said, quite unnecessarily.

Charlie gave her a mocking bow. "At your service, madam."

More Historical Romance from Jane Goodger

How to Please a Lady

JANE GOODGER

LYRICAL PRESS
KENSINGTON PUBLISHING CORP.
http://www.kensingtonbooks.com

Prologue

To be truly polite, remember you must be polite at *all* times, and under *all* circumstances.

—From *The Ladies' Book of Etiquette, and Manual of Politeness*

Rose was just beginning to fall into a peaceful slumber when she heard a woman scream.

Rose sat upright, her heart pounding, her eyes looking to her window and across the alley to the house next door, vacant up until last week and with a new occupant she knew nothing about. Another scream, long and drawn out and fairly bloodcurdling.

Her entire body shaking, she swept off the covers and headed to her door to fetch her maid, Stacy. Was it a murder? Since Rose's husband's death, she liked to have her lady's maid nearby, and so had moved her into a room across from her own.

"Stacy," she whispered harshly, opening her maid's door. "Come quickly. There's a murder being committed."

Stacy immediately roused herself, pulling on her wrap. "Should I get a lamp?"

"No, I don't want the murderer to see us. I heard screams coming from next door. I certainly do not want whoever it is to know there is a witness." Stacy followed her mistress across the hall and to the window that faced their neighbor's house, separated from them by an alley only a dozen feet wide. Rose's window was closed, but they could still hear the terrible sounds of suffering from next door, dreadful bone-chilling whimpers.

"This is terrible. We must *do* something," Rose said, her voice shaking. "Go fetch Robert and have him get the police."

"Yes, ma'am," Stacy said, her eyes wide with fright. She was turning to go when the screams took an odd turn, and Stacy stopped dead.

"Ma'am?"

"Yes, Stacy," Rose said with impatience. "Go. Time is of the essence."

"Ma'am, it's not a murder." Stacy let out a giggle. "It's, well, I do believe they're doing it."

The screaming took on a rather impressive operatic note—perhaps high C?—and Stacy giggled again. "He seems rather talented."

"Stacy, really," Rose said, her face turning a bright red. She knew because her cheeks were on fire, and she was grateful it was too dark for her maid to see. She couldn't imagine anything that happened in a bedroom to be so astoundingly pleasurable that it would cause one to make such a ruckus. Just as the note was trailing off, she felt as much as heard a low rumble of male satisfaction and, if possible, her face burned even brighter.

"Thank you, Stacy. You may return to bed. I do hope there will not be an encore performance," Rose said briskly.

"I'm thinking she's hoping there is one," her cheeky maid said before ducking out of the room.

"Don't be crass, Stacy," Rose called, sounding more amused than bothered.

Rose padded back to her bed and glared at her window, wondering about her new neighbors. She knew nothing about them, except they apparently enjoyed one another immensely. The street had been so peaceful since the Rutherfords and their brood of ten children had moved to the country. It wasn't only the noise that had been bothersome; it had been that their house had seemed so lively, whilst her own had been so terribly quiet on the evenings she and her husband weren't entertaining. It was the one thing she hadn't fully thought out when she'd married Daniel—the fact she would have no children.

Her neighbors on the other side were a wonderful couple with three small but well-behaved children. She had so hoped an elderly couple would buy the Rutherfords' home.

Pulling up the covers, she settled in. "Daniel, what do you think of our new neighbors?" she asked her husband, dead now for more than a year. She still talked to him, for he had been her dearest friend, and since he'd died, she'd had no one to talk to. Not really. She missed him terribly. Everyone had loved Daniel, and his death, so sudden, had left a large hole in her life.

She turned to her side, her back to the window, and fell asleep, only to be woken up one hour later to the sound of another murder.

> *Dear Neighbor:*
> *I would like to welcome you to our quiet little street. You'll find your neighbors very agreeable people and I wish you years of happiness in your new home.*
> *You may have noticed that our homes are quite closely situated. Perhaps you were unaware how easily sound leaps the alley separating our homes, but I can assure you that even with windows closed, voices travel quite well. I am a fan of opera, as many people are, no doubt. I do, however, enjoy performances in a more traditional venue.*

Rose smiled at that last sentence and could imagine Daniel chuckling. He had so enjoyed her wit.

> *Perhaps in the future you could move the performance to a more private location so as not to disturb your neighbors.*
> *Mrs. Cartwright*

> *Dear Mrs. Cartwright:*
> *Please accept my sincerest apologies for disturbing your evening. I was unaware sound traveled so well between our homes. I will attempt to curtail the noise, but as some aspects of the performance are beyond my control, I cannot make any promises.*
> *A*

Rose looked at the response, scrawled on the back of her own note (no doubt the cad didn't even possess stationery), and frowned. This was not the response she was expecting. Then again, what sort of response would she expect from a person who seemed to have no discretion?

That evening, Rose nearly dreaded going to bed. But she slept soundly the entire night through, waking up and smiling. Her neighbor had either not indulged or had chosen a different room. Feeling well pleased, Rose went about her day, not giving her new neighbor, whom she had yet to see, never mind meet, another thought.

"Oui, oui. Mon Dieu, mon Dieu, mon Dieu."

They, or rather, *he* was at it again. This was clearly another woman. A French woman with a throaty voice, who was apparently having as much fun as the opera singer had the other night. Rose was sitting at her vanity, sixty-two strokes into her one-hundred-stroke regime of brushing her hair, and Stacy was putting away her gown, when they heard the first obvious sounds of lovemaking.

Rose stood and marched to her window to look out. It was dark outside, but she could tell the window across the alley was open; hers was closed. And still she could hear the rapid French. *Touchez-moi là-bas. Oui. Là. Plus fort. Oui. Mon Dieu, mon Dieu, mon Dieu.*

"Do you speak French, ma'am?" Stacy asked, coming up next to her.

"Unfortunately, yes."

"What is she saying?"

Rose let out a long-suffering breath. "She's using the Lord's name in vain. Over and over." And with a rhythm that was impossible to misunderstand. Faster, louder, more frantic. This time, more than Rose's cheeks became warm. She backed from the window, stunned, as she recognized that she was becoming aroused from listening to the couple copulate. "Disgusting," she said, even though she didn't really think it was. And that, in itself, was perhaps the biggest surprise. She hadn't felt more than a tingle between her legs in years. What sort of depraved person was she that merely listening to another couple make love could excite her?

"I want to know about our neighbors. Neighbor. I think it's a bachelor. What can you find out?"

Rose stood in her kitchen with her cook, the aptly named Mrs. Faring, not only for her occupation but for the obvious fact she enjoyed eating her food as much as she did preparing it. Rose had no idea how old she was as she had few wrinkles, but the hair beneath her cap was iron gray. "How am I supposed to find out anything? I'm too busy in here cooking."

Mrs. Faring had never been a very agreeable woman, but she

cooked wonderfully and Rose had gotten used to her crustiness over the years. Her mother never would have tolerated such back talk, and Rose probably shouldn't either. But no one made raspberry tarts like Mrs. Faring, and she could never bring herself to fire the lady—especially since she seemed to know precisely when a raspberry tart was needed most.

"You could go over and borrow a cup of sugar. Strike up a conversation with their cook."

Mrs. Faring took on an expression of extreme affront. "What sort of cook would I be if I got so low on sugar that I needed to borrow a cup?"

Rose sighed. At the moment, she really didn't have another plan. She certainly couldn't go up to a bachelor's house and introduce herself. She supposed she could hover outside until she saw someone leave and pretend a chance meeting, but that sort of behavior was quite unfitting. She wished Daniel were alive. He would have gone over in a thrice, knocked on the door, and been best friends with the man within an hour.

"I'll go, Mrs. Cartwright." Annie, her kitchen maid, looked eager to get away from the cranky Mrs. Faring, who immediately took off her apron and hung it on a nearby hook.

"I'm going," the cook announced. "I'll make a neighborly gesture, ask if they know that the butcher on Seventh Avenue has better meat and fairer prices than the one on Broadway."

Rose smiled. "That's a perfect plan."

Twenty minutes later, Mrs. Faring returned, a smug smile on her face.

"What have you learned?"

"He's a bachelor. Annie, do you know who it is?"

Annie shook her head. "Do we know him?"

"We know *of* him. Half the gadgets in our kitchen were made by his company. C. A. Kitchen Tools. You should see his kitchen. It's like nothing I've ever seen before in my life, full of more gadgets than I thought existed." Rose smiled at her cook, who sounded like a young artist who had just visited the Louvre. "And the cook appreciated my help, you should know. They moved from another part of the city and she didn't know where she should shop," she said with a sharp nod.

"What else did you find out?" Rose asked, not really caring how the man made his living. "What's his name?"

Mrs. Faring's cheeks flushed slightly. "Wouldn't you know, I forgot to ask. I learned only that he is a bachelor, as you thought."

The information was disappointingly sparse. They now knew three things about her neighbor. He was rich. He was a bachelor. And he knew how to please a lady.

Rose wasn't certain why she was curious about her neighbor, or at least she refused to think about why, but she was. Terribly so. Usually servants were a bevy of good information, but alas, her own servants were of little help. And so, with a determination born of this strange curiosity, Rose climbed up the steps of the other neighbor, to her left, the Campbells, bearing a gift of raspberry tarts (it was worth the sacrifice to share) in a pretty little basket prepared by Mrs. Faring, who felt a bit guilty for failing in her mission.

The Campbells were a lovely couple who'd moved in a little while after she and Daniel had gotten married. Rose had actually briefly met Genevieve Campbell in England, but she had quite forgotten her until Genevieve recalled their meeting. Over the years, they had become wonderful friends; Rose was godmother to their middle child, Claire. Genevieve was one of those women who could charm the shell off a turtle, so if anyone knew anything about their new neighbor, surely she would.

The door opened after her knock, revealing the Campbells' unconventional butler, a beast of a man with a completely bald pate and a nose that looked like it had seen the inside of a boxing ring one too many times.

"Hello, Mr. Spark. Is Mrs. Campbell in?" She revealed the raspberry tarts inside her basket and the butler took one with an appreciative smile.

Mr. Spark stepped back without a word; he'd lost the use of his vocal chords during one particularly brutal fight and couldn't utter a sound. Meeting the Campbells' butler the first time had been a bit jarring for Rose, who had grown up with an impeccably trained staff, but it soon became clear he did his job well. Watching him give the staff orders was nothing short of amazing—it helped that he could write notes faster than most people could speak.

Mr. Spark led Rose to a sitting room, and a short time later, Genevieve entered, a bright smile of welcome on her face.

"I know why you're here," Genevieve said, her vivid green eyes sparkling as she sat down gracefully. "You've seen our new neighbor."

Rose laughed. "Actually, I haven't. Have you? The only thing I've learned is that he is a bachelor and creates kitchen gadgets." Among other talents. Just the thought caused her cheeks to flush.

"I've seen him but I haven't spoken to him or been introduced." Something about her manner made Rose curious. It was more what she wasn't saying than what she was.

"Oh?" Rose was trying valiantly not to appear too curious. Her interest in the man made no sense and, truth be told, was a bit embarrassing. She was just out of mourning, after all, and she'd never before shown any undue interest in a man.

Genevieve gave her a knowing smile. "I won't make you beg for details, dear, mostly because I know you never would. He's quite handsome. Tall. Blond. Striking, really. An Adonis."

"Genny," Rose said, slightly chastising. "You're a married woman."

"I can still appreciate a fine male form," she said, laughing. Then she spied Rose's basket and stopped midlaugh, as if someone had put a stopper in her mouth. "Do please tell me those are raspberry tarts."

"They are."

"Did you think to bribe me with those for information about our new neighbor?"

"Of course," Rose said without hesitation. "Besides, Mrs. Faring made too many."

"You should take some over to your new neighbor." From somewhere in the house came a delighted shriek. "Or I could give them to the children, at least the older two. They adore Mrs. Faring's tarts."

"That is a much better plan. It would be highly improper for me to deliver them to our new neighbor personally."

Genevieve creased her brow. "Would it? I don't see why."

Honestly, Rose didn't see either, but that wasn't the point. She was not going to introduce herself to the man who had been creating such a ruckus nearly every evening. Just the thought filled her with mortification. Now that she'd had time to think about it, she sorely regretted writing that witty little note of hers. Meeting the man behind his return note would be distressing, and she certainly did not want to give him any ideas by presenting him with a gift, even one as simple as raspberry tarts.

The two women turned toward the door as the sound of feet stomping down the stairs grew louder and louder, until her two older children ran into the parlor, stopping abruptly and nearly toppling over one another. "Hullo, Mrs. Cartwright."

"Hello, Thomas, Claire." Rose hid a smile, for both children were eyeing her basket.

"Shall I put them out of their misery?" Genevieve asked.

"Mr. Spark said Mrs. Cartwright brung—"

"—brought," Genevieve corrected.

"—brought a basket that might have raspberry tarts in it."

"And how did Mr. Spark know this?"

Thomas darted a look at Rose. "Because Mrs. Campbell gave him one."

"Would you like a tart?" Rose asked, quite rhetorically.

"Oh, yes, please!" Claire said. The two children hurried to the basket, Thomas taking two and Claire taking one—until she realized Thomas had taken two.

"One, Thomas, please," Genevieve said. "Then we'll have some left over for after dinner this evening."

Thomas replaced the tart good-naturedly.

"Why don't the two of you go out to the garden to eat those? I'll join you in a little while."

Rose took that as her cue to leave. "If I learn anything, I'll let you know. As I'm certain you shall do."

"Of course," Genevieve said, rising.

Rose walked down her neighbors' steps feeling a bit out of sorts. When she was a young girl and she'd felt like this, she would head to the stable and ride Moonrise until they were both exhausted. Of all the things in the world she missed since leaving England, her beautiful mare was at the top of the list, next to her brothers, of course. Daniel had suggested bringing Moonrise to New York, but Rose couldn't imagine her beautiful mare in the city. She'd be frightened by the traffic, and a ride in Central Park would have been far too sedate for her feisty mare.

Rose had nearly reached the gate in front of her home when a hack pulled up in front of the house next door—*his* house. She paused, her hand on the wrought-iron gate, and watched for the occupants of the hack to disembark. A man's fine boot appeared, then a leg, then a hand holding a top hat. And then, the man, his blond hair swept back from . . .

"Charlie?"

The man stepped down and turned toward her and Rose grinned, seeing the dear face of her former head groom. "Charlie!" Rose said, stepping quickly over to him, not hiding how delighted she was to see him. Charlie had accompanied her to America five years prior and she hadn't seen him since. Now here he was, looking fine in a tailored suit, and standing right in front of her.

"My goodness, Charlie, you're a sight for sore eyes. How *are* you? And look how fine you look," she said, holding out her gloved hands for him to take. He did, briefly, his blue eyes unreadable. He seemed neither happy nor sad to see her; it was almost as if he didn't recall who she was, which would be quite impossible.

"Mrs. Cartwright. I was sorry to hear about your husband's death. He was a good man," he said, his dear voice so familiar to Rose she nearly wanted to weep. His ready smile was absent and he sounded so formal, so un-Charlie-like, that Rose was momentarily taken aback.

"Thank you. I miss him every day," Rose said, swallowing down the sudden sorrow that was still difficult to hold at bay. She looked up at her neighbor's house, unable to hide her distaste for the owner. "What are you doing here? Do you work here? I've yet to meet my new neighbor. He's quite a mystery." Charlie was dressed so finely, she wondered if he might be her neighbor's new butler. Or perhaps a secretary. Charlie always had been smarter than a whip.

"I don't work here, Mrs. Cartwright," Charlie said, the oddest smile on his face.

"Oh?"

"I live here."

Chapter 1

The pleasure of your guests, as well as the beauty of the rooms, will be increased by the elegance of your arrangements; their beauty will be heightened by brilliant light, and by judicious management a scene of fairy-like illusion may be produced.

—From *The Ladies' Book of Etiquette, and Manual of Politeness*

Five years earlier

"**M**y lady, you look beautiful."

Lady Rose Dunford gazed at her reflection and smiled. She did not look like the same girl who had tumbled out of bed that very morning, dressed in her simplest gown and shabby old boots so she could rush to the stables to see if her favorite mare had begun foaling. The mare hadn't, of course. Charlie, their head groom, had assured her that Moonrise, so named for her lovely silvery coat, wouldn't produce a foal for at least another day.

But wouldn't it have been perfect, on this most perfect of all days, for the foal to arrive?

"Thank you, Sarah," she said, giving her hair a critical look. "You've done a wonderful job. Though I do hope the tiara my mother insisted I wear isn't overdoing it."

"Oh, no, my lady. It's quite befitting a future duchess."

A future duchess. She wanted to pinch herself to make certain she was awake. Rose Dunford, former hoyden and only girl in a family of males, was to reach the highest levels of the peerage in June, in just three months' time. Her poor mother had always bemoaned the fact that she had shown little interest in anything feminine, and yet she had attracted one of the most sought-after men in the ton.

Sarah took her ball gown from the bed where it lay and held it for Rose to step into. For some reason, this act seemed to finalize everything that had happened in her life in the eight months since she'd met Josiah Hartman, third Duke of Weston, at her come-out ball during the little season. Rose stepped into her ball gown and stood patiently as Sarah took up the tedious task of buttoning dozens of tiny seed pearls that held her shimmering pale peach gown together. Though not a bit vain, Rose had to acknowledge the gown did look rather well with her coloring—pale, unblemished skin, dark brown eyes, and nearly black hair. She was not au courant with her style or her looks thanks to a Spanish great-grandmother, but such things had really never mattered to her.

Rose touched her fingertips to the daring expanse of skin that showed above her bodice, frowning slightly. Barely out of the schoolroom, Rose was unused to wearing gowns that revealed so much flesh, though her mother reassured her the dress she now wore—indeed all her dresses—were perfectly modest. Still, Rose felt uncomfortable looking down and seeing mounds of flesh looking back up at her.

"It's not at all immodest, milady," Sarah said, clucking her tongue, having accurately interpreted Rose's frown.

Smoothing down skirts that had no need of smoothing, she thanked Sarah again and walked out of her room, her stomach feeling the effects of her nerves.

For a long moment, Rose stood atop Hallstead Manor's grand staircase and smiled at the hubbub below her. The house was brilliantly lit, and even from where she stood she could smell the heady scent of dozens upon dozens of roses, all white but for a single red rose in each arrangement. Roses. How ironic that Rose didn't much like her namesake flower, preferring the whimsical poppy, but in this choice her mother ruled and she had no say. Servants moved back and forth, making last-minute changes to the decor, wiping away imaginary dust from the furniture (her mother never allowed as much as a speck to remain for more than a day), and making certain each vase, each decoration was precisely placed.

Perfect. Like her life. For at eighteen years old, Lady Rose Dunford had managed to attract the pinnacle of society, the Duke of Weston. A widower, he had been the most coveted prize among all the single ladies of the ton for years. It was almost, her mother said coyly, as if he had been waiting for her come-out so he could finally make his interest known. Indeed, it was at her come-out that he'd made his intentions quite clear, asking for his first dance (a waltz), and then the next day showing up with a ridiculous bouquet of roses. Not altogether original, given her name, but she'd been thrilled nonetheless. Her mother had been beside herself with glee, trying and failing to hide just how thrilled she was that His Grace should show her daughter special attention.

The only daughter and youngest child of the Earl of Chesterfield, Rose would become a duchess in just three months. She was the envy of all her friends, and Rose could hardly believe her good fortune herself. She had no delusion that the duke had fallen in love with her. She knew it was because her father's property abutted the duke's and part of her dowry included a bit of unentailed land along their border. Still, it was lovely that she'd be so close to her family when they were a couple and visiting their country estate, and what girl in her right mind would be anything less than ecstatic that the Duke of Weston had singled her out?

The only problem, and it was such a small one, was that she hardly knew the duke. They'd shared two dances, one dinner (with two hundred other guests), and two well-chaperoned carriage rides. He seemed a nice enough man, rather too old for her (he was thirty-nine!), but he was handsome enough. Rose felt quite out of her element when she was with him; she hardly knew what to say to the man as he had little interest in the things that interested her. Besides, her mother had admonished her that talk of horses and breeding was not a topic of conversation for the drawing room.

Instead, Rose had said things like: "What a lovely day."

To which the duke would respond with such things as: "Nearly as lovely as you."

She'd nearly burst out laughing the first time he'd uttered such rot (her mother would chastise her if she knew she'd even *thought* the word *rot* to describe someone's speech). Rose intended to get to know her fiancé a bit more between the announcement of their engagement tonight and their wedding in June. It wouldn't do to marry a *complete* stranger, even if he was a duke.

"You look lovely, my dear." Her mother's eyes gleamed with

pleasure as she walked toward Rose. "And I knew that tiara would be perfect against your dark hair."

"Is His Grace here?" Rose asked, looking down toward the entryway.

"I suspect he is. He said he would arrive at eight o'clock and as it is half past, he is surely here. He seems to be quite punctual. No doubt he's sharing a bit of brandy with your father in his study."

Rose began walking down the long and curving staircase, liking the way her train flowed behind her, whispering softly as it fell from one step to the next. She didn't often wear trains—or tiaras for that matter—but tonight was special. Given that she would soon be a duchess, she figured she ought to get used to such finery.

"Moonrise may foal tonight," she said to her mother, who followed behind her. "Wouldn't that be wonderful?"

Lucille tsked. "You and your horses, Rose. Honestly. Please do not discuss your foaling mare tonight, I beg you. I wouldn't like to think we wasted our time and money on Mrs. Potts's finishing school."

Rose gave her mother a cheeky grin, which earned her a scowl. "I'll behave, I promise. I daresay I can act like a lady when the moment demands it. And I won't bring up Moonrise."

"See that you don't. It would hardly do to have His Grace change his mind at this late hour. The engagement hasn't been officially announced, my dear. And even when it is announced, you must be on your absolute best behavior and try to please His Grace. I don't want happening to you what happened to poor Penelope Dwyer." Penelope Dwyer, now known exclusively as "Poor Penelope," had been on the verge of nabbing His Grace not one year ago when something went awry. Her mother lived in fear that the same fate awaited Rose.

Rose looked down at the large sapphire on her left ring finger, recalling how three weeks ago, the duke had placed it there. As proposals went, it wasn't particularly romantic, for Rose's mother and father were in the room. They'd all decided a formal announcement would be made at an engagement ball that her mother could hastily put together. It wasn't such a difficult task, for the moment His Grace had shown Rose particular attention, her mother had begun planning the event. Her mother was positively in her glory with all the preparations; it was all she could speak of. Rose simply went along for the ride, like a leaf swirling in a stream, unable to control where it ended up.

Perhaps what made Rose most happy was that for the first time in her memory, her father had asked for a private meeting with her. Rose, the youngest and the only girl, was something of a curiosity to her father. He didn't quite know what to do with her, what to say. It seemed to Rose that her father hardly knew she existed. Until the duke first requested permission to court her. The way her father had looked at her then, it was almost as if he hadn't realized she'd been living in the same home as he all these years. And just that morning, he'd kissed her cheek and told her how proud he was.

Even though Rose felt she hadn't actually *done* anything at all, except perhaps been lucky enough to come of age before the duke found another wife, her father's words still made her swell with emotion. All her life Rose had felt a bit like an afterthought. Her brothers, so strapping and rambunctious, had garnered all the attention—good and bad. Rose had simply . . . been.

Now, this night, and for the rest of her life, Rose would be something special in the eyes of her father. Goodness, she would actually outrank him! This was not something she'd neglected to remind her brothers of, on more than one occasion, since the duke had proposed. They all agreed she'd been acting quite insufferable. Rose grinned at the memory. She had never felt like an afterthought with her brothers, particularly Stephen, who was closest to her in age. Marcus, Nick, and Adam tolerated her, but Stephen always included her in their adventures. Alas, he was at university and would be unable to attend the ball, though he'd written a very nice note wishing her well, then ending it with: *No matter whom you are married to, you will always be my favorite sister.*

Being the only sister, Rose was aware that the comment hadn't meant quite what it would have if there had been more females in the family, and though she recognized the joke (one oft-spoken), it still made her eyes prick with tears. She'd missed Stephen terribly since he'd gone away to Cambridge, and would miss him even more when she was a married woman.

Married woman. She still could hardly believe it.

She would join the ranks of the married. Of her four brothers, two were married and two remained steadfastly single. Stephen, of course, was still at university and far too young to contemplate marriage, and Nick had only just finished his studies. Marcus, the oldest at twenty-eight, had been married for two years, and Adam, still head-over-heels in love with his bride, for one. Rose had begun to tease Nick, reminding him that for the last three years a wedding had occurred and next year would be his turn.

"I think it's time to form the receiving line, my dear," Lucille said, returning from the ballroom, where she'd been making a last-minute check with the small orchestra they'd hired. "Sutton just informed me that our guests are beginning to arrive. Are you ready? You look ready. You aren't nervous, are you? I must confess I am. To be in such a spotlight. Did you see our guest list? And they all accepted. Even the prince. The *prince*, Rose. I can hardly credit it." Rose feared her mother might faint from excitement. Indeed, Prince Alfred, Duke of Edinburgh, was expected to make an appearance at the ball. Her mother had been struck dumb when she received his acceptance.

Nervous and rather giddy to be the center of attention, Rose stood next to her mother as their guests began arriving. It did seem strange the accolades they were expressing, as if Rose had done something magnificent rather than simply said yes. Lady Worther, kissing each cheek, told Rose how "absolutely happy" she was for her.

"She's so jealous she could spit," her mother whispered when the older woman was out of hearing. "She's been talking about Suzanna attracting the duke's attention for years, simply because the duke asked her to dance once."

Rose stifled a laugh and tried not to think about how her feet were beginning to ache. The duke, because of his lofty rank and position as guest of honor, led the receiving line, so Rose hardly had a chance to exchange more than a few words. He looked rather dashing in his evening formals, but Rose hadn't realized until that evening that His Grace was shorter than her own father. His slightly thinning brown hair was slicked back with pomade, and when he did look at her, his intense light blue eyes drifted down her person in a possessive way that made Rose feel slightly uncomfortable. Rose was completely unused to having a man look at her in such a strangely disconcerting manner.

While Rose had spent time with males, mostly her brothers, she had little experience flirting with men; it hardly seemed important to learn the art when the duke had begun his pursuit at her come-out ball.

"His Grace can't keep his eyes off you," her sister-in-law teased, her eyes twinkling with good humor.

Rose felt her cheeks redden. "I'm not used to such blatant male attention," she whispered. "I think it's this dress."

"It's what's in the dress," Georgette said, laughing lightly. "I think His Grace is impatient for his wedding night."

Rose gave her sister-in-law a quelling look, then ruined the effect by laughing. Rose adored Adam's wife. They'd just learned she was increasing and Adam was over the moon with happiness. After watching Marcus's disappointment at remaining childless, Georgette and her brother had been secretly worried they would suffer the same fate. Rose couldn't wait to meet her niece or nephew. Soon, she realized, she'd be having children of her own. It seemed impossible that she could be grown up enough to have children.

"I'll talk to you once the dancing starts. I have such gossip to tell you about one of our guests." Georgette, who at three months along showed no signs of her increasing, adored a good tidbit, and Rose could tell she couldn't wait to impart whatever it was she knew.

After nearly an hour, the receiving line dwindled and her mother went off to tell the orchestra to be ready to play the Grand March, a solemn and rather old-fashioned way to begin the ball, but her mother had insisted. Rose walked in on the arm of her intended, feeling everyone's eyes on her.

"You do me proud, my dear," Weston drawled as he pressed her hand, which rested in the crook of his arm.

"Thank you, Your Grace." She could feel his cool gaze on her and resisted the temptation to look into his light blue eyes, for she did have a tendency to blush hotly every time she did so.

"If you would do me the honor of dancing the first waltz."

She dared look up at him, and did indeed feel her cheeks instantly heat. "Of course, Your Grace."

Charlie Avery stood in the shadows and watched her, his heart aching as it always did whenever he looked at Rose. How could that woman in the stunning ball gown with her hair all done up pretty be the same little girl who had rushed headlong into the stables, braids flying behind her? He'd been ten years old, a stable boy and son of the head groom, when he first saw Rose, and even then he'd thought her the most adorable creature on earth. He ought to have been annoyed by her constant questions about the horses, about what he was doing, about why horses couldn't eat pudding.

Too many questions. Too many long hours while she watched him rub down her mare or help a foal into the world. Too many happy memories of them riding about the estate, often in the company of her brothers, who tolerated their little sister's sense of adventure. Years and years of memories. One day, when she was seventeen, he realized little Rose had grown up.

It had been the worst moment of his life.

She'd gone away to finishing school and he hadn't seen her in months. Hadn't really even given her much thought other than a vague sense that he missed her hanging about. Then she'd come home and headed almost immediately to the stables to say hello to Moonrise, her beloved horse. Maybe it was the way the late-day sunlight hit her face, or the blue dress she wore, or the expression of pure happiness on her face, or the way she closed her eyes and breathed in the scents of the stable as if it were the most wonderful smell in the world. But in that moment, he realized she was a woman and that the casual brotherly love he'd had for her was suddenly something much more. Of course he'd fallen in love with her. Who wouldn't?

She looked happy now, dancing with her future husband, no doubt charming the man the way she seemed to charm everyone *Holy God, she looks beautiful.*

"You know, if she knew how you felt about her, she'd find it embarrassing. Or worse, she'd pity you."

"Sod off, Harry," Charlie said good-naturedly.

Harry, one of Hallstead Manor's grooms, took a deep drag of his cigarette before tossing it to the ground and stamping it out with a heavy boot. "Just as well you're leaving," he said, his tone almost gentle, which made Charlie feel somehow worse. "She the reason? Just wondering. We're all wondering."

Was Rose the reason? Maybe falling in love with a woman he could never have was part of the reason he was going to America. But the bigger reason was that he didn't want to end up like his father, old and broken down, living on a tiny pension in a rented cottage. His uncle had gone to America ten years prior, owned his own home, had a good-paying job. If Charlie stayed in England, he'd be working in the stables until he couldn't work anymore. And he'd watch her marry another man, have his babies.

"No," he said. "I would have gone anyway."

Harry let him be, gazing in a window at a world so far removed, the dancers might as well have been on the moon.

"Gossip please," Rose said, coming up to Georgette. She was exceedingly warm and taking a break from the dancing.

Georgette was standing next to her best friend, Lady Barrington, a woman whose seemingly dour appearance was in sharp contrast to her good humor and lively personality. Indeed, when Rose had first met Lady Barrington, she hadn't been prepared for the older woman's sense of the absurd.

"This is my gossip so I believe I should be allowed to impart it," Lady Barrington said. Then she spoke directly to Rose. "Your sister-in-law says you are too innocent to hear this, but I said you're to be married soon enough, and I daresay you won't swoon."

"My, this does sound titillating."

"You've overdone it, Rebecca," Georgette said, sounding cross. "Now Rose will expect something more interesting."

Lady Barrington huffed, but otherwise ignored her friend. "Rose, do you see that dashing fellow talking to your brother? Tall. Dark. Exceedingly handsome."

Rose looked across the room and immediately spotted the man Lady Barrington was talking about. He was the handsomest man she'd ever seen in her life. Strong jaw, perfect hair, clothes tailored to perfection on his tall, lean form. "I see him," Rose said, trying to keep her voice neutral. She was engaged to be married, after all.

"He's an American," Lady Barrington said.

As gossip went, that wasn't terribly interesting, but Rose had a feeling there was more.

"Apparently he has high political aspirations. Already he works for the State Department, and for a young man, his rise has been quite mercurial. But he has a problem," she said mysteriously.

"Oh?" Rose asked, only because she knew she was expected to.

"He's not married. A man with high political aspirations *must* have a wife."

Rose wrinkled her brow. "Must he?"

"Not always," Lady Barrington said with a telling emphasis on the word *always*. "But it is certainly prudent when unsavory rumors begin circulating."

"Such as the one you are about to spread?" Rose asked, raising a brow.

Lady Barrington made a face, and Rose and Georgette laughed. "Don't ruin her fun, Rose. Go on, Rebecca."

She lowered her voice to just above a whisper. "It's said he's a sodomite."

Rose leaned forward. "What's a sodomite?"

Lady Barrington gave her a look, and Georgette said, "She's only a child, for goodness sake."

Georgette's friend waved a dismissive hand. "She's to be married in three months." She turned to Rose. "It's a man who prefers the company of other men."

This did nothing to clear things up for Rose. "Don't all men?"

Georgette looked like she was close to laughing aloud. "Not in the bedroom," she said succinctly.

Rose looked at them in confusion until her face suddenly cleared, and the two older women laughed aloud.

"Truly? But he's so . . ."

"Handsome. Yes."

"And manly," Rose said, tilting her head and looking at him. "I'm going over to meet him," she announced, and as she started walking off, Georgette grabbed her arm.

"Rose, don't say—"

"I won't. Goodness, what kind of a person do you think I am? I'm far more curious about America than I am about what he does in his bedroom at any rate." Rose had a bit of satisfaction at the stunned expression on the women's faces before making her way over to where her brother stood with the other man.

When Marcus spied her, he smiled and held out one hand, welcoming her. "The lady of honor," he said grandly. "Do you know, Mr. Cartwright, my sister in just a few short months will outrank me and will continue to do so even after the title becomes mine. Please allow me to introduce you to Lady Rose Dunford, soon to be the Duchess of Weston. Rose, Daniel Cartwright. He's on the staff of the U.S. ambassador, Edwards Pierrepont."

"Lovely to make your acquaintance and on such a celebration, Lady Rose," Mr. Cartwright said, taking her hand and making a small bow.

Rose's breath caught, for he was perfectly charming and extraordinarily good-looking, with a strong jaw, straight noble nose, and hazel eyes that were quite remarkable. "The pleasure is mine, I assure you," Rose said.

"Have you checked on Moonrise today?" Marcus asked.

"I have, but Mother forbade me to discuss horses tonight." She leaned in close. "Charlie says it won't be for at least another day. Her teats are full, though, so I think it may be tonight or tomorrow."

Her brother coughed and gave what appeared to be a look of apology to Mr. Cartwright. "Perhaps you should have followed Mother's advice and forgone talk of horses." He turned to the American. "My sister practically grew up in the stables and I fear is not shy about the subject."

"Why should I be shy? Certainly Mr. Cartwright understands where foals come from."

Mr. Cartwright laughed. "Indeed I do."

"I'm just glad Charlie's here for the foaling. 'Twould have been a pity had he already left," Marcus said distractedly. He was looking across the ballroom floor where his wife stood with a small group of young people.

Rose's stomach took a sharp and unexpected tumble. "What do you mean? Charlie would never miss the birth of a foal and certainly not Moonrise's."

"Didn't you know?" her brother asked. "Oh, I can see you didn't. At any rate, Charlie's off to America in a fortnight. Has some relative there with a nice position for him."

"He has a nice position here," Rose said, her voice small. She couldn't imagine their stables without him. He'd been the first person Rose had seen when she'd followed her brothers to the stable that long ago day. She still remembered how he'd looked, a strapping young boy with an easy smile, a curly mop of blond hair, and gentle hands, who hadn't minded a bit when she followed him about. It seemed completely incomprehensible that their stable would no longer have him there, and even more incomprehensible that when he left, she would never see him again, never be able to ask him questions or watch him rub down their cattle.

"He's quite set on going," Marcus said. "And I say good for him."

"Of course, we all want Charlie to be happy," Rose said, but she felt almost as if she'd learned her dearest friend was going away forever, not a servant.

"Who is this Charlie?" Mr. Cartwright asked.

"Our head groom. He's on to bigger and better things, I suppose," her brother said, as if losing Charlie wasn't devastating . . . to the stables and horses, of course. It was ridiculous that she should feel so sad; after all, she wouldn't even be living here in a short few months. Charlie was part of her childhood and she supposed saying good-bye to that idyllic time would be difficult. Tonight, though, she refused to become morose and dwell on sad things. She refused to allow anything to ruin her evening. Looking around, she felt a large sense of satisfaction seeing her smiling guests. Everyone seemed to be enjoying themselves immensely; it appeared all her mother's hard work was paying off in spades. Then she spied Lady Priscilla Whitmore, standing quite alone and looking less than happy.

"Marcus, do please ask Lady Priscilla to dance. I will not allow anyone to stand in a corner for this most important evening. She looks like a regular wallflower and I'm certain Eleanor won't mind."

"Eleanor *always* has a grand time and Lady Priscilla *is* a regular wallflower."

Rose flashed him a smile. "Not tonight."

Marcus laughed, then bowed, leaving her to chat with Mr. Cartwright. She adored his accent and had never had an actual conversation with an American. A school friend had married an American, but Rose had never had the opportunity to meet her husband before she departed for the States.

"I hear you are interested in politics, Mr. Cartwright," she said, thinking to begin the conversation with a topic he was certain to enjoy.

"Are you interested in politics, Lady Rose?" he asked with a small smile.

"Not at all. I was being polite."

Mr. Cartwright laughed aloud. "Thank you for your honesty."

"Actually, I'm much more fascinated with America. Where do you live?"

"New York City. Have you ever been?"

Rose shook her head. "No, but I hope to someday. I have a school friend who lived in New York for a time. She was a bit older than I, but we corresponded quite regularly after her wedding. She married a banker. Alas, I have lost touch with her. She lived on Fifth Avenue."

Mr. Cartwright jerked his head back as if shocked. "Not Caroline St. Pierre."

"Why yes. Don't say you know her."

"Know her! She was my neighbor for two years. They're in Philadelphia now. She was eight hundred eight and I am eight hundred twelve. A new couple lives there now. She's the granddaughter of the Duke of Glastonbury. Perhaps you know her; she's not that much older than you are."

Rose smiled. "Now you are surely jesting with me. I met her just this last season. Her Grace was quite enthusiastic about bringing Lady Genevieve out and she was the talk of London for a time." A sudden blush stained Rose's cheeks when she remembered more about Glastonbury's granddaughter. "She seemed like a lovely girl, but she did cause a bit of a scandal now that I recall. There was a story in an American newspaper. It caused quite a stir here."

"I must have missed it, and I'm not one to read society pages at any rate," Mr. Cartwright said, with the smallest hint of censure in his voice. "The Campbells are good neighbors and seem pleasant enough."

"I'm certain they are. I did not mean to imply the opposite, truly, but I was taken aback by how coincidental it is that you've had not one but two of my acquaintances as neighbors. I hope Caroline was a good neighbor."

"She was. I dined at their home several times and they at mine. I was sad to see them leave."

"Is New York very different from London?"

"Vastly. Everything is new there. Even the buildings that are meant to look old are new. We are such a young country, it's quite striking to be in a place where a new building is one built in the last two centuries."

"And which do you prefer?"

"They both have their charms," he said diplomatically.

"You truly do have a fine future in politics," Rose said, laughing lightly. "Do you wish to be president some day?"

"I'm afraid nothing as lofty as that."

"You will have a duchess in your corner, whatever you choose."

He smiled, and again she was taken aback by just how very handsome he was. "I am grateful. For now, though, I would be content with a dance. Will you do me the honor?"

Rose glanced at her dance card and nodded. "Of course."

The rest of the evening was like a pleasant dream. She danced with her father, who again told her how very proud he was, and Rose beamed a smile up at him. She'd never in her life felt so special, so loved, so full of hope for the future. As evening grew into morning and guests either left in their carriages or retired to their rooms, Rose sat next to her mother, who was exhausted but happy.

"I think the evening went quite well, Rose, quite well. His Grace remarked that you have comported yourself excellently all evening, and I think he is quite pleased with his choice."

"I'm glad. He seems a very pleasant man and I do believe we shall get on well." Rose wanted to believe her words, even though she still was more nervous than anything else around the man. It was his age, the way he looked at her, the way they didn't seem to have a single thing in common other than the fact they were marrying each other. While they were dancing their second waltz, she mentioned the possibility of going to the continent for their wedding trip, but he dismissed the idea immediately. "I do apologize, my dear, but going to the continent doesn't appeal to me in the least."

Rose swallowed her disappointment, for she'd been secretly hoping for a lengthy wedding trip where she would finally be able to see the things she'd only been able to read about. Rome with its Colosseum, Greece with its Parthenon, Egypt with its pyramids. Everything seemed so exciting, but it was clear her future husband had no interest in travel.

"Now all you have to do is plan the perfect wedding, Mother," Rose said with a tired laugh.

"I'm too exhausted to even give that a thought," her mother said. "I'm off to bed. We'll have a late luncheon to allow everyone to get a good night's rest. Goodness, it's after four in the morning. Good night, Rose. I was so proud of you this evening and the envy of every mother here." Her mother stood, then bent and kissed Rose's cheek.

"Good night, Mama." Her mother smiled; Rose hadn't called her mother Mama in years.

She watched her mother head upstairs to bed, but as sleepy as she was, Rose did not follow her. All night, Moonrise had been on her mind, so instead of climbing sleepily up to her room, she headed to the stables.

*   *   *

The sky was just beginning to lighten when Charlie stepped into Moonrise's stall to check on the mare. She'd been a bit restless the previous evening, and after he'd tortured himself watching Lady Rose with her new fiancé, he'd walked the horse around the grounds to settle her down.

"How are you this morning, girl?" he asked, placing a palm against the mare's neck and giving it a good rub. Moonrise nickered lightly, almost as if answering. And Charlie, who knew horses better than people, figured she'd just told him she was holding up but a little worried about the strange thing that seemed to be happening to her.

The mare was showing all the right signs that she'd be foaling within the next day. He wondered if Lady Rose would be able to be there to comfort her mare. Or would she be caught up in the festivities that surrounded her engagement? He knew, given a choice, Lady Rose would rather be by Moonrise's side, just as he knew if her mother demanded her presence in the house, she would not be present when the little foal came into the world.

Light footsteps on the stone floor drew Charlie's attention away from the mare. "Hell," he muttered, and leaned his head briefly against the mare's neck. He knew those footsteps, knew they belonged to the very lady he'd just been thinking about. He took a breath, trying to stop the sudden surge of longing that flooded him whenever he saw her. It was a damned nuisance. No matter how many times he braced for it, it came, unmanning and humiliating. Thank the Lord Jesus and all the Catholic saints that Lady Rose was completely oblivious to just how much he loved her.

"My lady," he said, steeling himself for the smile he knew would appear on her lovely face. "You're up early." He realized then she was still wearing her ball gown and looking far lovelier than a woman ought after dancing the night away. "Or is it late?"

"Late," she said, indicating her gown and walking to the stall. She placed her gloved hands atop the smooth gate and looked worriedly at her mare. "How is she?"

"We'll have a foal before the day is out, I should think. She's waxing, you see. And there's been just a bit of milk."

Lady Rose let herself into the stall and gave the mare a hug, completely ignoring the fact that her ball gown was brushing the floor, which wasn't entirely clean. Another sign a mare was about to foal

was an increased appetite and thirst, the results of which were difficult to keep up with.

"How's my beautiful girl?" she said, her voice deep and soothing.
She was still embracing the animal when she said, "I understand
you're leaving us, Charlie. I heard from Marcus this evening."

"Yes, my lady. It's off to America for me."

She looked at him then and his heart gave a bit of a tumble to see
her eyes had gone misty. "We all shall miss you. Terribly."

"Most of you are already gone, and with you marrying in just a
few months, it'd just be me and the horses left here."

She gave the mare a pat, then stepped away to stand by him, her
back to the closed gate. "Is that why you're leaving?" She gave him
a slight smile. "Because you've been lonely?"

Charlie cleared his throat and wished he could stop the telling
blush that stained his cheeks. "No, milady. There's opportunity for a
man in America. My uncle lives there, owns a house, has a good position. If I stay here, I'll never own anything but the clothes on my
back."

"Is that so important? Owning something?"

"I suppose it is when you don't own a thing."

She grinned. "Except the clothes on your back." She suddenly
wrapped her arms around herself as if she were cold. "Sometimes I wish
nothing would change. We all had so much fun when we were children,
did we not?"

"We did," he said. Yes, it had been fun, at least more fun than
digging horseshit out of stalls or shaving hooves. Even though all the
Dunford children were kind, he was never truly one of them, nor did
he expect to be. When they all went riding out, he would trail behind
with a picnic hamper strapped to the horse, always a servant. When
he was younger, he never questioned his role, never resented it. Now,
he did. Now, when he knew he could be something more, when he
thought of the possibility that someday someone might call him sir,
those memories burned in his gut, only serving to remind him again
and again that he was less. It was all made worse knowing that, as
head groom, he shouldn't have the thoughts he had about the young
lady of the house. He shouldn't spend nights awake thinking about
what it would be like to make love to her, having all-too-vivid
dreams of making love to her, waking up hard and aching and feeling
like a fool.

His father had worried about him, about all the time he spent with the Dunford children. They'd all come back to the stable, smiling and laughing, and he'd be left behind to take off the horses' gear, to wipe them down, to feed and water them. To clean up the piss and shit. He remembered one day when he was about sixteen, and they'd all been out, riding and jumping. Lady Rose hadn't been with them that day, and the brothers had taken off their clothes and jumped into the small lake on the north end of the property. He'd stayed dressed, looking at that cool water with longing. But he'd known it wouldn't have been right for him to join them. They hadn't even asked. That was the first time it struck him: they were not his friends, they were his employers. Though they were kind and polite, he meant no more to them than the horses they rode.

He'd ridden back to the stables silently that day, not bothering to join in with the brothers' banter. They returned, thanked him, and off they went to the house to enjoy their evening. And he went to work, alone and sullen.

"I wondered when it was going to start botherin' you," his father said, coming up next to him. Hell, Charlie had felt like crying, but he'd just nodded. It was only salt in the wound to find himself in love with Lady Rose. It didn't matter how many times he told himself of the foolishness of it, the futility, the idiocy. He loved her and he supposed a part of him always would, even when he was in the States and getting on with his life.

Just then Moonrise nickered loudly and kicked at her belly, making Charlie laugh. "She's likely wondering what that thing is inside her causing her discomfort and moving about."

"Poor thing. I wish there was some way to let her know all will be well. It will, will it not?"

Charlie allowed himself to look at her and was slightly relieved she was staring at the mare, her expression filled with worry. Her shawl fell from one shoulder, leaving it bare and allowing him to glimpse the gentle, smooth top of one breast. He immediately looked away, angry with himself for looking at her that way, for debasing her with his lust. And he did lust after her, nearly as much as he loved her.

"I've no indication of any difficulty," he said, his eyes on the horse. Good God, what if she had turned at that moment and seen him ogling her.

"That's good." She yawned. "Goodness, I am tired. I will try to come to the stables tomorrow, but we've a busy day planned. His Grace and I are picnicking and later we're having a small concert. But please do send word when the foal is delivered. I wish I could be here all day tomorrow, but alas, I have my duties."

"I will certainly send a message to the house when she safely delivers her foal," Charlie said.

"Thank you. Good night, Charlie. Or rather, good morning." She let out a light laugh and Charlie watched as she left the stall and walked toward the house in the early morning light.

Chapter 2

"My dear, you hardly need a chaperone."

"Grandmama always cautions about such outings. She says it gives a man permission to do things he oughtn't, that a man alone with a young lady cannot control his, um, base urges." Rose's cheeks flushed and her mother laughed.

"I'm certain His Grace will be able to spend an hour or two alone with you on a fine summer's day without losing his head," her mother said. "And if he should try to steal a kiss or two, it's perfectly acceptable. But only a kiss or two, young lady. It is up to a lady to call a halt to any unwanted advances, though I hardly think His Grace will give you any reason on that account. He's a gentleman of the finest ilk."

Rose nodded, but her stomach was a jumble of nerves. She honestly didn't even think the duke would try to steal a kiss, but she also had no wish to be alone with him. She was such a nervous ninny when she was with him, and having another person there would give her a great deal of comfort. In less than three months, she would be alone with him every day, so she supposed she should get used to his company. "We have so little in common, Mother. What shall we talk about?"

"Not about Moonrise," her mother said sternly.

"And not about politics or science or traveling, either. Did you know His Grace has no wish to travel, when it is something I longed to do when I married? I thought a wedding trip to the continent would be wonderful, but he is solidly against it."

Her mother patted her shoulder. "Every marriage has compromises, dear. And as for conversation, ask His Grace about Mount Carlyle. Every man loves to talk about his home, the improvements he's made and the ones he's planning. It shall be your home, after all. and your curiosity would be a natural thing and a good topic of discussion."

Rose smiled, grateful her mother had given her such wonderful advice. "Thank you, Mother. That is perfect."

"I'd rather not discuss my plans for Mount Carlyle," His Grace said, his tone brooking no argument. "Discussions of architecture and construction are tedious, and I'm quite certain you wouldn't understand at any rate."

They'd decided to picnic by the lake, a fair distance from the house, which meant an interminable amount of time to try to come up with something they could discuss. The path to the lake was lovely, and since it was a warm day, quite pleasant. Weather was always a safe topic of conversation, Rose supposed.

"I'm so glad the weather cooperated with us so we might enjoy our picnic, Your Grace."

The duke looked about as if just noticing what a fine day it was. "Indeed."

"I thought last night was lovely, did you not?"

Weston walked five paces before answering. "It was a middling affair, though I did want to discuss something with you. I've found it's best to air grievances quickly."

Rose looked up at him, mildly surprised. "You have a grievance, Your Grace?"

"Indeed I do. It's about your behavior last evening. I do realize you are young." He gave her a tight smile, his eyes sweeping quickly down her form. "But when you are my wife, I would appreciate it if your attention was on me, not young swains."

Rose stopped, and the duke stopped as well, facing her. "Whatever do you mean?" She thought back on the evening, on her "behavior," and could not think of a single incidence where she hadn't acted like any other woman in the room. She did dance with men other than His Grace, but then she was expected to.

"You are a natural flirt. Men can misinterpret such a"—he paused and looked at her again, his eyes coldly assessing her—"talent. While I enjoy your charming personality, I would hate to think that other men might take your charm as invitation."

Rose's cheeks flamed, and not from humiliation, but from anger. "Sir, I'm certain you misinterpreted what you saw. I hardly know how to flirt, and I certainly would never behave in a manner that would invite unwanted attention."

His Grace chuckled, but there was little humor in his expression. "Now I've made you angry. You must not be."

"I am not angry," Rose said, and tried to calm her ire. "Simply taken aback."

His Grace turned and began walking down the path again, and Rose followed, staring at his back with more than a bit of dismay. She knew it was good to spend time with the man before they married, but she worried that the more she got to know him, the less she liked him. That would never do.

"Your Grace, I do wish to please you," she said, not wanting their argument to ruin their day.

He stopped again in the path and turned, slowly, to look at her. "Do you?" he asked softly, his eyes again drifting down her body and making Rose uncomfortable. "I should like to have a wife who wants to please me."

Rose was horrified that he'd once again misinterpreted her. She was young and terribly naive, but she knew when a man looked at a woman the way the duke was looking at her that he was thinking carnal thoughts. Worse, His Grace thought *she* was thinking carnal thoughts.

"Of course I do," Rose said, not knowing another way to respond. The way he was looking at her made her skin crawl.

"My last wife, God rest her soul, was a timid creature. She didn't care for the benefits of marriage," he said, putting telling emphasis on the word *benefits*. "She was quite young when we married, as are you. I should not like another timid wife."

Rose was quite certain her cheeks had never burned so brightly. He saw and laughed. "So innocent," he said, lifting one hand and touching her cheek, and she willed herself not to move away. "I find it quite charming. Innocence. But only in small amounts." He dropped his hand and studied her, his hooded gaze resting on her chest for so long, Rose had the urge to cover herself, but she forced herself to look at his face, not wanting to be timid.

"Yes, you will do nicely. See?" He looked down, and Rose was horrified to see he'd taken himself out. His . . . thing . . . fully erect, jutted obscenely from his trousers.

"Sir!"

"You have made me hard, my dear. And now you must take care of it."

"We . . . we are not yet married. It . . . this is improper, Your Grace." She swallowed, unable to again look at the large red thing protruding from his pants.

He laughed again, and Rose wanted to slap him. "You'll be a virgin on your wedding night. Have no worry. But I need release now and you will accommodate me. You will please me, Rose." He placed one hand hard behind her neck; the other held his man thing, stroking obscenely.

"Please, Your Grace." Rose tried to pull away, but his crushing grip on her neck made it impossible.

"Yes, please Your Grace," he said, chuckling. He pressed on her neck, hurting her, squeezing with one beefy hand as he pushed her downward. "Get on your knees, my dear, and put me in your mouth."

Chapter 3

Thus the first rule for a graceful manner is unselfish consideration of others.

—From *The Ladies' Book of Etiquette, and Manual of Politeness*

"I hear those American girls love a man with an accent," Bucky said, jostling Charlie as they stood just outside the stables. Bucky was all of eighteen and, having lost his virginity just one week ago to one of the chambermaids, his thoughts were solidly on one subject. "Get 'em tipsy and they'll do whatever you want." He made an obscene gesture, and Charlie laughed because Bucky was a harmless bloke who didn't mean a thing he said. The youth was so smitten with that little maid, he'd already begun thinking of marriage.

"I'll be working too hard to have time for a girl," Charlie said. "At least at first. That's the thing in America; work hard and you make more money. Here, you work hard and it's always the same. Doesn't matter if you work hard or dawdle around all day like you, a man still gets paid."

"You have to find a girl, Charlie," Bucky said, ignoring the insult, his eyes going wide. "Or are you going to be too busy mooning about a certain lady."

"Sod off, Bucky," Charlie said lightly. Harry had a big mouth. He'd confided in him a few months back after pulling down one too many whiskeys and sorely regretted it. Everyone knew he was a fool for Lady Rose now, even this young whelp.

As an apology, Bucky pulled out a flask and held it out to Charlie. "Sure, why not," Charlie said, grabbing the flask, taking a small swig and handing it back to Bucky. He didn't want to drink too much, not with Moonrise about to foal.

"Oh, shite," Bucky said, his eyes wide as he pulled the flask down and quickly put the cork back in. "Company."

Charlie followed Bucky's gaze to see Lady Rose hurrying toward the stables, her cheeks flushed from the exertion of walking so fast. She looked . . . hell, she looked like she was running from a swarm of spiders. Behind her, the duke walked toward the house, and Charlie's eyes went from the duke to Lady Rose, sensing something was wrong.

"Hello, boys," she said as she neared them. She held out her hand and Bucky reluctantly handed over his flask. "Thank you." Then to Charlie's surprise, she pulled the cork, took a long pull, swished it about and spat onto the ground before taking another pull and swallowing it. As if she'd done nothing stunning, she corked the flask and handed it back to Bucky, who stood there mutely, gaping at her. Charlie watched silently, noting with growing alarm that she was shaking, that putting that cork back in the flask was far more difficult for her than it should have been.

"Bucky, go check on the horses in the pasture."

"But . . ."

"Now, Bucky," Charlie said as he watched Lady Rose walk into the stable and head toward Moonrise.

Bucky walked away, mumbling beneath his breath, but Charlie ignored him. Something was wrong. Something had happened. A lover's quarrel? He looked to where the duke walked, now a small figure stepping up the shallow stairs to the veranda. When he reached the top, he turned and looked toward the stables, and something in Charlie's gut churned.

He walked into the stable and saw her standing outside Moonrise's stall, clutching the railing. She was trembling visibly and he realized when he reached her that the odd clacking noise he could hear was her teeth chattering—even though the day was quite warm.

"Are you quite well, my lady?" Charlie asked, looking at her intently.

She took a short, audible breath, then turned to him and smiled. "Of course," she said, smoothing down her skirts. Charlie's eyes followed the motion, noting the grass stains by her knees. His gaze immediately went to her face, but she looked away, training her eyes on the mare. "How is Moonrise?"

He studied Lady Rose a long moment more, finally deciding to not press further. It wasn't his place, and if she didn't want to tell him what was troubling her, he certainly couldn't force her to tell him. "You'll have a foal by tomorrow morning."

She smiled, then leaned her chin on the hands that rested on the gate. It was such a familiar sight, to see her like that. How many times had he been working on a horse, trimming hooves or grooming one, only to look up and see her just like that, silently watching what he did?

"Then I'll see you in the morning, Charlie."

He turned sharply to her, for he could have sworn her voice broke, as if she was crying—or trying not to. But she only smiled and turned away before he could determine whether there were tears in her eyes. "My lady," he called as she walked away.

But she simply waved her hand without turning, calling out, "To-morrow, Charlie. Take care of her for me." It wasn't until she reached the outside that she turned and smiled. "I'm counting on you." Then she spun around and walked quickly to the house.

Rose spent a near sleepless night, trying not to think about what had happened with the duke but finding it impossible. She was set to walk out with the duke again and the thought of being alone with him was making her physically ill. He was to be her husband and she couldn't even bear to be alone with him. What would it be like when they were man and wife?

When she was dressed, she headed immediately to her mother's room. She hadn't any idea what she would say, but she could not go on without telling her mother of her doubts. She could never tell her what had happened. It was mortifying and humiliating, but she decided she could tell her mother she was having grave doubts about the duke and about the wedding. Three months had seemed like for-ever not two days ago; now it seemed as if she were teetering on the last step and would fall into marriage in a blink of time.

She knocked on her mother's door and entered to find her mother sitting before her vanity, her maid putting the final touches on her hair.

"Don't you look lovely, dear," her mother said, rising and walking over to her to adjust one sleeve. "His Grace will be here in less than an hour, but you do appear to be ready."

"Mother, I would like to talk to you about the duke." Rose darted a look at Peggy, her mother's maid.

"You may go, Peggy, thank you."

Her maid gave a quick curtsy before leaving, closing the door quietly behind her. When she had gone, Rose blurted out, "I think I've made a terrible mistake."

Her mother laughed and waved a dismissive hand. "Wedding jitters. We've all had them."

"It's more than that," Rose said, swallowing thickly. "Yesterday, when we were walking, he . . . the duke . . . made improper advances."

Her mother gave her a look of amused commiseration. "Oh, darling, you look so worried. A few stolen kisses between an engaged couple is nothing to fret about." She turned to sit back down at her vanity, but then her gaze sharpened and she looked at Rose through the reflection. "He didn't . . . You are still . . ." She let her voice trail off, but Rose knew what she'd meant.

Rose felt her cheeks redden. She longed to tell her mother the truth, but it was just so shameful. And what if her mother dismissed it as nothing? Or worse, blamed her for inciting his passions? She'd been taught for years that it was up to the woman to let a man know where the boundaries were, yet she hadn't stopped him. She hadn't struck him or really even tried to push him away once it had started.

"Nothing like that." Somehow, it was worse, but she couldn't bring herself to say it aloud, not to her mother, who trusted her, who was so very happy that the duke had offered his hand.

Her mother looked visibly relieved. "Then there's nothing to worry about, Rose. Men sometimes have a difficult time controlling their baser feelings, and it is up to us women to keep them in check. If he tries to do more than steal a kiss, you are to tell him in no uncertain terms that it will have to wait until your wedding night. After you're married, I'm afraid you will have to submit to his baser whims. But we'll talk more about that on the eve of your wedding, shall we?"

Rose stood behind her mother, feeling ill. The picture her mother painted of marriage was nightmarish. He would do that and more when they were married. He would humiliate and hurt her and she could do nothing, say nothing? No wonder his first wife had always looked so pale.

She thought of her brother Adam and Georgette, so clearly in love, so happy together. She'd seen them kissing when they thought no one was watching and it had always seemed like such a lovely thing. So obviously not all marriages were frightening, nor were all men like the duke. Or maybe there was something wrong with her? Maybe she was supposed to have found pleasure in what he'd done? She shuddered at the thought.

"Who's walking on your grave?" her mother said on a small laugh.

Rose forced a smile. "Do you think you could accompany us on our walk today, Mother?"

Her mother gave her a chastising look. "Rose, you must not be silly about this. He is your intended and has already expressed his distaste of chaperones and being treated like a schoolboy. We dare not upset him at this critical time. Besides, Lady Simmons is arriving shortly. Now, go get ready for your duke, dear, will you? And please stop fretting."

Thirty minutes later Rose stood outside the formal parlor, listening to the sound of her mother and Weston talking to one another. She knew if she crossed that threshold, she would be sentencing herself to being alone with the duke. And she also knew if she didn't, her mother would be angry and fetch her. She steeled herself and entered the parlor, unable to give the duke even a passing glance. She dreaded what she would see in his eyes.

"You have another lovely day for a walk," her mother said pointedly.

Rose darted a look at the duke, who observed her with bland amusement. When she'd first met him, she'd thought him quite dashing. Now the sight of him made her physically ill. What was she going to do? How could she face a lifetime with a man she couldn't bear to look at? "Mother, I'm quite tired from yesterday's walk."

"But you didn't even reach the lake. Cook commented that you and His Grace never got as far as the lake. All that food wasted."

"I ate when I returned," Rose pointed out, not wishing to argue. "And we walked quite far enough even if we didn't reach the lake."

"I wish for a walk." Both women turned to the duke as if they'd forgotten he was in the room. "Yesterday's walk was so . . . bracing."

Oh, God. Rose wanted to run from the room, wanted to scream out what His Grace had made her do, what he had said after he'd made her do the despicable act. *Do not disappoint me, Rose. I do not want a timid wife. Perhaps it is not too late to call things off. . . .*

He knew what he'd been saying, what he was threatening. Please me or pay. Please me or I will ruin you by ending the engagement, by throwing you aside. He'd acted as if he were in his right to do what he did, that her reaction was childish and supremely distasteful. Was what he'd demanded something that was his right to demand? She was young and naive, and she had displeased him. And so, to her shame, she'd apologized, explained that she had never even been kissed, surely it was wrong for her to do something so . . . intimate without the benefit of marriage. He'd laughed and chucked her lightly under her chin as if she'd just spoken the most adorable nonsense.

She prayed he wouldn't expect her to do it again. Rose looked at him and he had that same hooded gaze he'd had yesterday and a secret smile that told her he knew what she was thinking.

"Perhaps you would like to join us, Mother," Rose repeated, trying not to let her voice show her desperation.

"I cannot, dear. As I told you, Lady Simmons is visiting this afternoon and I must attend her."

"Let's take our walk, shall we?" the duke said, rising and holding out his arm, indicating the door that led to the terrace.

Rose walked to him and tried to smile, for whose benefit she could not have said. When they reached the terrace, Rose looked up, praying for threatening clouds. Though the sky was not as bright as the previous day, the sun continued to shine through a milky layer of clouds that at the moment didn't seem to have a drop of rain in them. In the distance, she could see a field of poppies, swaying cheerfully in the gentle breeze, but the sight of her favorite flower did nothing to lift her mood.

"This is a walk, not a death sentence. You annoy me with your missish behavior," Weston said.

"I am a miss, sir, after all."

He looked at her with annoyance. "You should learn early on, my

dear, that you will not argue with me. You will obey me in all things—
all things—and you shall do so without complaint or hesitation. We
can have a pleasant life together if you resign yourself to those simple
demands. I am not an ogre, Rose, but I am a powerful man who will
not tolerate an incompliant wife. Do you understand?"

Rose stared straight ahead, her hands fisting. "I understand, Your
Grace."

She saw from the side of her eye that he was looking at her, probably gauging whether she told the truth.

"I would like for us to be happy," he said, his voice gentler, causing Rose to look up at him. "I do believe we are well suited. I pay
you a compliment, my dear, and I am giving you the greatest of hon-
ors by asking you to be my wife. Do you not think a dozen other
young ladies would step forward if our engagement were broken?"

"I do not wish that, Your Grace," Rose said. Oh, but she did, she did.

"Good. You have pleased me. And you shall please me even more
momentarily, I am certain of it." He held out his arm and she took it,
looking for all the world like a woman without a care. As they walked
toward the path that would lead to the lake, Rose looked to the stables and wondered whether Moonrise had foaled. Charlie hadn't sent
word, which worried her a bit. As if her thoughts conjured him,
Charlie appeared at the large door and stood there, watching them,
and Rose had the terrible urge to break away from the duke and run
toward him. He lifted his head slightly, but she was too far away to
see his expression. Then he nodded, once, and Rose smiled and
looked back toward the path. Moonrise had had her foal, and for that
small moment, she was filled with a bit of joy.

"Bucky, watch the foal. I'm going for a walk."

Bucky, who was cleaning up the mess from the birthing, looked
up, surprised. "You want me to watch her?"

"You're ready. And I need a walk."

"I'd think you'd need your bed more than a walk," he said.
"When's the last time you slept?"

"I think I need a bath more than a bed," Charlie said, looking
down at his clothes. He'd washed the blood and fluids from his face
and arms, but his clothing was still a sight. At the moment, though,
he wouldn't have cared if he were covered in blood from head to toe.

He couldn't stop thinking that something had happened yesterday, something between the duke and Lady Rose. If he was wrong, no harm. But if he was right, she would need him and he'd be damned if he didn't try to protect her.

Charlie went out the back of the stables through a small paddock, walking quickly to the railing and leaping over the fence effortlessly. All night, the image of Lady Rose's pale face had haunted him. Maybe he was a fool, maybe he was so much in love that he saw something where there was nothing, but his gut was telling him she should not be alone with the duke. The couple had been walking toward the path that led to the lake, and he was quite certain that's where they'd been headed. He cut through the forest, keeping his eye on the path, seeing occasional flashes of color from Lady Rose's yellow dress through the trees and brambles. He walked parallel to them, ignoring the prickers digging into ungloved hands and even through his thick pants. The brambles were a curse on this land, always making a stroll in the woods an uncomfortable affair.

He decided he would keep his distance until he was satisfied that she was safe. He had no business taking a stroll in the middle of the day, especially when a foal had just been born. The longer he followed them, the more foolish he felt. Clearly, they were only a couple taking a walk together. Was it real concern for Lady Rose that kept him going or his ridiculous jealousy? he wondered, trying to be honest with himself. The day was cool, but tramping through the woods without the benefit of a path was making him sweat from the exertion. The couple was, perhaps, a hundred yards from where he watched them, no doubt chatting about their upcoming nuptials. What the hell was he doing, following them? He was about to turn back to the stables in disgust, when they stopped in the path, then moved closer to the forest on the opposite side of the path from where Charlie stood, holding his breath, watching them. Then he recognized, even from that distance, the obvious movements of a man unbuttoning his pants. Holy God. And Lady Rose stood there, frozen. Terrified.

He'd kill the duke if he touched her.

In a matter of seconds, Charlie assessed the situation and weighed his options. He wanted her safe. He wanted the duke dead. But, of course, that could never happen. Charlie knew he would swing from the nearest gallows if he laid a hand on the duke. And so he did the next best thing—he started singing loudly and quite badly the first song he could think of.

"Mary had a little lamb, little lamb, little lamb. Mary had a little lamb whose fleece was white as snow—"

He stopped abruptly, as if shocked to find himself in the company of Lady Rose and His Grace, but wanted to whoop out in joy, for his ploy worked. The minute he started singing, the duke turned and made short work of buttoning his trousers and Lady Rose sagged with relief.

"I do beg your pardon, Lady Rose, Your Grace. I did not mean to offend your ears with my singing," Charlie said good-naturedly.

"What the hell are you doing out here, boy?"

"Charlie is our head groom, Your Grace," Lady Rose said, her voice shaking slightly, and Charlie used all his willpower not to make a fist.

"I don't care who he is and I certainly don't expect an introduction," the duke said, his cheeks red, likely from anger or frustration. Charlie didn't give a damn.

"I'm actually glad to have stumbled upon you, Lady Rose. You see, Moonrise had a foal early this morning. I sent word to the house but you had already left on your walk. She's a lovely little filly. Would you like to see her?"

Lady Rose immediately looked to the duke as if asking permission, and Charlie tensed. If the duke denied her, what could he do? Join them on their walk? Insist that the lady return with him to the stable?

"I would so love to see her, Your Grace. Shall we?" And Lady Rose simply turned and began walking back to the stable, leaving the duke staring impotently at her back before glaring at Charlie and reluctantly following.

Charlie trailed behind, keeping a good distance between himself and the couple, but not so far as to let the duke believe they were alone. He stared at his back, wishing he could do more, wishing he could pummel the bastard within an inch of his life. Never in his life had he had such a strong urge to commit violence upon another man. He could picture himself smashing his fist into the duke's face, putting his hand around his throat and squeezing until the life seeped out of him. But Charlie realized he valued his own neck far more than the duke's. He whistled softly as they walked, his eyes never leaving

Rose's slim form, his heart breaking for her. She'd looked so damned scared standing there. What if he hadn't followed them? What if he'd turned around? What would have happened?

As they neared the stable, Lady Rose picked up her pace, and Charlie jogged to catch up to the pair. He wanted to be there when she first set her eyes on the pretty little filly. She was nearly pure white, though she would certainly darken like her mother in a few months

The three entered the stables, stopping momentarily to allow their eyes to adjust to the dimness of the interior. A tiny bit of orange fluff, one of five kittens from the latest litter, caught the corner of Charlie's eye as it wiggled its little bum, ready to pounce on its prey—His Grace's boot. The kitten pounced, and the duke looked down, annoyed.

"How sweet," Lady Rose said, just before the duke shook the animal off him rather roughly.

Charlie scooped the kitten up and smiled reassuringly at Lady Rose, holding the creature against his chest before leading the couple toward the new foal, who was nursing enthusiastically and making small sucking sounds. Bucky stood outside the stall watching, and Charlie motioned his head, silently telling the younger man that he could leave.

"What a good mum she is," Lady Rose said softly, her eyes filling with tears. "Such a pretty baby." She turned to Charlie and smiled at him just as the duke stepped between them, blocking Charlie's view of Lady Rose.

"Charming," the duke drawled. "Is this her first foal?"

"Yes," Lady Rose said. "It's so wondrous, isn't it? How the foal knows just what to do and how Moonrise is so accepting of her. It's miraculous, really."

The duke chuckled. "Hardly a miracle. Shall we return to the house?"

"I did wish to stay here and watch the foal for a bit more," she said.

Charlie hung back, watching the couple, feeling uneasy and tense. It was strange to see her with a man, and stranger still to see her so subdued. This was not the woman he knew, the one who dashed in and out of the stable, who would take up a brush and begin grooming the nearest horse simply because she wanted to.

"But I wish to return to the house," the duke said, his tone biting. "This outing has been less than pleasant and I certainly don't want to spend my day standing in filth and staring at a horse."

"Of course, Your Grace."

The duke turned to leave and spied Charlie standing there, staring at him with clear dislike. "You, boy, don't you have duties to attend to?"

"The foal is my duty, Your Grace."

The duke let out a beleaguered sigh. "The foal, the foal. No doubt if I don't let you stay, you will sulk. You may stay, Lady Rose, but I do expect to see you at luncheon. Surely you do not plan to eat out here."

Lady Rose gave a small curtsy. "Of course, Your Grace. Thank you. I will see you for luncheon."

Something snapped inside Charlie at that moment, though anyone looking at him wouldn't have known. It was as if a glass vial containing a black emotion he'd never before experienced shattered, allowing that dark poison to surge through his veins. Hatred, hot and dangerous. If Lady Rose hadn't been standing there, he was not certain he could have kept from launching himself at the duke and thrashing him within an inch of his life. As if sensing his thoughts, Weston gave Charlie a hard stare before leaving and Charlie stared right back.

"Count yourself fortunate that you are not in my employ, boy."

"I do, sir, thank you."

The duke's nostrils flared at the insult, but he left without another word.

After the duke left, Charlie carefully placed the kitten back on the ground and stood beside Lady Rose as she watched the foal. She was a sweet little filly, already sturdy on her skinny legs.

"Moonrise did well," he said into the silence.

When Lady Rose didn't respond, he looked at her, dying a bit inside when he saw a tear trailing down one cheek. He'd never felt so helpless in his life.

"Charlie." She turned her head to him, her hands still clutching the stall, pain so clear in her eyes it hurt. She shook her head and looked back at the foal.

"Is there something you wanted to say, my lady?"

Her breath hitched and she shook her head again, swallowing

fiercely, as if trying valiantly not to cry. God, he wanted to draw her into his arms, to take her pain away, to tell her she would be all right. For a moment, it appeared she couldn't breathe at all, and then, in one swift movement, she launched herself against him, clutching at his shirt, her forehead pressed against his chest. "Oh, Charlie," she cried, and began sobbing wetly against him as he stood there, arms akimbo, completely unsure what he should do.

"I can't, I can't," she said over and over, until Charlie couldn't take it anymore. He put his hands on her shoulders, closing his eyes when he felt her slim body shaking with her cries.

"Shhh," he said, not knowing what else he could say. He didn't know precisely why she was crying, but he had a feeling it had something to do with the ass she was expected to marry.

She pulled back slightly, her eyes and nose red from crying, and looked up at him, and it was all he could do not to bend his head and kiss away her tears. "I'm sorry," she said, her voice thick

"It's perfectly fine, my lady. I'm often called upon to comfort ladies who break into tears."

She let out a watery laugh; then her eyes filled again. This time, she stepped back, out of his arms, and brushed the tears away with her gloved hands. "I'm just being silly. Just tired from all the festivities."

She turned abruptly away to stare blindly at the foal which was rooting around the hay curiously, its muzzle becoming covered with bits of straw.

"My lady," Charlie said hesitantly. "Did something happen yesterday? Something . . . bad?"

She stilled. "Whatever could you mean?" If she hadn't looked so wretched, Charlie would have laughed aloud at her gallant attempt to pretend she hadn't just been in his arms sobbing.

"Did he hurt you?" *Please say no. Please, God, say no.*

But she let out a small sob and Charlie thought he'd go mad from the rage coursing through him. And then, the blood drained from his face when he saw purplish marks on her neck. "You're bruised," he said, his voice shaking with a sickening combination of anger and horror.

"Am I?"

"Your neck. Jesus, like fingerprints. I'll kill the bastard."

"No, no, Charlie," she said, turning toward him again, her eyes wide, desperate. "It wasn't like that. He didn't . . ."

"He sure as hell did something. And I saw what he was doing today, my lady. I saw."

"Oh, God," she cried, covering her eyes with her hands. "It's not what you think. He . . ." She made a poor attempt at gathering herself together. She took a breath. And another. "I'm perfectly well, Charlie. Just prewedding jitters."

Charlie recalled the previous day, Lady Rose coming into the stable, grabbing the whiskey, taking a mouthful. Spitting it out. Rinsing her mouth. And today, that bastard unbuttoning . . .

"I'll kill him."

Her eyes flew wide. "No, Charlie. It was nothing. Nothing."

It was his time to close his eyes briefly, because he didn't want her to see the violence coursing through him. He knew what that man had done to her. He couldn't imagine someone forcing a girl to do what the duke had obviously done, someone as sweet and lovely. "I'm so sorry, my lady. So sorry that happened to you." He wanted to draw her into his arms, but he couldn't. He was the head groom, not her friend, not her anything. "You should tell your mother."

"There is nothing to tell," she said, her tone dead. "And if anything had happened, it wouldn't matter. Don't you see?" She lifted her chin. "Everyone is counting on me, on this marriage. I hardly think they'd care about anything as long as I was well enough to walk down the aisle."

Charlie started to take a step toward her, but stopped himself. "They'd care, my lady."

She shook her head. "I don't have a choice."

It was on the tip of his tongue to beg her to go with him to America, but he remained silent, feeling nearly as helpless as she did. *Run away with me. Marry me.* Just having those thoughts created a wave of humiliation so strong he was staggered by it. Marrying the likes of him would only bring her more shame.

Instead, he said, "Tell your mum, my lady. Show her your neck."

Her hand went to her neck, hiding the bruises from him, and her expression changed, grew hard. "I told you nothing happened and you are not to make presumptions. You are not to speak to a soul about this, do you hear me, Charlie? If you say a word, I'll make certain you're dismissed immediately."

Heat rushed to his cheeks. "I'm leaving in less than a fortnight, so I hardly think it would matter if you dismissed me, my lady." He gave her a tight smile, as glad that she had put him in his place as he was hurt by her words.

"Your promise, Charlie."

"I will not tell anyone. I promise."

Chapter 4

Many have done so, and having, with that view, been tempted to accord unwise indulgences and to overlook serious faults, they have found that, far from gaining the love of their servants, they have incurred their contempt.

—From *The Ladies' Book of Etiquette, and Manual of Politeness*

Rose walked back to the house, suddenly fiercely glad Charlie was leaving. How would she ever be able to look at him again without feeling mortified? He knew what had happened, had seen the duke unbuttoning his pants. It was humiliating. It didn't matter that Charlie was angry with the duke. Why had she broken down like that, throwing herself into his arms? She wished with all her might that she'd just left the stable without saying a word.

Charlie had been so kind, letting her water his shirt, letting her lean on his solid strength. All her life he'd been a quiet presence, someone who represented home as much as her own parents. Those long months she'd spent in finishing school had left her so homesick, just the smell of hay would make her smile and her eyes prick with unshed tears. Wrapped up in the scent of hay was all that was Charlie, who never complained or judged or did anything except make her laugh and teach her how to care for Moonshine. When she'd returned from finishing school and seen him, seen how he looked at her, all grown up, a lady in truth, part of her had felt a bit of a thrill. He never looked at her like that again, because she suspected he knew even more than she how impossible it would be to bridge the gap of their birth. But he was always kind.

And how had she repaid his kindness? By threatening to dismiss him. What a wretched person she was.

She was about to climb up the shallow steps to the veranda, but turned around and headed back to the stable to apologize. She might not have a chance to see him again before he left; it would be terrible to have him go with this between them. When she entered the stable, she saw him throwing great forkfuls of hay into one of the stalls. It was a job the head groom usually assigned to an underling, but Charlie was undertaking the task with ferocity, his shirt clinging to him, his curling blond hair dark along the edges from sweat.

"Charlie." He shoveled another great bit of straw, then stopped, his back toward her, heaving from the exertion of his work.

He turned his head slightly. "Yes, my lady."

Impertinent and not at all like him. He was angry, she could tell.

"I came back to apologize."

Rose bit her lip and watched as he slowly turned around. "Thank you."

A good and meek servant would have bowed and insisted there was no need to apologize, but though Charlie was a good servant, he'd never been meek. He looked at her, his blue eyes dark, and wiped the curls away from his forehead, revealing his strong brow.

"Will that be all?" he asked.

Rose swallowed. "Yes. No. Oh, Charlie, I won't be able to bear it if I know you are angry with me."

He sagged a bit, leaning on the pitchfork. "I could never be angry with you. I am angry with what happened. I'm angry I can't hurt the cur for what he did to you. I'm angry because you will marry him and you will likely be unhappy for the rest of your life. And there is nothing I can do about it. I'm angry because I am powerless to help you. I'm so angry, my lady, I can hardly breathe."

"Oh."

"And I'm angry that you . . . that I . . ." He let out a breath.

"You're quite angry, Charlie," Rose said, letting out a small laugh.

"Yes. But not with you, my lady. Do you understand?"

Rose nodded, feeling worlds better. "You look tired, Charlie. When did you last sleep?"

He gave her a smile. "Two days ago."

"I order you to bed. I can still do that, you know. You haven't left for America yet."

"Yes, my lady," he said, giving her a small bow.

Rose turned to go. "Have a good rest, Charlie." She walked back to the house, her spirits slightly higher, but the closer she got, the worse she felt. His Grace would be in their house, for she had not seen him leave and his horse was still in the stable. Would he stay to dine with them? She prayed not, even though they had invited him. Just the thought of trying to be pleasant to the man was enough to make her want to run away. For a fleeting moment, she pictured herself climbing into a carriage and telling the driver to go, go anywhere. To Scotland, anywhere far away. It was a wonderful image, but one as foolish as it was impossible.

She would marry the duke.

"I can't marry the duke." This she announced to her mother five minutes before they were scheduled to go down to dine. She might have said "the sky is blue" for the reaction her mother gave her. "Did you hear me, Mother?"

"I'm glad you stopped in before luncheon, dear. I wanted to talk to you about Mr. Avery."

"Charlie?"

Her mother gave her a tight smile. "That's what I want to talk to you about. He is a servant, not a friend. You are to call him either Mr. Avery or groom, certainly not by his given name. His Grace mentioned that he thought you were a bit too familiar with Mr. Avery and I can now understand his concern."

"His concern?" Rose looked at her mother in utter confusion.

"He felt Mr. Avery was entirely too impertinent today and suggested I dismiss him immediately. Of course, I will not. That being said, however, I would have given it consideration if Mr. Avery wasn't already leaving."

"Mother, I've known Ch—Mr. Avery—since we were both children. I've always called him Charlie."

"No longer."

"I call my maid by her given name."

"That is entirely different. Certainly I don't have to give you a lesson in how to treat servants. You are being purposely obtuse, Rose, and I don't like it."

Rose dipped her head slightly. "I apologize."

"As for that ridiculous statement you greeted me with earlier, it doesn't warrant discussion. Shall we go down to luncheon?"

"Yes, Mother."

"Oh, don't look so gloomy, Rose. It's hardly becoming, and the duke has decided to stay for luncheon so that you might spend a bit more time together. He is being quite accommodating and I do wish you would do the same."

It would be just the four of them, as all of the lingering guests from the ball had departed that morning and her brothers had returned to their own homes or, in the case of Marcus, London. When she reached the footman who stood outside the dining room, she took a bracing breath and schooled her features into something more pleasant than the terror she knew was in her eyes.

Luncheon was tolerable, only because she sat across from the duke, who was seated at her father's right. The two men were occupied in a discussion about hunting, and Rose let them talk, giving her meal undue attention. She could hardly bear to look at the man without her entire body convulsing in a shudder. What if he wanted a stroll in the gardens after they were finished eating? What could she say? Just the thought made her want to run from the table. This would never do. She was not an overly timid girl, and yet around this man she acted like a frightened mouse. All during the meal she rehearsed in her head what she would say to him, for she planned to let him know that his behavior was abhorrent and that there would be absolutely no more unseemly acts on his part.

After luncheon, once her father and His Grace had returned from their cigar and they were all gathered in the main parlor, Rose gathered her courage. "Mother, would it be possible for me to have a moment of privacy with His Grace?"

"Of course," Lucille said, and nodded to her father. The two departed posthaste, leaving her behind with the duke, who chuckled beneath his breath, at what she had no idea.

"How delightful that you've requested some privacy, my dear," he said, his tone silky.

They both still stood, having risen when her parents departed, and Rose took a step back, horrified that he had misinterpreted her reason for a private interview. "Your Grace," she said, keeping her gaze level and her voice strong, "there is something I need to discuss with you."

He inclined his head, bidding her to continue, an amused look in his eyes, as if he found her seriousness utterly charming. "I find your behavior these past two days unacceptable and disturbing." Her cheeks heated just at the thought of what he'd made her do. "It will not happen again. Not before our wedding. It is more than improper; it is sinful."

He stood there, looking at her with that terrible hooded gaze and half smile, but said nothing.

"If anything untoward should happen again between now and our wedding day, I will inform my mother, and she will most assuredly tell my father." There, she'd laid down the gauntlet. She stared at him, proud that she'd found the courage to confront him. Rose had considered his reaction, guessing he would be angry or sullen. But he seemed merely curious. He propped his chin on one fist and tilted his head slightly.

"And then what do you suppose would happen?"

"I'm sure my father would . . ." Her voice trailed off, because she truly couldn't imagine what her father would do.

He surprised her when he threw back his head and laughed. Pulling out a handkerchief, he dabbed at his eyes as if what she'd said was so delightful it had brought him to tears of mirth. "Oh, dear, my sweet little innocent child. Your mother knows."

"What? No, she doesn't, I—"

"She may not know the particulars of our passions, but she definitely *knows*. Or at least hopes."

"What do you mean?"

He walked up to her and laid a hand beneath her chin, like some benevolent uncle. "What mother of your acquaintance would allow her unmarried daughter to walk unaccompanied to such an isolated spot as your lovely lake?"

"She trusted you," Rose said, but even as she said the words they sounded somehow false to her. She *had* thought about that, had wondered, but had accepted her mother's explanation without question.

"Trusted. Hmm. Odd way of showing trust, if you ask me, my dear. By allowing you to walk out with me quite, quite alone, she ensured you would be essentially compromised by me. It was, let us say, a bit of an insurance policy. Your mother is not a stupid woman and I am certainly no fool. But I want you as a wife. I want access to that delectable little body of yours and that hot little mouth." His gaze drifted lazily down to her lips. "And don't for a second believe your mother didn't know precisely what she was doing, what she was allowing. Count yourself lucky, my dear, that I do enjoy the anticipation of taking you on our wedding night. Such a lovely tradition."

Rose felt bile rising up in her throat. "You are loathsome."

He laughed again. "I appreciate a girl with a bit of fire," he said, but then his eyes grew hard. "Just be certain not to overdo it. A wife must obey her husband without question. That is all I ask." He looked at her and chuckled. "How distressed you look. Like a child who's had her candy taken away."

Rose fought not to cry. Or scream. "I would ask that you refrain from improper behavior until our wedding, Your Grace." She hated the way her voice sounded, hated that what he'd said about her mother sounded like the truth. Her mother would do anything to ensure this wedding took place, and Rose now suspected she would get no help from that quarter.

"Very well," he said, with a dismissive wave of his hand. "I'm off to London and it is unlikely I'll return much before the wedding. Will you miss me, my dear?"

When she remained silent, he laughed again, but his eyes narrowed and Rose sensed he was angry beyond measure.

"Mother, I am curious." Rose sat on her mother's bed, watching as she brushed her golden hair, now slightly dulled by strands of gray.

"About what, dear?"

"About why you allowed me to walk alone with His Grace. It was highly improper, duke or no."

Her mother let out a sigh and placed her brush on her vanity. "I see nothing improper about an engaged couple taking a walk."

"But it *is* improper, and you know it. Was it because you feared he would break the engagement?"

Her mother let out a laugh that was decidedly false. "How silly you've been lately. One moment claiming you don't want to marry at all, then complaining about propriety. You would be ruined forever if you broke this engagement." Lucille turned to look at her daughter. "You do know that, don't you? You are aware of what your life would be like should you break this off?"

"I don't want to break it off," Rose said, her cheeks flushing with her lie.

"I should think not. Once you are married, this will all seem inconsequential. You will be a duchess." She sighed. "Sometimes I have to pinch myself to think my own daughter will be a duchess. Every girl dreams of such a match. I did as a girl. Of course, an earl is very fine for most girls, but I was the daughter of a duke. It was a bit of a set down for me. But I was one of five girls and the youngest, and my mother took the first proposal without a single thought what it would mean to her own daughter."

Rose had heard the story many times over the years but had never heard such a bitter note in her mother's tone. "Did you not love Father at all?"

Lucille laughed. "You are so young, Rose. No, I did not love your father. I suppose I admired him a bit. He was handsome and this estate is lovely. I don't know what this modern talk is about love."

Rose, looking down at her slippered feet that dangled from her mother's bed, said, "I understand what marriage is, Mother. I never had any illusions I would love my husband. But I thought perhaps I would not be repulsed by him."

"Repulsed? My dear, the duke is quite handsome."

"Do you really think so? I do not find him so."

"It's of little consequence at any rate. We all grow old. Look at your father now. Old and fat."

Rose laughed, for her father was indeed quite fat. But she quickly sobered, thinking what lay ahead. Years and years with a man she loathed, whose touch repulsed her. Would that change? She thought not.

"Good night, Mother. I shall endeavor not to be so silly in the future."

Lucille smiled. "I do hope not. Weston is a great man and your father and I are beyond honored to have him choose you as his bride. You should be honored as well. I know it's frightening to you, Rose, but do try to think of the family."

Rose nodded, but inside she felt a sickening panic grow. All she could think of that night as she lay in bed was escape.

Chapter 5

Never look back! It is excessively ill-bred.

—From *The Ladies' Book of Etiquette, and Manual of Politeness*

"I'm coming with you."

Charlie, lying on his stomach on his bed and lost in concentration over one of his drawings of machinery, looked back to find Lady Rose standing at the foot of the bed, her eyes wide, a large and overstuffed carpetbag clutched in her hands. "Where do you think you're going?"

"To America. With you. I can't marry him, Charlie, and I see no other way out. I have money," she said, patting her bag, her eyes wide and determined. "Not much, but enough to get me to New York."

Charlie pushed down the sudden joy that filled him. Her brothers would kill him if he let her join him on the ship. Hell, they'd probably kill him before he set a single foot onto the ship. He threw back the covers, for he'd been planning to head out early to make his way to Liverpool the next morning, then immediately drew the blanket back over him when he realized he was dressed only in his smalls. "Would you mind, my lady?" he asked, looking down at his naked torso. She seemed glued to the spot, her eyes pinned to his chest. Then she spun around, muttering an apology.

"You can't come with me, my lady," he said, tugging on his trousers. "You must know how foolish that would be. Your brothers would catch up to us and that would be the end of me."

Her head dipped. "I can't marry him, Charlie."

No, she couldn't. And it wasn't only what he'd done to her. Charlie had a chum who worked at Weston's estate and he'd asked a bit about the duke, about what the staff thought of him. What he'd heard made his blood burn. The duke, it seemed, had a fascination with the young maids, and there had been more than one who'd left in tears after being found in the bastard's bed by the housekeeper. The maids lived in fear of him and were cautioned to stay away lest they lose their position. "But it weren't their fault. Not always," his friend had said. "Some of 'em were good girls, and they're ruined now. Hell, Charlie, one was only fifteen."

But bring Lady Rose with him? In steerage? She couldn't travel alone; that would arouse too much curiosity, and no proper lady would ever travel alone. He looked at her standing at the foot of his bed, her hair pulled back in a simple bun, her coat plain and unadorned. She looked perfectly ordinary. She looked, Charlie realized, like a young woman who might be seen with a man such as he. This was no spontaneous decision, he realized; she had planned this all along, counting on his soft heart to save her.

And hell and damnation, she was right. He couldn't say no to her, not with her looking at him with those big brown eyes filled with more hope than she should have in such a situation.

"Your brothers—"

"—will never know. How could they? No one would think that I had run off with you. The last place they'll look is Liverpool. They'll check with all my aunts, then my grandmothers. And by the time they are about to go into a full panic, they'll have received the telegram I plan to send from Liverpool right before we depart. Please, Charlie. They need never know I have an accomplice. They'd never think that I would be with you."

Charlie gave her a hard stare. "And what of when we're on the ship? What then? Do you plan to sleep in steerage with the other women? Or will you be traveling first class by yourself? Do you realize what could happen to a girl traveling alone like that? They'll think things about you, bad things. What of your money? Your clothes. Certainly they're not all like what you're wearing now. And when you get to New York, where will you go?"

At this last question, Lady Rose smiled. "I have a plan for that, too. I've thought of everything, Charlie." She frowned. "Except for the ship part. Couldn't I stay with you?"

Charlie tugged on his shirt, the fabric snapping with his frustration. He wanted to help her, he truly did. But he was going to be in steerage with hundreds of other men, not crammed in a small room with a woman. A desirable woman whom he happened to love more than life itself. "I'll be in steerage with the other lads," he said.

"Oh." Then she pulled out a pamphlet, and Charlie instantly knew what it was—his pamphlet for the White Star Line. She held it out, one finger pointing to the print. "It says here that they accommodate married couples."

Charlie's entire body stilled, and for a count of five, he couldn't take in a breath. "You want us to marry?" he asked cautiously, hating that rush of joy that had him sitting abruptly on his bed, for in that moment, his legs couldn't be trusted to hold him. "I'd be more than happy to, my lady, if need be."

Lady Rose let out a laugh. "Goodness, Charlie, you should see your face. The situation is not *that* desperate. We could *pretend* to be married."

Charlie forced out a laugh, feeling foolish. "Of course. Scared the living daylights out of me." What the hell had he been thinking?

"I would never do that to you, Charlie," she said softly. "My plan is to marry Daniel Cartwright. He's an American who was just here for my engagement ball. He's a delightful man with a promising career in politics and he needs a wife. I will be that wife."

Charlie raised one brow. "Does he know that?"

"Not yet. But I'm confident I can convince him. Please, Charlie, say you will let me come. I can't bear the thought of marrying Weston." Her eyes filled with tears, and had it been any other woman standing there, he would have thought she was trying to manipulate him. But he knew she truly loathed and feared Weston. The man was a pig, and Charlie knew he would do anything in his power to protect her from him.

"Fine," he said, sounding angry. "You can come with me. But when we get to New York, you're on your own, understood?"

Lady Rose grinned. "Understood."

"And you know where you're going when you get to New York?"

She nodded. "I have his address. Oh, thank you, Charlie." She hugged him and he thought he just might die if he didn't wrap his arms around her, but he didn't, and so he did die, just a little bit.

The sun was rising when they arrived at the Cannock station. Rose pulled a veil down, hiding her face, trembling with fear that someone would recognize her and immediately tell her parents that she was traveling unchaperoned with a strange man. That alone would instantly ruin her. Charlie purchased their tickets, refusing to allow her to pay her way, and returned to sit by her as they waited for the first train of the day.

They sat outside the wooden building upon a bench, the morning mist drifting toward them from across a stretch of grass. It was chilly and damp, and Rose was glad she'd worn a nice warm wool coat, but she secretly wished she also had the lovely mink muff that she'd left behind.

By the time the train finally pulled into the station at ten minutes past seven, her muscles ached as much from the stress of fearing someone would see her as from trying to stop her shivering.

"The train will be warm," Charlie said, looking straight ahead as if the mist fascinated him. It was strange to be with him without a horse between them. Though she'd known him all her life, Rose suddenly felt as if she didn't know him at all. On this gray morning, his eyes looked more blue than she remembered, and a fine stubble of beard, darker than the blond curls on his head, made him seem even more foreign to her.

She shivered again, and he turned toward her, concern in his eyes. "Would you like my coat?"

Rose shook her head. "It's not the cold as much as I'm frightened to death that someone will recognize me."

"I wouldn't recognize you if I stared right at you," he said, obviously trying to cheer her. "Anyone who knows you would never suspect you would wear such an ugly dress."

Rose immediately looked down at the serviceable brown dress that she'd "borrowed" from Sarah on the pretense she needed something plain to wear to the stables. "It's not that ugly," she said.

"Compared to the fancy things you usually wear, it is," he said, leaning toward her and speaking low. "Besides, that veil hides your whole face. You look like some sort of specter."

"Good. Better I be completely invisible. I daresay by the time we embark, my nerves shall be completely frazzled."

He frowned. "You ought to try to sound like someone from the working class. You talk like that in steerage and everyone's going to know you don't belong."

"Oh," she said, drawing out the word. "Ya mean I should 'ave talked like this, then? Like I never 'ave seen the inside of a 'ouse?"

Charlie chuckled. "That was awful. Just talk like yourself. You can be a former lady's maid who thinks she's better than she ought to be."

When the train finally arrived, Rose stood immediately, impatiently waiting for the few people who were disembarking in Cannock to do so. She held her reticule in one hand and her large carpetbag in the other, until Charlie took it from her, saying, "You may not be a lady, but I can still be a gentleman."

She grinned at him and handed over the bag, which was quite heavy. She'd crammed as much into it as she possibly could, including a sapphire necklace she couldn't bear to part with as it had been a gift from her grandmother, who would no doubt collapse in horror when she learned what her favorite granddaughter had done.

The train ride from Cannock to Liverpool was blessedly quiet. Thankfully, the pair didn't see anyone they recognized at the station, and once they were on the train, Rose finally relaxed. She refused to consider what her parents would think, what the duke would do, how her brothers would react. She prayed she'd be on the ship and looking back at England by the time they realized she was gone. Whenever she felt panic building inside her, she pushed it down. She could not allow herself to think about how she could very well be ruining her life. Certainly when she'd detailed her plan to Charlie she'd sounded confident, but she was so far from that state she nearly broke out into hysterical laughter. Every time the train stopped, she had to force herself not to run off the train and take the first one back to Birmingham. She would sit there, still, clutching her reticule in her hands until she heard the engineer call for everyone to board, and only then would she trust herself not to jump from the train.

Charlie was silent and brooding, no doubt thinking about how angry her brothers would be if they discovered he had been her accomplice. Rose didn't believe they would find out; she would never have put Charlie in that sort of position. The entire train ride, she kept reminding herself: *It's not too late. You can go back and no one will ever know.* The ship wasn't leaving until that evening at high tide, which meant she had until six.

"Charlie."

"Yes m'la—I'll have to stop calling you that, you know. If we're pretending to be married, I'll have to call you by your given name. I do apologize."

She waved a hand at him. "Don't be silly, Charlie, I completely understand." Still, it would be strange to have him call her Rose, but she imagined she'd have to get used to it. Soon, if all went as planned, she'd be simply Mrs. Cartwright, a far, far lesser title than duchess. That was if she didn't change her mind. "Charlie, am I doing the right thing?"

"You're doing the right thing, but I'm not certain you're doing it the right way. I don't know why you couldn't talk to your mother."

Rose looked out the window at the passing scenery. "You don't know her like I do. She never would have let me break the engagement. I told her I wanted to break it off, you know, but she became quite cross with me."

Charlie looked at her solemnly. "Then you're doing the right thing. I just pray to God your brothers understand. Don't think for a second they won't come after you."

"I know they will, but by then it will be too late. I'll already be engaged to Mr. Cartwright and your name will never be mentioned. I'm so grateful for your help, Charlie."

Charlie let out a sound that Rose supposed was an acknowledgment of her gratitude. She knew she was putting him in a terrible situation; she only prayed her brothers, particularly Marcus with his terrible temper, never found out.

Chapter 6

In the street a lady takes the arm of a relative, her affi-
anced lover, or husband, but of no other gentleman, unless the streets are slippery, or in the evening.

—From *The Ladies' Book of Etiquette, and Manual of
Politeness*

Charlie, who had never been to a city larger than Birmingham and
only on the rarest occasion, found himself a bit overwhelmed by
the activity and smell of Liverpool. He'd had plenty of doubts when
he'd agreed to let Lady Rose accompany him, but getting jostled and
stepping carefully to avoid God knows what on the streets, he felt
those doubts triple. This was no place for Lady Rose, and he was
completely out of his element, a country bumpkin in the bustling city.

The train station was just a short walk from the port where their
ship was berthed. He'd purchased his ticket in steerage weeks ago
and could only hope the ship could accommodate another passenger.
He wasn't sure what he'd do if there was no room left.

"Shall we get a hack?"

Charlie shook his head. "The conductor said the port is only five
blocks, so we can walk. It'll be good after sitting on the train for so
long."

Lady Rose—no matter how hard he tried, he could not think of her
as "Rose" as it was far too familiar—gamely followed, relinquishing
her heavy bag to him. The truth was, he had very little money to spare
and he certainly couldn't ask a lady to pay his way.

"My, this is even busier than London," Rose said, and something
in her voice made Charlie stop and turn to her. She looked so damn

young and lost, and he wished more than anything he could make everything better for her. She stood, her dark hair coming loose from her hastily repaired bun, her brown eyes looking up at him, and tried to smile. It was that pathetic little smile that tugged at his heart the most.

"Here, grab my coat. That way we won't be separated." Charlie felt unaccountably pleased when she immediately took hold of his coat. He liked the tug of her hand; it gave him a sense of protectiveness, as if he were finally doing something to make her safe. Less than ten minutes after they departed the railway station, Charlie was looking up at the *Adriatic*, a steamship that would take him—and Rose—to their new lives.

"We have to go to the ticket clerk and purchase another passage," Charlie said, looking around until he spied a sign for the White Star Line. All around them, passengers struggled with luggage, sometimes entire families with even the smallest children tugging bags and trunks behind them. The first-class passengers stood out, for they carried not a single bit of luggage; they had servants for that. He looked back at Lady Rose and smiled wryly. Despite her simple gown, it was clear she wasn't like the rest of the steerage passengers, who looked world-weary and disheveled. Lady Rose had an air about her born from years of training that marked her as a member of the upper class. That, and the fact she was wearing a pair of expensive kid gloves that no one in steerage could ever afford.

As they waited in line, Charlie bent down so he could whisper to her. "My lady, I think it would be best to take off your gloves."

She looked down at her hands. "Whatever for?"

"Because they mark you as a lady. And because I wouldn't put it past any of these passengers to steal them from you. Those gloves are worth more than some of these people make in a year."

"Oh, of course. But do you really think someone would steal them?"

"In the blink of an eye. If you have any other valuables, you ought to give them to the steward for safe keeping."

She quickly removed her gloves, and Charlie let out a small groan, for she had revealed delicate, white, unmarred hands decorated with a lavish sapphire ring and an opal that seemed to sparkle unnaturally, as if it were lit from within. At least that's the way it seemed to Charlie.

"Put one of your rings on your left hand, my lady," he said low. "Then turn it so the stone doesn't show. See? Now it looks like a simple wedding ring. Put your other ring in your sack."

Lady Rose gave him an affronted look. "It's not a sack, it's a reticule."

"A fancy sack, then," Charlie said, teasing.

She grinned and held out her left hand, and seeing that band of gold made his chest hurt again. "We're officially married," she said with a grin, and he looked away toward the ticket counter. Stupid to feel a tug in his chest when she said that. He could almost hear Harry chuckling at his foolishness.

"I need another ticket for third class," Charlie said when they reached the clerk. "I decided to get married." He looked back at Lady Rose and winked.

The man glanced at Lady Rose, then shook his head. "Booked solid. Every berth in the married section is taken, nearly a full ship. Can't say I'd want to be in third class with one thousand other souls aboard at any rate. Sorry, mate." He looked down at his log, then to Rose, and said, with odd reluctance, "I could separate you. You with the men, her with the women."

"No," Rose said, clutching at Charlie's sleeve. The clerk noticed the gesture and smiled, likely thinking his "wife" couldn't bear to be apart from him, newlyweds that they were. "What other accommodations does the ship offer?" she asked, sounding like exactly what she was—a lady. The clerk's brows jumped upward and he took a closer look at Lady Rose, as if he might see the blue blood flowing through her veins.

The clerk looked down at his log, brows furrowed. "You're in luck. I've got one second-class cabin available, but it will cost you twenty more quid."

"Twenty," Charlie repeated, feeling slightly ill. That was more than half a year's wage and a large portion of what he was carrying.

"Charlie," Rose had said quietly. "May I have a word?"

He stepped back from the window, just far enough to talk to Lady Rose without the man overhearing. Charlie could picture Marcus going up to this very window and making inquiries about Rose and learning quickly that a lady traveling with a scruffy blond man had indeed booked passage on the *Adriatic*. "Could you please sound less . . ." Charlie struggled for a word, until he finally settled on "hoity-toity."

"Hoity-toity?" Lady Rose repeated. "Did I truly?"

"Yes, my lady, you did. You do know Marcus will murder me if he realizes I have helped you. Any one of your brothers will, of course, but I think Marcus would be particularly brutal. The less attention you can draw to yourself, the better."

She lifted her chin. "And perhaps you should remember to call me Rose. I daresay there are very few husbands traveling in second class who call their wife lady."

"It's difficult," he ground out.

"So is everything about this trip, but we shall manage. Now, please allow me to pay for our passage. While I don't believe I have the funds for first class, I see no issue with you allowing me to pay for second class. After all, you are doing me a very great favor and this is the least I can do. And to be honest, Charlie, I've read terrible accounts of steerage and I cannot tell you how relieved I am that we won't be forced to travel that way."

Hot shame filled him, but he wasn't about to let his pride stop him from allowing her to purchase a second-class cabin. At least Lady Rose—*Rose, Rose, Rose*, he thought with frustration—could avoid the humiliation of the physical exam if she was in second class and would have a bit more privacy.

In the end, he let her pay, knowing it was for the best; she wouldn't stick out like a sore thumb quite as much in second class as she would have in steerage, where passengers slept together in one large room. And if he were honest, sleeping in a large room with a few hundred unwashed men wasn't something he particularly looked forward to either. But he did wonder which would be worse, sleeping in a roomful of unbathed men or sleeping in a tiny room with sweet-smelling Rose.

Rose stood at the rail, clutching it with gloveless hands, her knuckles even paler than her face. *Go back, go back, go back*, she screamed to herself. There was still time; the gangplank was still letting passengers on board, many in tears as they left behind loved ones. Rose's eyes were dry; she was too terrified to cry. She'd sent a telegram minutes before they'd boarded: *I am safe STOP Cannot marry Weston STOP Will wire when destination reached STOP.*

She wondered how long it would take for her parents to receive the telegram and whether they were already in a panic looking for her.

She hadn't left a note, hadn't wanted anyone to know she was gone. No doubt her maid had been the first to realize something was amiss. Sarah had probably been curious, wondering if Rose had gotten up early to go to the stables. Rose had done that on numerous occasions. Did they even know she was gone yet? Or was everyone making assumptions? They'd know soon enough.

Her mother would be devastated, her father livid. And the duke, oh God, it didn't bear thinking. What would a man like Weston do after being humiliated so? She wanted to be glad of her escape, but at that moment, watching as the crew prepared to pull back the bridge onto the dock, she couldn't even revel in that thought.

Rose looked down into the dark, swirling waters of the Mersey, idly wondering if she would survive a jump. When the bell rang, a delicate sound above the murmur of the passengers, the engine came to life, a great deep rumble like some animal stretching and awakening, vibrating beneath her feet. And then the ship began to move and real panic set in and her breathing became shallow. Charlie stood next to her, a calming presence, and once in a while he'd look over, no doubt worried that she was about to do something rash—or more rash than running away. Oh, Lord, this was a horrible mistake.

"We should probably go to our cabin," Charlie said after a time.

She turned to look at him, and she knew her panic was clear in her eyes. "Oh, Charlie, what have I done?"

If she had asked that question thirty minutes ago, he would have likely replied, "Nothing that can't be undone." But now, with the sun setting behind Liverpool and the ship pulling away from port, gaining speed—it was already too far away to safely swim to shore—there was no reversing her decision. "You've saved yourself," he said.

Bless him for saying that. His words, spoken so matter-of-factly, calmed her as nothing else could. She was saving herself. Yes, she was leaving behind a terrible mess, and she doubted her mother and father would ever forgive her, but it was worth it to not have to marry Weston. She had to keep telling herself that. Rose took a bracing breath. "Let's go see our cabin, shall we?"

The mood of the other passengers was solemn and Rose sympathized. They were more like her than she realized, all leaving home, all likely believing they might never see their loved ones back home again. A young couple who stood in front of them while they waited to be directed to their cabin seemed especially sad. The woman leaned heavily upon her husband as she wept.

"It'll be all right, Charlotte, you'll see. We'll come back when we can," her young husband said, but his words only caused the woman to cry in earnest. The man looked back at her and Charlie, giving them an embarrassed smile. "She's got four sisters back in York, you see."

"I have four brothers," Rose said, feeling her throat close up. She swallowed and pushed down the sadness; it would never do to put on such an emotional display in public. If she cried, which she prayed she would not, she hoped to do so in complete privacy. Already she'd made a cake of herself in front of Charlie and she'd vowed that would not happen again.

The young woman turned, her eyes red and watery, her nose pink. She looked the picture of misery.

"I do apologize for making such a scene. I didn't even think to cry until the engines started and then I couldn't stop," she said, laughing a bit. "I'm Charlotte Browne. With an e. And this is my husband, Roger."

"Pleased to meet you, Mrs. Browne. We are Mr. and Mrs. Charles Avery of Cannock." Rose gave Charlie a smile, proud that she'd handled the introductions so flawlessly.

They all stepped forward, closer to the steward. "What takes you to America?" Roger asked. "We're settling there with my brother and his wife. He has a haberdashery in Boston. Not buttons and such. Men's clothing. It's different in America. Don't know why, but there it is. My brother is an excellent tailor and he has a very fine business and could use my help. They left two years ago and convinced us to join them."

"Convinced *you* to join them," Charlotte pointed out good-naturedly. It was obviously something that had been pointed out before, because Roger took her jibe in stride.

"She was excited up until a few minutes ago," Roger said. He draped his arm around his wife, an easy gesture that made Rose slightly self-conscious. She and Charlie were supposed to be married, but they were acting like virtual strangers. Then again, she'd never seen her parents touch one another unless it was absolutely necessary, such as for a dance or to disembark from a carriage, and they'd been married for thirty years.

When Charlotte and Roger were busy with the steward, Charlie leaned in close and whispered, "Are you feeling better now?"

"I'm quite fine, thank you. And but for a momentary lapse, I've been fine this entire trip. Thank you for your inquiry."

He chuckled, deep and low, and something about that laugh made her feel slightly off. "You ought to pay attention to Mrs. Browne. She acts the way a person in second class ought to act."

"I have no idea what you could mean," she said, lifting her chin.

"Ticket, please," the steward said. He was dressed in a smart navy uniform, his shoes polished to an impressive shine, which Rose found oddly reassuring.

Charlie handed over his ticket and the steward directed them to their stateroom.

Rose knew, of course, that their stateroom wouldn't be as luxurious as she was used to, but she couldn't stop a gasp of dismay when she saw it. It was hardly bigger than her wardrobe at home. Two narrow bunks with thin, straw-filled mattresses were crammed on one side, the floor space so limited, Rose had to turn sideways to walk from one end to the other. There were no blankets, no pillows, no window.

"It's meant only for sleeping," Charlie said loudly over the sound of the engines, which felt as if they were beneath her feet. He heaved his bag onto the top bunk, situated uncomfortably close to the wooden ceiling; he would not be able to sit up properly once in bed. He put her carpetbag at the foot of her own bunk. "I expect we'll spend much of the day topside."

Rose felt as if she were slowly being torn apart, as if someone was pulling at the delicate thread of a seam, revealing more and more of her fear. Even Charlie, her dear friend, seemed like a stranger to her. This space was too small to share with a big man like Charlie. It was almost as if she were seeing him for the first time, his large size, his scent, which reminded her of home. In this cold cabin, she could even feel the heat from his body. It was downright uncomfortable and completely unwanted.

She didn't want to feel anything.

"Charlie," she said, sitting abruptly on the hard mattress. "I think I'm about to cry. Would you mind very much leaving?"

She looked straight ahead, staring at the wall, and noticed then that someone had carved a small heart with two sets of initials. It was such a sweet gesture, one likely done by a man who was truly married to the love of his life. She could sense Charlie looking down at her, no doubt with a furrowed brow. She'd seen that look a hundred times when he was caring for one of the horses that had taken ill.

"Of course, my lady." And he made for the door.

"Do not call me that," she shouted, standing so abruptly, she smacked her head—hard—on the top bunk. "Bloody hell. Bloody, bloody, bloody hell." She rubbed her smarting head and glared at Charlie as if it were his fault her head was hurting. "I'm not your lady. I'm no one's lady anymore." She took a breath, horrified that she'd shouted and cursed, horrified that Charlie was now looking at her as if he had, indeed, bludgeoned her. "I'm sorry, Charlie. My nerves are frayed and . . . and . . . you've been so kind and I'm just a horrid person who is breaking her parents' hearts and who is going to America to marry a man who probably doesn't even remember who I am."

"I'm sure he remembers you, my l—" He shook his head hard. "Rose. I'm sure he remembers you. Hell, I can't do it, my lady. It's wrong."

She stood in front of him, hands on her hips. "Say my name, Charlie."

He looked down, his cheeks ruddy. "Rose."

Rose placed her hands on his face and gently lifted to make him look at her, and he met her gaze, his eyes holding some strong emotion—likely anger—before he took a step back and she dropped her hands. "Rose," she said.

"It's a boundary I don't want to cross," he said, sounding slightly put out. Ah, so he *was* angry.

Rose let out a small laugh. "My goodness, Charlie, we're unmarried and sharing a cabin. I think we've crossed the biggest boundary already."

He smiled slightly and finally gave a sharp nod. "Fine. Rose it is."

"Or Mrs. Avery, if you will." She grinned at him, expecting him to smile, but he became even more grim-faced.

"Do you still need that cry?"

Rose thought a moment and shook her head. "Perhaps later. What about you, Charlie? You've left behind your father, and I know you have friends back in Cannock."

"Dad understands." He looked away, and Rose knew it must have been difficult saying good-bye to his father.

Rose hadn't said good-bye at all. Guilt came flooding back, making her almost ill. She would write her family when she reached New York and pray everyone forgave her.

While he waited for Rose to join him in the dining hall, Charlie made fast friends with half a dozen shipmates and saved one young mother by fashioning a rattle out of two spoons for her cranky baby, who was happily banging the contraption against the wooden table where they sat. The fare was edible, if not especially flavorful. But it was plentiful.

The dining area was large enough to accommodate the fifty second-class couples. Already, Charlie felt himself in rather good company, having met a law clerk, a secretary, and a man who claimed he was the finest butler in all of Britain. His wife, a patient woman with a ready smile, rolled her eyes in good humor. "He has a position already," she said, patting his arm. "The son of our master set up house there with his new bride and we've accepted the position. He paid for our ticket, don't you know."

"Could have paid for first class," her husband muttered.

"And have us think we're better than we are? Oh, no, I'm quite happy in second and thankful we're not in steerage." She shuddered.

"Yes, but I can smell it," the banker said, and they all laughed. Charlie laughed, too, but only to be polite. He was only one wealthy lady away from being in steerage, which was where he really belonged.

Mr. and Mrs. Browne came to dinner a bit late, and Charlie wondered if the glow in Mrs. Browne's cheeks told the reason why. He envied them their easy love for one another and he wondered if he and Rose would actually make people believe they were married. He was so damned nervous around her, feeling like some kind of imposter. It was bad enough he had to call her by her given name (his father would want to thrash him within an inch of his life), but to share such a tiny cabin with her was beyond improper.

"Where's Mrs. Avery?" Mrs. Browne asked when she saw him.

"She wasn't feeling hungry, but I expect she'll be out soon," Charlie said, even though he really had no idea whether Lady R—Rose—would be out at all. If he were to slip up in front of these fine folks, he'd kick himself and hard.

"Here she is," said Mrs. Browne, as if she were seeing an old friend.

"Hello." Just the sound of her voice did something to him. How the hell was he going to survive being in the same cabin as her for eight long days?

He thought he'd steeled himself for the sight of her, as he always did when he had advance notice, but she looked so lovely in this unlovely place, he couldn't help but stare. How could she look like a queen wearing an ugly gray dress buttoned up to her chin?

"Have I missed dinner? I thought I didn't have an appetite, but it seems I am quite famished now. What is on the menu?" As one, everyone looked at Rose, then back at Charlie, and he could almost imagine what their thoughts were: How on earth did that man manage to get that woman to marry him?

Charlie didn't sound completely uneducated, but he didn't sound as if he'd been to Oxford or had a tutor or been drilled in comportment either. Hell, had Mr. Browne just sat up a tad straighter? He counted himself lucky that he knew how to read and had learned basic sums. He was not the sort of man a woman like Rose should be with and he had a feeling everyone at the table knew it. Rose looked from person to person, a pleasant smile on her face. "Have I missed dinner?"

Charlie stood and noticed the bemused and curious looks of the other men at the table. None of them, not one, had stood when their wives appeared. But damn if it didn't look like they were all about to launch themselves to their feet. Thankfully, Rose sat next to him and, to his surprise, grabbed his hand and held on as if she might slip away. He looked at her and for the first time realized she was nervous. This girl who had been to balls, who had spoken easily to people at the highest levels of society, who had been engaged to a duke, was nervous. He squeezed her hand gently, trying not to dwell on the fact it was soft and smooth and felt perfect in his.

Within a few minutes of her sitting, a young uniformed man placed a plate of beef stew in front of her.

"It's not awful," Charlie said, and felt like he'd slain a dragon when he earned a small smile. "You probably need this back if you're to eat properly." She turned toward him and let out a small laugh when he placed her right hand onto the table near her fork.

"So, Charlie, what are your big plans when you get to America? Heading west or staying in New York?"

From the corner of his eye, Charlie could see Rose turn to him, no doubt curious about his reasons for leaving. Or perhaps not. She'd never asked him about his plans.

"My uncle works in a restaurant there and he's promised me a job. He's recently made maître d' at Delmonico's."

Rose's face lit up. "I've heard of it," she said, seemingly delighted that she could add to the conversation and apparently forgetting that, as his wife, she would already have been privy to this information. "My friend Caroline wrote me when she first moved to New York. It's a marvelous place and attracts the highest level of society, such as it is in New York." Charlie widened his eyes and tried to convey what he was thinking. It was something like: *shut up now.* Rose saw his expression and snapped her mouth closed. "Of course," she said, with a nervous smile, "we could never afford to dine there. I understand it's quite dear. Caroline married well, you see." Her voice sort of drifted away and Charlie held back the urge to chuckle.

"You didn't know where Mr. Avery was working before now?" Mrs. Browne asked her, her tone light, almost teasing.

A telling blush tinged Rose's cheeks. "I'd forgotten," she said brightly. "Details like that flitter in and out of my brain all the time." She laughed and everyone at the table joined in.

"Perhaps I'll be able to bring home some food from the kitchen and it will be almost as good as sitting down in one of their fancy dining rooms," Charlie said.

They all shared their stories, some expressing a bit of concern over tales of high unemployment, but most seemed to have a well-thought-out plan. Charlie wondered if that was the case in steerage. He knew he was lucky, for he would have a job the moment he stepped off the boat, but scores of others would be on their own. His uncle had written in great detail of the difficulties facing immigrants since the panic two years ago in '73.

After supper, Charlie suggested they go on the deck; the air below was stagnant and, if not completely foul, then unpleasant. Many of the other passengers were on deck, too, but it was rather cold and most didn't last long.

"I very nearly ruined everything, didn't I?" Rose asked when they were standing alone at the rail.

"But you covered nicely, my ... wife." Charlie let out a silent curse. Calling Rose my lady was so ingrained, it was beyond difficult to break the habit.

Rose wrapped her arms around herself, pulling her coat close. "It's rather chilly."

"We'll go below soon."

"I don't mind. The air is so clean. It reminds me of vacationing in Brighton when I was a girl." She was silent a long time before she said, "I'm not doing very well, am I?"

"You're doing fine."

She shook her head. "No, I am not, but I shall try harder. Charlie, why are you going to work in a restaurant? You're a groom, the finest one in Birmingham. Did you not enjoy your work?"

Charlie looked down at his hands gripping the railing. "I did. Very much. But I suppose I wanted more. I never would have been anything other than a head groom, and I'm only twenty-five. Now I can be or do whatever I want."

"And what do you want to be?"

"Rich," he said without hesitation. "Very, very rich."

Chapter 7

Be careful in conversation to avoid topics which may be supposed to have any direct reference to events or circumstances which may be painful for your companion to hear discussed. . . .

—From *The Ladies' Book of Etiquette, and Manual of Politeness*

Though Rose was exhausted, she could not sleep. The throb of the engine and the absolute darkness inside the cabin were driving her a bit mad. Because of the danger of fire, oil lamps were not allowed lit after nine at night. At home, a lowered gaslight was always lit, providing a sliver of light beneath her door, and the only noise she was likely to hear was the sound of crickets outside her window. And she was cold, even wearing her jacket. One would think the ship would provide the bare necessities, such as a blanket and pillow, but those luxuries were reserved for first class.

"Charlie, are you awake?"

"No."

She smiled. "I do apologize, but I cannot sleep and I was wondering how you were managing it. It's the engine, you see. The noise."

"You'll get used to it."

Rose stared up at the bottom of his bunk, unhappy with his reply. She would not get used to it and supposed she would not sleep for eight nights.

"Charlie."

He grunted, and that was enough to encourage Rose to ask her question.

"Are you frightened?"

She heard a rustling sound and a *thump* as Charlie jumped down from his bunk. "I am a bit," he said, his voice so close she knew he had to be sitting on the floor next to her, his back to her bunk. "But I'm excited, too. My uncle wrote that a lot of blokes don't have jobs and I'm one lucky son of . . . lucky man. It will be strange not being in England; it's all I've ever known. In New York, there's all kinds of people. Italians, Germans, Irish, Greek. English, too. All there to find a better life. Sometimes I think there might not be enough better life in America so that we can all find it."

Rose turned on her side and reached out her hand to touch the top of his head. When she was very small, she use to beg Charlie to let her touch his hair and he almost always relented. She called it dandelion fluff because his blond curls were so fluffy and soft, and would pretend to blow the seeds away and make a wish. It was comforting in a way to reach out and touch that softness, that familiar sensation. "You have such lovely hair," she said, moving her fingers as if she were lightly kneading bread. She blew and closed her eyes. "I just made a wish."

He chuckled before saying, "It's a curse. But girls do seem to like it, so I suppose I'll keep it."

She batted him lightly on the head. "Charlie Avery, such vanity. And you shouldn't speak of other girls when you're here with your wife." She laid her hand on his head again. "It's not fair you should have such lovely soft curls."

"You have curls," he pointed out, his voice sounding oddly hoarse.

"But not as pretty as yours," she teased. She was silent for a moment, mulling over all her troubles, her fears. "It's a distinct possibility that Mr. Cartwright will send me packing and I'll return to England in disgrace."

"Is that your biggest fear?"

"No," she said, removing her hand from his hair. "Being forced to marry Weston despite my running away. That's my biggest fear."

Charlie turned so that his arm rested on the bed. It was so dark in the room she couldn't even see the glint of his eyes, but she could sense he was looking at her. "I won't let that happen," he said in a tone she'd never heard him use before. "If I had the power, I would make sure he never married anyone."

Rose frowned. "I daresay there isn't much you could do if Mr. Cartwright does send me away, though I can't imagine Weston would still want me after this humiliation. If he finds out. There is a distinct possibility I'll be home before he even knows I'm missing. He mentioned he was going to London for several weeks and wouldn't return until just before the wedding. Knowing my mother, she will do everything in her power to keep my disappearance from him."

"Surely your parents cannot keep it a secret for too long."

"They are very determined for me to marry Weston. He's a duke, Charlie. I very much fear I've made a terrible enemy; I pray my parents do not bear the brunt of my actions. It was a selfish thing of me to have done."

Rose felt her hand suddenly engulfed in his. "You mustn't say that, Rose. You are not some sacrificial lamb to be offered to that ogre. Is it selfish to want to be happy?"

"At the expense of everyone else, yes."

He pressed her hand against his beard-roughened cheek and Rose stilled. It felt lovely and safe, but somehow far too intimate in this small, dark place. Fortunately, he dropped her hand quickly and turned back around so that he was facing the wall again. Rose hesitated before touching the top of his head again, but the lure of those soft curls was just too much.

"This man you're wanting to marry. Is he kind?"

Rose smiled. "He seemed so. And Marcus likes him, and you know how difficult he is to please." She rested her head on her hand, wishing she had thought to bring a pillow. "I realize it seems a bit mad to travel across the ocean expecting to marry a man one hardly knows."

"Just a wee bit," Charlie said, sounding as if he were half asleep, but when she dropped her hand from his head, he gave a small protest until she returned it.

"Do you think this is a terrible sin, Charlie?"

"Touching a man's hair is perhaps the most sinful of things. So, yes."

"Ha," Rose said. "You know what I meant. I meant me, sharing a room with you. Pretending to be married. Lying. All sins."

"But not bad sins, Rose. Not sins that will make God too angry. And I think He'll understand your reasons."

"This is the most sinful thing I've ever done. Oh, I forgot disobeying my parents. Thou shall honor thy mother and thy father. I'm breaking a commandment."

"A commandment created by man, not by God."

"Charlie, that's not true. Is it?" She could tell he shrugged. "I'll pray extra hard. If I were a Catholic, I'd just tell my sins to a priest and that would be that. Sometimes I think the Church of England should implement something similar. I suppose if God wants to punish me, He'll make me return to England and marry Weston."

Charlie chuckled. "Rose."

"Very good, Charlie," Rose said. "That's the second time you've called me Rose this evening. Yes, what is it?" She could feel him breathe, in, out, in, out. Whatever he wanted to say was apparently not easy.

"What happens between a man and a woman who love one another, or who are at least kind, can be lovely. I wanted you to know that so you wouldn't fear your wedding night if this man does agree to marry you. I don't want you to be afraid."

Rose's throat squeezed shut, more from the way Charlie said those words, with quiet conviction and a concern that truly touched her, than from the words themselves. If the rumors about Daniel Cartwright were true, she would not have a wedding night, which was exactly why she'd chosen him. She'd spent long hours lying in her bed, trying to think of a way out of marrying the duke. Many young women married men they did not care for. But not many married men they feared.

Weston did not love her and she most certainly did not love him. But did that give her the right to do what she had done?

"I'm not afraid," Rose said finally. "Not now."

She was lying, Charlie knew she was. He let it go because he was hesitant to say anything that would stop her soft, warm hand from caressing his head. He knew she didn't realize it was a caress. Likely, it was just as calming to her as it was to him, but he was damn sure it wasn't nearly as erotic. If she knew that her simple innocent touch was driving him mad with need, she'd never touch him again. It was the worst sort of torture, but one he was willing to endure. For a lifetime. He could stay where he was forever, sitting on this cold, damp floor, listening to her talk as she threaded her hands through his hair. He closed his eyes and tried not to picture her hand other places, but he was no saint. Then again, maybe he was.

Charlie had been taught the art of pleasing a woman—and it was an art—by a young widow who found him, as she put it, full of endless energy. For a long time, Charlie thought all women were like Rhonda Smithers, finding as much pleasure in the bedroom as he did. And Lord above knew he did. He hadn't been with Rhonda for more than a year, since she'd left for Cornwall to care for her ailing mother, and as he wasn't one to seduce innocent women or cuckold married men, it had been a while since he'd enjoyed the pleasure of a woman.

"Charlie, how do you know?"

Charlie tensed a bit. "Know what?"

"You know, with a woman. I didn't know you had a sweetheart."

"I'm twenty-five years old, Rose."

She let out a sound that very much resembled a snort. "That's not an answer."

"That's all the answer you're getting."

She pulled his hair just enough to sting, and he smiled. When they reached New York, they would say good-bye, and it was unlikely they would ever see each other again even if she frequented Delmonico's with her new husband. He'd be working in the kitchens and storeroom, not out front, though his uncle had said if he were "as pretty" as his father was when he was young, the owner just might promote him to waiter. Charlie had no desire to be a waiter or anything at Delmonico's for long; a man didn't get rich working in a restaurant.

That first night aboard ship set the pattern for much of the journey. The two would talk late into the night until exhaustion finally overtook Rose and she was able to fall asleep. Charlie would take up his position on the floor, their heads close together so they wouldn't have to shout, and talk about what they thought New York would be like, books Rose had read, their childhood adventures. So many conversations started with Rose saying, "Remember the time . . ." Many times, Charlie hadn't remembered until she related the story.

"Charlie."

She'd been silent for perhaps ten seconds. Rose knew she was likely driving the poor man crazy with her talking, but he never complained or hinted she was bothering him. She simply couldn't bear to lie there listening to the throbbing engine. She'd imagine it sounded as if it were saying something, like Go home, Go home, Go home. And no matter how much she tried, she couldn't make it stop.

"Yes, Rose."

She smiled. There was something about the way he said her name, a certain hesitation that told her he still resisted calling her by her given name.

"Remember the time I caught you in the loft with our governess?"

"Now that's one I remember. You saved me from a terrible mistake, Rose. I was only seventeen and Miss Talbot had found herself in a difficult situation."

"Do you mean what I think you mean?" she asked, more shocked than she could express. Miss Talbot had been such a stickler about propriety, and as a little girl, finding her alone with Charlie hadn't really been Rose's concern. Finding her sitting on a pile of hay in the middle of the day when she was supposed to be preparing Rose's lesson was the true shock.

"Yes. She was let go shortly after, remember?"

"Do you mean to say she was already enceinte and she was trying to make you think that you . . . Oh, that's terrible. Why you?"

Charlie laughed. "Because I was seventeen, had a decent enough position, and I was ready and willing. And she was a very desperate lady."

"Really, Charlie, have you no shame?"

"*I* wasn't doing anything wrong," he said with mock affront. "She was trying to entrap *me*."

"But you were willing. That sort of activity outside the confines of marriage is a sin."

"Not a very big one and not one very many people avoid. And of course, who wouldn't be willing?"

"I wouldn't," Rose said, sounding a bit more morose than she'd meant.

"You'll change your mind about all that, no doubt."

Rose wondered if she would. It was highly unlikely, given that just the thought of kissing a man made her slightly ill. Unfortunately, every time she tried to picture it, she saw Weston's leering face, his too-thick lips, his . . . She squeezed her eyes closed as if that would banish the images. It was just as well she wasn't going to have to worry about kissing and men and all that bedroom activity. If Mr. Cartwright was indeed not interested in women. What would she do if it turned out all those rumors were wrong and he still wanted to marry her? Not two days ago, she'd congratulated herself on being the cleverest woman she knew when she'd come up with her plan. "I do believe my mind is made up," she announced with certainty.

"That's because you've never wanted to be with someone. When you do, you'll change your mind."

"I never will."

She heard a rustling sound that meant Charlie was turning to look at her. "What about when you are married?"

Rose's face heated. "I really do not want to discuss this any further," she said, sounding very prim. "It is a highly improper conversation."

"Even with your husband?" Charlie asked, clearly teasing.

"You are not my husband, thank God." Charlie turned around suddenly and Rose had the feeling she had hurt him. "I didn't mean that to sound quite so awful."

"No matter. I've thicker skin than that." But he sounded off, and Rose frowned.

"I'd make a terrible wife in truth, Charlie. I don't know how to cook or clean or do any of those other things a husband demands." Rose found herself wincing. She had not meant that to come out quite the way it had, and found herself quickly explaining to a silent, inscrutable man. "That's not what I meant. It's not that I wouldn't want to. With you. But of course I don't. It's nothing against you. You're a fine-looking man and I imagine any woman would . . . Oh, God." She slapped a hand over her mouth to stop herself from saying more.

"My lady," Charlie said, putting things to rights by using her title. "I know what you meant."

"Do you? Because I don't. Oh, Charlie, I'm so confused."

He chuckled, and Rose resisted the urge to give him a smack.

"You've been through something, Rose," he said quietly. "And it's going to take some time to get over it. But someday quite soon, you'll be back to your old self, kissing your beau and looking forward to walking out with your new fiancé."

Rose snorted. "Kissing a beau."

Charlie turned back around and said quite near, "What is so amusing?"

"Nothing," Rose said quickly.

"You've never been kissed, have you?"

"Of course I've been kissed."

"Where?" Charlie demanded, clearly not believing her.

"At my ball," she said with a small sniff. "And other places, of course."

"Not where as a place, but where on your person? Cheeks and hands don't count."

"Oh," Rose said, slightly crestfallen. "Then I've been kissed a dozen times at least."

"Liar."

"Charlie Avery, how dare you say such a thing? You are hardly in a position to know whom I have kissed and whom I have not kissed."

"True enough," he said, sounding rather grumpy.

Rose let out a sigh. "I was lying. I haven't been kissed." This was said so quietly, Rose was fairly certain he wouldn't be able to hear her.

"I thought so."

She stuck her tongue out at him even though it was far too dark for him to see. "It's all a bit of nonsense at any rate. Kissing and romance and all that. It's nothing I'm interested in. Not one bit. When Weston showed interest in me, I was so relieved I wouldn't have to participate in the husband search any longer. I pity girls who fancy themselves in love."

"Do you really?" He sounded almost sad.

"Of course. For one, it's impractical, especially for the aristocracy. Marriage is a business matter, an arrangement. Love only complicates everything."

"You sound like you're repeating something you've heard a dozen times, Rose. You cannot truly believe that. What of your brother and his wife?"

"Marcus?"

"No, Adam. He and his wife seem to like each other enough."

Rose pursed her lips; Charlie was right. Adam and Georgette loved each other madly. Marcus, on the other hand, did not seem nearly as happy in his marriage. Still, she recalled his courtship and it certainly had seemed as if he and his fiancée had adored one another. "I suppose they do," she said reluctantly. "But they are newly married. I rarely see couples who've been married for any length of time staring into one another's eyes like lovesick calves. I've never seen my parents touch each other in affection and certainly never saw them kiss."

"That's too bad," Charlie said softly. "Kissing is lovely."

Good God, now all Charlie could think about was kissing her. Kissing her long and deep, thrusting his tongue into her mouth, tasting her. She had the most beautiful mouth, soft and pink. He didn't know how many times in the past year he'd caught himself looking at her mouth. Thank goodness she was blissfully unaware.

It seemed as if everyone on board ship knew he was completely gone over his "wife" except for the lady in question. Roger Browne had nudged him on more than one occasion when he'd caught Charlie staring at Rose with less than pure thoughts. "You don't have to wait until bedtime to use your stateroom," he'd said with a wink. Charlie had given the man a weak smile, envying his married state fiercely. Imagine having a wife who was willing any time he was? Who loved him and couldn't wait until they were alone. More than once, he'd seen the Brownes give each other a look, and then disappear after saying a polite farewell.

It was such a mistake to look at Rose, to imagine kissing her, because his body would react in an obvious way, leaving him aching and uncomfortable. He simply couldn't stop himself. He needed some release, but privacy on board ship was nonexistent and he certainly couldn't take care of himself with Rose in the same room. Charlie was on edge, and talking about kissing was enough to make him harder than hell, enough to make him more reckless than he should be.

"Maybe your first kiss should come from a friend and not a beau." Damn, he'd actually said that aloud.

Her silence was answer enough. He'd no doubt disgusted her. Had he forgotten who he was? He was not her friend, he was her servant. His mortification made him physically ill. Maybe she hadn't heard him?

"Do you think so?"

It had been a full minute between his comment and her answer. A full minute of gripping his legs with shaking hands, so horrified was he that he'd actually uttered those words aloud. And now she had answered him. In a matter of speaking.

"It would mean nothing, you see. Probably a very bad suggestion." He held his breath, his entire body taut, not knowing what he wanted her to say. Of course, he wanted to kiss her, but he wanted to *kiss* her, not pretend it was some sort of lesson. Then again, he really wanted to kiss her no matter what the reason.

"Yes. Very bad." She didn't sound at all certain. "But if we did kiss, at least I could honestly say I'd *been* kissed. Should anyone ask."

The relief that Charlie felt was nearly dizzying. "Very true. And I'll let you kiss me, so there will be no doubt about who is kissing whom."

"Oh, Charlie," she said, almost sounding weepy. "You are the kindest man I know."

Guilt gnawed at him, but not enough to change his mind. For nearly two years he'd imagined what it would be like to kiss Rose, and now he finally had his chance. He turned, his left arm resting on her mattress, the other straight by his side, right hand pressed flat against the rough wood floor. Then he felt her hand, just one, spanning his cheek, her fingertips at his jaw so that she might pull him toward her if she wanted to. Instead, she moved forward, keeping him still, until her nose butted up against his, making her laugh.

"You have to tilt your head just a bit," he said, trying to keep his voice from shaking. He closed his eyes, even though it was black as pitch in the room.

"Tilt," she whispered, her mouth so close to his, it was all he could do to keep that hand planted firmly on the floor and not drag her to him. And then, heaven on earth found him when her lips touched his, soft, hardly felt, but by God the most glorious thing that had happened to him in his adult life. She withdrew and he could almost picture her face, with her brow likely furrowed. It had not been much of a kiss. "There, we've kissed," she said, but she was still so close he could feel her soft breath against his face.

"Have we?"

"Haven't we?"

"We've touched lips. We have not kissed."

"Isn't that the same?"

Charlie chuckled. "Let's try again. I'll show you, just a bit, and you can stop anytime you'd like." *But please, please don't stop, at least not too soon.*

This time, she pulled him toward her and planted her lips against his. "Now what?" she asked against his mouth, her voice slightly muffled, and he smiled.

"You're smiling. Don't laugh at me, Charlie."

"No. I wasn't."

He moved his mouth, just a bit, just enough to show her how it was done, this kissing stuff. He pulled at her lower lip and he thought he heard her gasp, but the engine noise was too loud and he couldn't be certain. He teased her, first her bottom lip, then her top, then slanted his head a bit more, deepening the kiss just a bit, just enough to show her but not enough to frighten her.

When she moved her lips against his, finally, finally, he fisted his hands to keep them where they were, for his body was screaming to pull her close. She sighed—he felt it more than heard it—and he pulled back more for self-preservation than anything else.

"There. See? It's not awful." He knew his voice sounded hoarse, his tone gruff, but he couldn't utter a gentler sound at the moment.

"No, not awful," she said, sounding far less affected by the kiss than he. "Thank you, Charlie."

Thank you, Charlie. It felt like a punch to his gut, those words. Because they were uttered precisely the way she would have thanked him for saddling her horse or handing her up. Thank you, Charlie.

He had to leave, had to get out of this room where his stupid desires, his foolish dreams seemed to be laughing at him. What the hell had he been thinking? That he could trick her into kissing him and then she'd fall head over heels in love with him and want to marry him instead of some wealthy American stranger?

He stood and climbed up on his bunk, staring blindly at the ceiling, and waited perhaps five minutes before saying, "I'm going to get some air, my lady. I'll be right back." He jumped down from his bunk and walked out of the tiny cabin, not aware that he'd called her my lady until the door was shut. How quickly he reverted to the servant when he was treated like one. In that moment, as he pressed the back of his head painfully against the stateroom door, he hated himself. He hated what he represented, he hated his lust and love for

Rose, he hated the fact he was poor, that his hands were rough, that his boots were dull and worn. Charlie stalked around the common room, finally settling at a table, alone in the dark, unwilling to return to the stateroom where he would have to listen to her lilting voice, breathe in her perfect scent, wish he could lie next to her.

Thank you, Charlie.

Bloody hell, if he wasn't the biggest fool on the face of the earth.

Chapter 8

Your mode of address to servants must be decisive, yet mild. This should be tempered with kindness, when circumstances call it forth, but should never descend to familiarity. For no caution is more truly kind than which confines servants strictly to their own sphere.

—From *The Ladies' Book of Etiquette, and Manual of Politeness*

Thank you, Charlie.

Was that truly what she had said? Perhaps she could have said, "Thank you, Charlie, for confusing me utterly, for making me doubt my plan, for making me feel things I've never felt before and no doubt will never feel again." It wasn't his fault. She was the one who'd asked for a kiss, and it had been glorious. The fact that it had been glorious and she was thinking about kissing Charlie again only made everything more confusing. One didn't kiss the Charles of the world. They were as off-limits to her as she would be to them.

She had always been aware, on a certain unemotional level, that Charlie was a good-looking man. But it had very nearly been like having handsome brothers. She could acknowledge her brothers were stunningly good-looking, like appreciating a painting. She simply had not thought of Charlie in that way. Until now. Until he'd pressed his beautiful mouth—and it *was* beautiful (another thing she hadn't truly noticed)—against hers and kissed her. Perhaps the most horrible thing was that she wanted another kiss. And that would be so, so wrong.

Rose gnawed on her knuckle, horrified by what she was feeling.

She was also excruciatingly aware that Charlie had called her my lady before he'd left, a marked reminder that what they'd just done was not to be repeated. Level heads would have to prevail, and she thanked goodness that Charlie possessed a far more level head than she. Had he left because he was embarrassed by the kiss? Remorseful?

Sometime during the night, Rose fell asleep, only to be awakened by Charlie entering their stateroom and announcing breakfast was being served. She sat up carefully, rubbing her bleary and burning eyes, and scowled at Charlie for no other reason than that he looked entirely too chipper this morning. She wasn't even certain if he'd returned during the night and gotten any sleep at all. He certainly looked well rested. And handsome, with that glorious curling blond hair, scruffy three-day beard, and the most piercing blue eyes she'd ever seen. . . .

What was *happening* to her? She'd known Charlie her entire life and never thought of his eyes as piercing.

"Every morning it's nearly impossible to get you up and we nearly miss breakfast, which, if you haven't noticed, is the only meal of the day worth eating."

"I'm up," Rose said, sounding grumpy and tired—because she *was* grumpy and tired. She stood and was face-to-face with Charlie, her eyes perfectly even with his beautiful mouth. Ridiculously, she found it difficult to breathe.

"My lady."

She immediately looked up, blushing hotly. "Rose, Charlie." She lifted her chin and pretended her insides weren't a jumble of nerves.

"Rose, that kiss. I should like to apologize. It was wrong."

Rose shook her head. "I kissed you, if you recall. No apology is necessary." He took a step back, as if he was afraid she might launch herself at him and press her mouth against his. "Of course, it won't happen again. It was improper, given our circumstances."

Charlie stiffened, but Rose forged doggedly ahead. "I do appreciate the effort, Charlie, truly I do. I wouldn't want you to think I am unappreciative. I also realize kissing me is outside the purview of your responsibilities and I recognize that if anyone needs to apologize, it should be I, for having put you in the position of being unable to refuse my request."

Charlie said something beneath his breath and his blue eyes

snapped with what looked a lot like anger, but he was so quick to recover, Rose couldn't be certain.

"I beg pardon, Charlie? I didn't quite hear what you said."

"I don't want there to be any misunderstanding, Lady Rose. I kissed you because I wanted to, not because you asked me to. When I kissed you, I was not your servant, I was a man who wanted to kiss a woman. More fool I. If you'll excuse me."

Ah, so he was angry. Quite angry. Rose watched in dismay as he spun around and stormed out of the stateroom, leaving her behind with her mouth slightly open in shock. She ignored his anger, his hurt, everything he'd said except one thing: *I was a man who wanted to kiss a woman.* For some reason Rose didn't want to examine too closely, she smiled and her mood brightened considerably. And she was starving.

During the first few days of the trip, Rose kept mostly to Charlie's side, but as the days progressed she found herself more and more in the company of the women on board, and in particular Charlotte Browne. Rose, as any young lady would, was well-schooled in the fine art of being a lady. As such, her needlepoint skills were excellent and she was pleased to teach Charlotte some of the more intricate stitches she had learned. The older woman was pleasant company and Rose felt guilty about lying to her. She was thankful Charlotte planned to live in Boston rather than New York, for that meant there was far less chance they would ever run into each other. How would she explain her "new" husband if they chanced to meet?

The two would spend long hours on the deck talking about their families. Charlotte with her four sisters and Rose with her four brothers, had endless stories to tell. It was rather nice to share her life with someone who didn't know her, and it was profoundly comforting to talk to her about her brothers and introduce them one by one. Being on a ship produced an honesty and forthrightness that Rose had never experienced before. She had always been careful not to put anyone she knew in an ill light, but Charlotte didn't know any of the characters in her story, so Rose found herself divulging things she wouldn't have dreamed of telling someone back home.

"Marcus is terribly unhappy, I think," Rose said. Odd, she hadn't really ever thought about Marcus as being unhappy until she started talking about him with Charlotte.

"Oh?"

"It's his wife. She's quite nice and pretty and very friendly."

"She sounds awful," Charlotte said, laughing.

Rose pressed her lips together, unused to saying anything unkind about anyone. But it somehow felt so good to be honest for once.

"I think she's a bit too friendly. With everyone. She adores being the center of attention."

Charlotte's eyes grew wide and she stopped stitching. "With men you mean?"

Rose furrowed her brow and examined a flower she'd just added to her project. "I have no suspicions whatsoever and feel awful even hinting at any impropriety, but yes. She's constantly surrounded by men and I think Marcus pretends not to care, but he does. I can see it in his eyes." She stopped a moment, wondering if she should divulge her greatest concern about Marcus's wife. "And I fear she drinks rather too much."

"Oh, dear."

"I thought she would be perfect for him. He's the oldest, you remember, and so full of responsibility and his duty. Eleanor was light and air. She made him smile more than I ever remembered seeing him smile growing up. But now . . ."

"Now?" Charlotte prompted.

"He almost never smiles. I fear she's broken his heart."

"That's terrible. Marriage can be so wonderful; I can vouch for that. But I have seen couples that seem so wrong for one another."

Rose was quiet for a long moment, idly wondering if Charlotte thought she and Charlie were right or wrong. It was a silly thought, but Rose was curious. "What do you think of Charlie and me?"

Charlotte burst out laughing. "Let's just say I can tell you two are newlyweds. He reminds me of Roger when we first got married. I remember my mother telling me, 'He's smitten with you, Charlotte. I don't think I've ever seen a man as smitten as that one.' And of course, she was right. He was. And I was. We still are," she said softly. "He's a wonderful husband." Charlotte winced a bit and kneaded the back of her head.

"Perhaps we should stop our needlepoint lesson today."

"I have developed a bit of a headache. If you don't mind, I think I'll take a little nap."

Rose stood. "Of course." Rose buttoned up her coat and walked to the railing, where the wind was strong and had a decided bite to it. All the nooks and crannies on the deck were filled with those well enough to partake of the air. Below, many poor souls were sick and dared not venture forth on deck. Neither Rose nor Charlie had suffered anything but the mildest discomfort, but others had not fared so well. She wondered if Charlotte were finally succumbing to seasickness.

They had just three days left before reaching New York. By now, Mr. Cartwright had likely gotten over the shock of receiving her telegram announcing her imminent arrival. She'd been brief and vague about her visit, writing only that she would be arriving in New York on April twenty-ninth and would be going directly to his residence "to discuss a matter of great importance."

Her parents had no doubt determined that she had departed for some parts unknown, for the telegram would have told them that it had been sent from Liverpool, but her name would not be on the ship's manifest as she was listed only as Mrs. Charles Avery. She prayed whoever was sent to fetch her didn't look at the manifest too closely and recognize Charlie's name. They would be looking for Dunford and would not find that name aboard the *Adriatic*.

Rose stayed on deck as long as she could, until the cold wind forced her below. The second-class salon was filled with couples, playing cards or cribbage. In one corner, an older man had brought out a violin and was playing softly to a small group. She found Charlie surrounded by a group of men, apparently fascinated by whatever he was doing. Edging closer, she craned her neck to see what was so interesting, only to discover that Charlie was holding one of his inventions—a device he'd created to remove horseshoes. Charlie was always creating odds and ends with the help of the village blacksmith. He would draw a picture and the blacksmith would create it. Charlie had created a dozen tools that made his life easier caring for horses.

"You should get a patent for that. It'd make you rich."

Charlie snapped his head around to search for the man who'd spoken. "And why would getting a patent make me rich?"

"If you have a patent, you could make more and no one could copy your idea."

"And where would I get the money for the materials and the labor to build them? I doubt I even have enough money to pay for the patent." Charlie laughed. "I'll tell you what, though, that's an idea I'm going to put away for later. Who knows, maybe this little thing will make me a rich man. And if it does, I'll have you to thank and make sure you get your share. What's your name, sir?"

The young man blushed. "Arthur Slater. I'll hold you to that."

Charlie laughed again. "I'm afraid that promise is a bit like a rooster promising an egg, but it's nice to think about, now, isn't it?" The men chuckled and Rose smiled, feeling unaccountably proud of Charlie. He looked up then and caught her eye, his smile slipping a bit before he recovered. "If you'll excuse me, lads, my wife is here to fetch me."

He walked toward her, looking at his horseshoe tool thoughtfully, as if he'd never considered it might have any value to anyone else but him. As they walked toward the other end of the dining hall, Rose said, "I didn't really come to fetch you. I was curious what you were talking about that was so interesting to the other men. I had no idea men could be fascinated by a tool."

"Neither had I."

"I think you should try to patent it, Charlie. I can think of no reason you should not."

"Perhaps," he said, sounding dispassionate, but he took another long and thoughtful look at the tool before shoving it into his pocket.

That night, Charlie had the most erotic dream in his memory and woke up to the blackness of the stateroom with a painful erection and no way to assuage it. He was almost embarrassed, for in his waking moments he never would have allowed himself to think such carnal thoughts about Rose. Oh, he had carnal thoughts, but his dream had been downright indecent; he hadn't known his mind could actually conjure the images it had, at least not with Rose as the centerpiece of this lust. Now he'd be tortured with those images—real or not—in his waking moments and he knew it would be some time before he'd be able to get those thoughts out of his head. Hell, he could practically still taste her, the dream was so real. She had been so responsive, coming around him over and over, hot and pulsing, pleading with him to keep pleasing her. When he'd awoken, he'd been very near release. For several long minutes he relished the aftermath of the images, finally letting out a groan of pure frustration. He would never have her that way, never bury himself inside her, feel her slick heat, taste her arousal. Tease her nipples with his tongue.

"Jesus," he said, rather too loudly.

Rose sat up and Charlie winced at the clear sound of her hitting her head against the bunk. "Charlie, what's wrong?"

She stood so her head was even with his, and by God, it took more strength than he knew he had not to put his hand behind her head and kiss her until the dream came true. He could picture her, her brown eyes drowsy from sleep, her hair pulled back in a messy braid, her lips soft and plush. He said another silent curse. "Just a nightmare," he said gruffly.

He'd hoped that would be enough explanation and Rose would settle back to bed. It was a futile thought.

"It must have frightened you quite a lot. What was it about?"

"I don't remember."

Rose laughed, clearly not believing him, and for one small moment he weighed telling her precisely what his dream had been about. Perhaps then she would stop pestering him.

"You don't have to tell me if you don't wish," she said pertly.

"I don't."

"Good night, then." She didn't move, and he could still feel her soft breath against his face. "Are your eyes open?"

"Yes." Why was she torturing him?

"Funny how we do that in the dark. We cannot see, yet we open our eyes as if we can."

He grunted and was tempted to roll over and give her his back, but he stayed where he was, mere inches from her soft mouth, telling himself he was a fool to even think about kissing her again. Foolish, foolish thoughts that would lead to nothing except more frustration.

"I'm wide awake now," she said unnecessarily. "Mrs. Browne was ill today and I didn't see her for dinner. I do hope she will be better tomorrow. I missed her company. She did look rather ill."

"I'm sure she will be."

"I wonder what everyone is doing back home," Rose said, not taking the hint that he wanted to sleep. "Do you think my brothers are scouring the countryside looking for me?"

"No doubt Marcus got on the next ship to America to chase after you."

She gasped, and he wished he hadn't said what he believed to be the truth. "Marcus is not stupid, Rose, and when they received that telegram from the Liverpool office, I'm certain they put two and two together."

"That means they know I'm with you."

"Probably," Charlie said, feeling slightly ill. He knew he was just fooling himself that her brother wouldn't have gone carefully over the manifest of every ship to leave port the day they'd set sail. "I only pray he doesn't think we actually got married when he sees Mr. and Mrs. Charles Avery. Or maybe it would be best if he did think we got married. Either way, I'm a dead man for sure."

"Don't say that. I won't let him hurt you. And Marcus certainly wouldn't murder you. He might want to, but he wouldn't."

Charlie laughed. "And how are you going to stop him?"

She laid a hand against his cheek and he closed his eyes, hating that such a simple touch left him reeling. "I'm so sorry to put you in this situation. Once I explain that you saved me, he'll understand."

It wouldn't matter if he had saved her; the only thing that would matter to Marcus was that he had thoroughly compromised his sister by staying in the same cabin with her.

"Of course, it won't matter, will it?" she asked, sounding a bit lost. "Being here, with you, in the same cabin. We didn't think things through, did we, Charlie? I was so afraid, I wasn't thinking about my reputation; I just didn't want to be alone. Marcus will never understand. In my entire life, I've never acted so rashly. I'll die if you are the one who is punished, Charlie. I swear I won't let that happen." She pulled him toward her and pressed a quick kiss to his mouth, sealing a promise he knew she wouldn't be able to keep, even if she tried. She pulled back, just enough so their lips weren't touching. "I'm compromised."

She said it simply, without inflection, and Charlie tensed. "Yes." It was the truth, after all.

"So I suppose it doesn't matter, does it, if I kiss you again?"

He lay unmoving, every muscle in his body singing with a new kind of pain. "I think it does matter, *my lady*." She laughed, softly, rejecting his feeble attempt to remind her who they were, who he was.

"No." She kissed him again, softly. "It doesn't. Besides, it's only a kiss. What harm can that do?"

He ought to show her, he ought to show her what a real kiss was like, what a man who was dying to bed a woman would do to a woman who was practically offering herself to him. She wasn't, his mind screamed, at the same time his cock sprang to painful life and pressed against his breeches.

"Kissing can lead to other things, my lady. Things you may not like."

She was quiet for a long moment and he felt her withdraw slightly, as if repelled by his subtle reminder of Weston. And then, damn her, she kissed him again, her lips so soft against his, teasing him, making him want to respond with every fiber of his being.

"You forget yourself, my lady," Charlie said coldly, desperately.

"No, Charlie." She sounded breathless and her hand on his jaw tightened slightly. "You don't understand. You're helping me to forget."

Bloody hell, if she knew what her words, what her touch was doing to him, she'd stop. Then, without thinking, he reached down, grabbing her beneath her arms, and hauled her up on top of him, ignoring her shriek. She lay prone upon him, her breath harsh against his face, but she wasn't struggling. "You want me to help *you* forget?" He sounded nearly incredulous. "By God, Rose, what will I do to help *me* forget?" And then he kissed her, the way he longed to, pushing up his hips so there would be no doubt what her innocent little kisses were doing to him. Damn her, but she wasn't repelled. She deepened the kiss, allowed his tongue into her mouth with a groan.

With a will he didn't know he possessed, he gentled, shifted, and turned so that she was no longer on top of him, but rather against the bulkhead on her side. He let his hand sweep down her body, from her shoulder to her back, and then to her round buttock, so smooth and lovely beneath his hand. Only a thin bit of muslin separated his palm from her flesh, a thought that had him stifling a moan. One of her hands went to the back of his neck and held him there as if he would escape. The other was trapped between their bodies and tantalizingly close to his aching cock.

"I'm just a man, Rose. And you're a lovely woman, giving me kisses, telling me to do things I have no right to do. I want you, Rose, in all the ways a man can want a woman. But we cannot. We cannot." He kissed her, as if contradicting his words, sweeping his tongue into her sweet, sweet mouth, relishing the way her breath caught, the way she shyly pushed her small tongue against his.

She pulled back slightly and let out a soft breath. "I know. I'm sorry."

He chuckled. "Now, what have you to be sorry about?"

"As a woman, as a *lady*, it is up to me to put a halt to things. But I have let you take liberties with myself, liberties I should not have allowed at all. I . . . I wouldn't want you to think . . . We are from different worlds, after all."

Charlie stiffened and swallowed—hard. He knew what she was saying, knew it had to be said, but that did nothing to stop the hot humiliation that washed over him. "I'm not thinking about anything"— he said, turning and easing himself off the bunk—"except getting a taste of some fancy tail."

"I've made you angry."

"No," Charlie said, sounding angry even to his own ears. "No," he repeated more gently. "This circumstance, it makes it easy to forget who we are. What we are. I do apologize, my lady. I will not forget again."

"Charlie, that's not what I meant. Well, not entirely. Oh, Charlie, please do not be angry. Please."

He dropped his head, feeling suddenly unaccountably weary. "I cannot be angry with you, my lady."

"Rose."

"I think that's something we'd best forget. When in company, I will call you Rose or nothing at all. But when we are in this room and when we are alone, I will call you whatever I damn well please, and it pleases me to call you my lady," he said. "It's best. My lady."

"Very well." She sounded every bit the lady she was, and Charlie knew, if he was to maintain even a bit of control over his baser impulses, he'd best remember that.

Rose lay awake long after she returned to her own bunk, feeling slightly embarrassed by her behavior and downright awful about making Charlie angry. She didn't know what had come over her. Curiosity, no doubt, and a real wish to discover if she were repelled by all men. Obviously, she was not. Certainly, she'd proven that point if no other, proven she was practically wanton, if she were honest. Or perhaps it was just Charlie and that he was a friend, familiar, safe, someone who would never hurt her. She couldn't imagine kissing another man, not even the very handsome Daniel Cartwright, whom she planned to marry. If he'd have her. Which he no doubt would not.

Stupid, silly girl. What was she going to do when she reached New York? It had all made perfect sense when she was lying in bed, her heart racing with fear. She would escape. She would go to New York, ask Mr. Cartwright to marry her, and he would, eternally grateful that she'd shown up, practically unannounced on his doorstep, to offer her hand in marriage. It all seemed so comical now.

Almost certainly, Mr. Cartwright would pity her, but he would no doubt send her packing and she would head back to port and take the first ship back to England, where she would spend the rest of her ruined life in her parents' near-forgotten property on the Yorkshire moors. She wouldn't even qualify as a companion, not with such a soiled past. She was beyond ruined.

At odd moments, ever since she'd made the fateful decision to run away, her body would be swamped by fear. It would travel from her head to her toes, a black wave of dread that would leave her reeling. No matter how many times she tried to push such thoughts away, the wave would hit her and she'd be left feeling quite ill. It was as if she stood at the top of a steep hill and pushed a granite ball down toward a cherished piece of art. She watched with terrible anticipation, knowing there was nothing she could do to stop what she had done. The moment the ship had left port, she could not reverse her decision.

Rose looked up at the bunk above her, wondering if Charlie slept. She didn't understand what was happening to her, and with Charlie of all people. He was her servant, at least he had been. Not two weeks ago, if she had even thought about kissing Charlie, she would have been horrified. There were some lines one simply did not cross, and she had leapt over that line with pure abandon.

Perhaps the worst of it was, she wanted to again. She wanted to kiss him, to touch him. She liked Charlie, perhaps too much. He was right, of course. Being forced to share small quarters, pretending to be married, created a false intimacy. She remembered when she was sixteen, putting on the play *Romeo and Juliet*. She was Juliet and a young lord by the name of Samuel Lansing had played her Romeo.

They had gotten caught up in the drama of the play and very nearly fallen in love. But once the play and the summer party was over, it was as if someone waved a wand and that feeling disappeared almost immediately. That's what was happening between her and Charlie. She didn't truly have feelings for him. She couldn't.

And yet, even now, when she thought about saying good-bye, her heart ached far more than it should.

Chapter 9

Avoid, at all times, mentioning subjects or incidents that can in any way disgust your hearers. Many persons will enter into the details of sicknesses which should be mentioned only when absolutely necessary. All such conversation or allusion is excessively ill-bred. It is not only annoying, but absolutely sickening to some, and a truly lady-like person will avoid all such topics.

—From *The Ladies' Book of Etiquette, and Manual of Politeness*

The ship had been following the coast for three days now. When the passengers had first spied land a collective shout had arisen, and those who were well enough to be on deck rushed to the starboard side to see what America offered. For three days, it hadn't offered much more than rocky shores and wooded fields. It was certainly a letdown after all they'd heard about this Promised Land. Lately, Rose had taken to wandering listlessly about the ship, missing the company of her friend, Mrs. Browne. Neither she nor Charlie had seen the woman for two days. Rose sat on the opposite side of the ship from Charlie, huddled out of the wind by one of the lifeboats, while he watched the shore.

They were one day from New York and activity along the shore had increased. Houses and larger buildings could be seen from the ship, and the waters had become dotted with fishing boats. Charlie was standing by the rail watching the men fish, though they were too far away to see what sort of fish they were catching, when Roger came up next to him, placing his forearms on the rail, one fist clenched tightly in the other. Charlie looked from Roger's hands to the man's face, knowing immediately something was wrong.

"I could go for some nice haddock about now," Charlie said, testing the waters. He'd found on this trip that Roger was not a talkative man, and when he did talk, it took him a while to ease into what he really wanted to say. And by the way he was kneading his hands together, Roger was a man who wanted to say something.

Suddenly, Roger pressed his fists against his mouth, stifling an awful sound of anguish.

"What's wrong, man? Is it Mrs. Browne? Is she still unwell?"

Roger dropped his hands, kneading, kneading, his eyes bleak and unseeing on the horizon. "She died, Charlie. Yesterday," he choked out. "It weren't nothin'. Just a bad cold, we thought. Didn't even think to call in the doctor. And then, like that, she turned and didn't wake up."

Roger looked at him with red-rimmed eyes filled with terrible grief, and Charlie put a firm hand on his back. "I'm so sorry, Roger. My God."

Roger searched his face, almost wild. "I haven't told anyone, Charlie. I don't want them to know. I don't want them . . ." His throat closed on the last word and he turned away, his hands frantically moving against one another. "I don't want them throwing her overboard. I want to take her to America. She wanted this—despite the tears, it was what she wanted." He swallowed, trying to control his emotions. "I want to bury her in America. I couldn't let them take her. They might, mightn't they?"

"I don't know," Charlie said. "But I won't say a thing, Roger, not if you don't want me to."

"Looks like she's sleeping, it does. Just like she's sleeping." Roger stifled another sob, gripping the rail hard, as if he could stop his grief if only he could hold on to that rail tight enough. "I can't go home," he said bleakly. "I can't go home without her."

A passenger walked by and Charlie took his hand from Roger's shaking back, not wanting to draw attention to Roger's obvious grief. "Can I do anything to help?"

Roger gave him a quick glance. "What's there to do? Just don't tell anyone, please. Not even Mrs. Avery. Promise."

"I promise."

* * *

Charlie left Roger standing by the rail, unable to offer the man any words of comfort that would make a difference. He walked along the deck, nodding to people he knew, his cheeks turning ruddy from the cold wind. He found Rose huddled, shielded from the worst of the wind, in a corner by a lifeboat. She looked up when she saw him and smiled, and just that innocent smile made his chest hurt.

"I wonder where Mrs. Browne is? She can't still be ill," Rose said. Her hair, usually so neat, had escaped its pins so that long strands whipped about her face. It was April, but it felt more like February, and a few snowflakes flew, stinging cheeks and making the gray Atlantic seem even more forbidding.

"I saw Mr. Browne earlier. She's still a bit under the weather and not up to seeing visitors."

Rose frowned. "Poor thing. She must be terribly bored Perhaps I'll check in on her later."

"I wouldn't," Charlie said. "Mr. Browne was quite certain his wife was not up to a visitor. He did apologize, as he knows the two of you have become friends."

Charlie's heart gave a little tug as he watched a smile form on Rose's lips. The two women had been inseparable for most of the trip, the close quarters making for a fast friendship. He couldn't bear to tell her the news, and was relieved that at least that burden had been taken from him by his promise to Mr. Browne.

"She has become very dear to me," Rose said. "I'll no doubt see her tomorrow when we reach New York. Can you believe it, Charlie? America. I'll have to pinch myself when we reach shore."

She put aside her needlepoint and blew on her hands, even though she was wearing a pair of gloves. "I do hope it's not always so cold. Goodness, it feels like winter, not spring."

"I talked to one of the crew and he said this cold snap is unusual. It can snow in April, though, just as it can snow back home. The climate is quite similar, in fact."

A gentleman walked by at that moment, his feet slipping perilously on the slick deck, and Charlie stepped out to steady the fellow. "Steady on," he said, realizing almost immediately the man was unsteady for more reason than just the light snowfall. He reeked of alcohol.

"I'm fine, good fellow. Just fine." And Charlie watched, chuckling under his breath as the man weaved down the deck.

"Was he inebriated?" Rose asked, sounding shocked.

"I believe so." Charlie laughed aloud at the look on her face.

"It's not amusing to be tipsy at ten o'clock in the morning, Charlie."

He shook his head. "I had no idea you were a prohibitionist."

"I'm no Frances Cobble, but I certainly don't advocate public intoxication." Rose sighed.

"Who is Frances Cobble?" Charlie asked, slightly put out that she'd thought the lady was so notorious that he would know who she was.

Rose's cheeks flushed slightly. "She's really an insufferable woman who blames all of society's ills on working-class men who drink. I heard her lecture once, and she inspired tremendous fervor amongst her followers. I agree that too much drink is a dangerous thing, but to point out the weakness of only the lower classes seemed rather wrong to me."

"So, my lady, you are a champion of the lower classes."

Her brown eyes snapped. "Do not mock me, Charlie. If I was prejudiced against the lower classes, which is what I believe you are implying, I wouldn't have agreed to accompany you on this trip."

Charlie nearly choked. "You begged me to allow you to come," he pointed out, trying to sound reasonable.

"Yes, I did. But as a woman who is not prejudiced, I was the one who considered it the less evil option."

Charlie became quite still. Because he knew if he allowed even one muscle to move, he would lose the small bit of control he had over his temper.

"I think this is coming out all wrong," Rose said in a small voice. "Each time I try to explain myself, I sound more and more like a hopeless snob. You know that's not how I truly feel, Charlie."

He looked at her a long while, enjoying the fact she began to squirm a bit in her seat. "I don't know what you feel," he said finally. "You are the product of your upbringing, as am I. The only difference between you and me, my lady," he said as if her title was a curse, "is that I fully believe a man's value should be weighed by more than who fathered him."

"Of course," Rose said, her cheeks flushing.

"You agree?"

She lifted her chin regally, a motion that incensed Charlie even more. He knew why he was getting angry, as much as he knew he shouldn't. But why did she so completely dismiss him as a possible husband, even at her most desperate hour, even when he very well might be her most logical choice? He was a man she knew, whom she liked, but a man so completely inappropriate, even her situation hadn't been quite desperate enough for her to consider him. He knew he was being unfair to her, but it still hurt to know she thought so little of him. "I do agree. You know I do. You're just trying to be ornery, Charlie, and I do wish you'd stop."

"And yet, you would never consider—" He stopped himself, thank God. Wasn't it humiliating enough that he'd already offered to marry her and she'd dismissed his suggestion as if it was the grandest joke, as if such a suggestion was so absurd she never thought, not for one second, that he might have been sincere?

"Never consider what?"

He dipped his head, shielding his eyes from her, for he had a terrible feeling they showed too much. He knew he was upset about Mrs. Browne, about seeing Roger's grief. He was raw and tired and in love with a woman who didn't see him as more than precisely what he was, a servant. Who the hell did he think he was?

Jesus, he'd let this charade muddle his head and make him think things he had no business thinking.

"Charlie? Why do I have the feeling I've made you angry again?"

He chuckled, more at his own stupidity than her words. "Have you ever considered not marrying? Perhaps getting a position?"

Rose looked up at him and wondered if he knew how superior he sounded. Yes, she would simply hang out a sign and get a job. As a woman with no skills other than French and needlepoint, she no doubt could apply to any position and live quite well in a strange city. Was that what he believed? A man had so many more options than a woman. She *had* considered working but, other than servants and shopkeepers, she'd never known another woman with an occupation. Did Charlie think she should be someone's maid? Or perhaps work in a textile mill?

"I have thought about finding a position," she said, and she could see the surprise on his face. "I thought I might look for a position if Mr. Cartwright sends me packing, which no doubt he will do. The problem is I have no skills and no references." Rose hadn't been brought up to do anything except run an efficient household as the lady of the manor, and she would have done that quite well. She knew how to host a party, write polite invitations, deal with servants and shopkeepers—all skills that had been drilled into her since she was out of the cradle. She knew how to play the pianoforte, was excellent at needlepoint, and could carry on a lively conversation when she needed to. She could dance fifteen dances, knew which garment to wear at which time of day, and how to eat a ten-course meal without appearing like someone common. She knew, she realized, how to be what she was—a lady. And with those dubious accomplishments, there really was only one position for which she was even remotely qualified, that of a governess, the most dreaded position of any woman who had any upbringing or education.

"I thought perhaps a governess, but I have no references and very few funds to hold me over until I do find a job. I'm afraid I'll have to return home. I even thought I might sell my jewelry, but the only piece I have of real value is my sapphire necklace. Do you remember it? I wore it on the night of my engagement." She let out a soft sound of dismay. "I can't sell that, Charlie. It was my grandmother's. She's the only one in the family I even like."

A gust of wind whipped around the deck of the ship, finding her despite her relatively sheltered spot. It was so cold and her head was starting to ache from bending it so long over her needlepoint. "I think I'll go below. I'm afraid it's too cold for me. Perhaps I'll take a nap. I'm awfully tired. Perhaps that's why I'm so cranky." She gave Charlie a small smile, hating that he seemed to be still angry with her, though she hadn't any idea why.

"Here," he said, taking off his own jacket and wrapping it around her. It was so warm and smelled so good, of Charlie and home, and Rose suddenly felt as if she might cry.

"Thank you, Charlie." She stood looking up at him, so close that if she got on her toes and leaned forward just a bit, she could kiss him. It would be wrong, of course, even if they were a married couple, for everyone knew how coarse such displays were. Her mother would have been mortified by the public affection some of the men showed their wives on board, arms slung over their shoulders, kissing and holding hands. Rose had been taught such displays set apart the classes, but when Rose saw Mr. Browne putting his arm around Charlotte, she hadn't been offended. She'd been envious. What must it be like to have a man not care who was watching, to have him look at her as if she were the most important thing in the world?

Charlie stepped back, and Rose was grateful he was sensible enough not to encourage her. She could not be sensible, not when it came to Charlie. How had that happened? When had Charlie gone from a dear employee to someone she thought about in ways she'd never thought about another man.

About the time you kissed him, Rose, she told herself.

Chapter 10

A man servant is rarely grateful, and seldom attached.
He is generally incapable of appreciating those advan-
tages which, with your cultivated judgment, you know to
be the most conducive to his welfare.

—From *The Ladies' Book of Etiquette, and Manual of
Politeness*

They reached Castle Garden near the tip of the island of Manhattan the next day as snow swirled around them. Those in first and
second class boarded another, smaller boat, leaving the passengers in
steerage behind to be processed by immigration.

"They have to check them for disease," Charlie explained as their
smaller group was politely escorted from the ship to the ferry that
would bring them to their destination.

Rose, who hadn't been feeling well since the previous day, was
grateful they wouldn't be forced to stay behind with the third-class
passengers, who looked on as they departed with no small bit of envy
and some hostility. Though she was exhausted, she hadn't been able
to sleep. The excitement of the day, the noise of the engine, and all
her worries combined to make sleep impossible. It was no wonder
she was feeling less than well. Her head ached and, despite the frigid
air, she was perspiring beneath her winter coat.

The passengers were excited to finally reach land, and the tears
she'd seen when they'd departed England were nowhere to be seen
now. Which made her think of Charlotte, whom she'd hadn't seen in
three days. She craned her neck but was unable to spot her friend's
familiar red hair amongst those moving about on the ferry.

"Where are the Brownes?" Rose asked, but Charlie was apparently too far ahead of her and didn't hear. He found them a cozy spot to sit inside, their small amount of luggage at their feet. Rose leaned against the bulkhead and looked out a thick window coated with salt, which made it impossible to see anything of the shore. She'd gotten a glimpse of the Castle Garden depot, half expecting to see some sort of castle. Instead, she saw only a large brick building that reminded her of the hospitals for the poor in London. The area surrounding the building seemed bleak indeed, with hardly any vegetation to speak of other than a few scraggly trees, still bare from winter, shuddering in the icy wind.

Rose toed her carpetbag and frowned; she'd left so many cherished belongings behind in her haste to escape. Dozens of gowns and shoes, books and bits and pieces of her life she likely wouldn't see again. Charlie hadn't brought much more than she had, and he'd planned his trip for months. Many of the other passengers had large trunks that had to be carried by stewards from the boat to the ferry, which caused only a small delay. It was clear the men had done this many times before, for they were quick and efficient, stopping to listen to questions from passengers and responding with courteous assurance.

As they sat waiting, Rose's eyes felt unaccountably heavy and her head nodded sleepily.

"You can put your head on my shoulder if you like," Charlie said, leaning toward her, his voice low.

"I couldn't," Rose said, hearing her mother's voice in her head that a lady would never show such weakness in public, nor such demonstrative behavior to a man who was not her husband. She didn't see Charlie's frown, the way he shifted away from her. She leaned her head against the cold bulkhead, clasping her gloved hands in front of her. Her eyes burned, she was so tired.

"Are you unwell?"

Keeping her eyes closed, she said, "Perfectly well, thank you."

Charlie chuckled, though she didn't know why. He would do that sometimes—oftentimes, now that she thought of it—and she never knew why. "Why are you laughing at me?" she asked sleepily.

"Because you could be attacked by a shark and you'd still sound like a lady," Charlie said fondly.

"That's because I am a lady, Charlie. I cannot be what I am not, you know. No more than you can." She said this last so softly, she was quite certain he couldn't hear her. It wasn't that she didn't want him to hear; it was that she simply wanted to sleep.

Rose hadn't realized she'd drifted off until Charlie woke her by jostling her a bit. She forced her eyes open, feeling as if someone had given her a bit too much sherry. Her head felt thick and odd.

"We've arrived, my lady," he said close to her ear, and she smiled because the man still refused to call her by her given name. "New York."

He said it like a prayer, and in a way, Rose thought it was. She was pinning all her hopes on this city, on one man she'd met at a single ball. "New York," she repeated, hoping that if she said it like a prayer, it would have the same power.

"You're flushed, my lady. Are you certain you're well enough to travel?"

"Oh, yes," Rose said, rallying. "Quite well enough, given we've reached our destination. Have you seen the Brownes? I did so want to say good-bye to Mrs. Browne and perhaps exchange addresses with her. I thought I'd have plenty of time for that."

"Perhaps they are on another boat, since they are headed to Boston."

"Yes, of course."

The ferry docked at the East River Pier, and the passengers, despite the frigid and now thickly falling snow, gathered on the deck, anxious to finally set foot in their new home. The snow made it difficult to see the city's skyline, but Rose was able to make out the dim shape of buildings. The port was bustling with activity despite the poor weather, and Rose wondered if hiring a hack in America was the same as hiring a hack in London.

And then, they started moving, a line of people shuffling down the gangplank. Rose's stomach was a jumble of nerves. In just a short time, she'd be standing on the front step of Mr. Cartwright's home, announcing her arrival. She'd sent a telegram, so he knew to expect her, and she fleetingly wondered if he might have even thought to meet her getting off the boat. She looked around the crowded pier, but didn't see anyone she recognized among the dark shapes standing near the gangplank. She had a sudden and awful feeling that she wouldn't recognize him even if he were standing there. Would he recognize her? She would have laughed if she hadn't been so frightened by that thought.

She walked with Charlie, side by side, until they stepped onto the hard dirt. Charlie smiled broadly. "We did it, Rose," he said, laughing aloud and putting a hand on each side of her face. For a second, she thought he might just kiss her, right there in front of the passengers and possibly her future husband. But he dropped his hands and looked toward the city, unable to hide the pure joy he was feeling at reaching their destination.

"Charlie. My God, you've become a man." A distinguished gentleman approached them, and Charlie immediately rushed to him, giving him a strong embrace. "How was your journey?"

"Uncle George, I didn't realize you were coming to meet me. What a pleasant surprise. I'd forgotten how much you look like my father. When I first saw you, I thought my father had put on his best suit and decided to come to America, too."

"People thought we were twins. How is the old man?"

"Well, sir, and he sends his regards." Charlie turned to Rose and made the introductions, and if his uncle found it strange that she was accompanying his nephew, he didn't show it on his face. "Lady Rose, my pleasure," George said with an elegant bow, which Rose found unaccountably comforting, as she'd secretly feared men in America wouldn't know how to behave properly.

"Uncle George, I need to escort Lady Rose to her destination. You don't mind, do you?" he asked, bending to pick up her bag.

"Mr. Avery," she said, using her firmest tone. "You've done quite enough for me. I shall never be able to repay the debt I owe you for acting as my escort on our journey. I wouldn't dream of delaying you further. Please, there is no need for you to bring me to Mr. Cartwright's home. I'm perfectly capable of climbing on and off a cab. But thank you."

Charlie looked uncertain, but Rose had a feeling he didn't want to delay starting his new life by first bringing her to Fifth Avenue.

"You know his address?"

"Eight hundred twelve Fifth Avenue," she said immediately, having stated that address over and over in her head on their journey.

"Are you certain? It would be no imposition, my lady."

"Perfectly certain, Mr. Avery. Look, there is a line of cabs right over there." She held out her hand and Charlie shook it, and something in Rose's heart shifted just a bit. This was not right. This was not how she was supposed to say good-bye, not as if they were two acquaintances who meant nothing to one another. But with Charlie's uncle gazing on and looking a bit impatient about standing out in the foul weather, that brief shaking of hands would have to do. "Thank you, Mr. Avery," she said, looking in his eyes and trying to convey to him just how much it had meant to her, having him keep her safe.

"Of course, my lady." He turned to go, then stopped and looked back. "If you need me, send word to Delmonico's, will you?"

She forced a smile, because at that moment she felt unaccountably like weeping. "I will."

Walking away from Charlie was far more difficult than she would have imagined. It was so strange; saying good-bye to him seemed far worse than leaving home, and she had to stop the insane impulse to chase after him. Instead, Rose adjusted the grip on her carpetbag, lifted her chin, and walked to where a line of hacks waited. Beneath her feet, the snow had turned to a thick slush, mixed with mud, and her practical shoes no longer seemed so practical. As she walked, her shoes proved little protection against the cold, and her stockings and skirts were drenched by the time she reached the first hack. She was not ten feet from the line of hansom cabs, when she stepped in and out of a particularly deep patch of mud, leaving one shoe behind.

"Oh, bother," she said, standing for a moment on one foot as she determined her best course of action. She placed her carpetbag beside her, with her reticule on top, then leaned precariously over to retrieve her shoe. With a bit of triumph, she lifted the mud-covered shoe from its mooring, then plopped it on the ground in front of her and shoved her soaking and freezing foot inside.

"There," she said with satisfaction. She would look a pure mess when she reached Mr. Cartwright's home, but there was nothing she could do about it at the moment. She'd worn her best dress (a far cry from what she'd worn back home, but presentable enough), and now it was stained with mud and water and her shoes most certainly ruined. She bent to pick up her bag and stopped, her heart sinking with dread.

Her bag was gone. Her money, her jewels, her clothes, everything. Rose looked wildly around but saw no one absconding with her things, and no one nearby appeared to have seen anything. Turning, she looked for Charlie, but he'd long since departed the pier with his uncle. Oh, why had she decided to be stubborn about his accompanying her to Mr. Cartwright's?

She stood there for a long moment, feeling completely alone.

With a heavy sigh, and digging deep inside herself to find a stiff upper lip, Rose trudged toward the only cab left still empty; the others had quickly filled with the ship's passengers. It would be humiliating, but she'd have to ask Mr. Cartwright to pay her fare.

"Hello, sir, are you available for transport?"

"I am. Where are you going?"

Rose gave him the address and moved forward to board the conveyance.

"That'll be two dollars."

"Very well. I'll pay you when we reach the destination," she said, waiting for the gentleman to lower the stair so she might board.

"No money, no ride," the man said, folding his arms rudely and looking behind her where an elderly couple and a younger woman waited for another cab to appear.

"Dear sir, I said I would pay you when we arrive, and I will," Rose said, smiling tightly. The man looked her up and down, then shook his head. No doubt she didn't look like the sort of person who would be able to pay cab fare.

"This way, folks," the man said to the people standing behind her, who hurried to take the cab. Within a few moments, their fare was paid and they were on their way, the cab driver shoving his hat down on his head to protect it against the bitter cold and snow. Leaving Rose behind, standing in the slush, feeling unbearably cold, her cheeks red from the biting snow.

Rose waited for a few minutes for another cab, but that driver gave her the same answer. There was nothing left to do but walk. She stopped a dock worker and asked directions, and was vastly relieved that Fifth Avenue was an easy walk down Broadway, "Not more'n five miles." She could walk five miles, certainly. If only she didn't feel quite so ill, it would have been an easy jaunt. As it was, she knew it would be difficult, but no more difficult than anything else had been these past few weeks.

Rose took the scarf that she'd bundled around her neck and lifted it up a bit so it protected her ears from the wind. It was April twenty-ninth. Imagine this sort of weather, and nearly May. She hadn't been here long, but she already hated America.

Charlie sipped his beer and tried to pretend to be happy. His uncle was over the moon about having him travel to America and wanted to hear all the news from back home. George lived not four blocks from the pier, but he wanted to get out of the weather and headed directly to the nearest bar. It was apparent from the greeting he'd received when they'd entered that stopping at a bar "for a little taste" was something he did often. As they settled at the smoothly polished bar, George asked a dozen questions about Hallstead Manor. To be honest, the last thing Charlie wanted to talk about was Hallstead, but as George had spent his youth there in the very same stable where Charlie had worked, he wanted to know all.

"And what was Lady Rose doing, traveling with you like that? Her parents know? I can't imagine they would approve. Where was her maid?"

Charlie couldn't stop the blush from tingeing his cheeks, and of course his uncle didn't miss his discomfort. "She's traveling to be with her fiancé," Charlie said, glad he'd been able to tell his uncle, if not the complete truth, then something quite close.

"Getting married, is she? To an American? Usually it's the other way around. American girls heading across the pond to marry some title."

Charlie grunted noncommittally. He felt hollow inside, as if something important were missing—or had been forcibly removed. Funny, he'd had such stupid hope that Rose might actually see him as a man worth marrying, even before he'd decided to move to America. He'd have cruel fantasies of her looking at him and finally realizing that she loved him as much as he loved her. In those fantasies, she'd left Hallstead and they'd lived in a smart little cottage with enough land to raise horses. How he could have ever thought that Rose would accept such a simple life was beyond him. And to be fair, she had no way of knowing he loved her; even his suggestion about marrying her had sounded like a bit of a joke. The irony of leaving England to get away from Rose only to have her live in the same country was not lost on him. Harry had once asked him if she was the reason he was leaving and he'd lied. She *had* been the reason.

Now, she was gone forever. She'd either marry Cartwright or go home. Either way, he'd probably never see her again and certainly would never feel her soft mouth against his. It would have been better not to have those memories, which would likely torture him for years.

"You start work Saturday," George said. "Just kitchen work for now. Sweeping and washing dishes. But if you're like me, you'll be running the place before long."

"I appreciate the chance," Charlie said sincerely. He knew how difficult it was to find a job like the one his uncle was offering. He took a sip of his beer, thinking only that it wasn't nearly as fine as the ale back home at the Boar's Head Inn.

George, Charlie was quickly finding out, was a man who liked to talk, and his favorite subject was Delmonico's. The food, the staff, the building, the chef, the clientele. As maître d', George had a bit of power over the wealthy patrons who visited the restaurant, and it was clear he relished it. It was he, after all, who could determine if a reservation could be made, a special room reserved, a highly visible table procured. "The mayor himself knows me by name," George said proudly.

But he'd never invite you to his house, now, would he? Charlie would never say such a thing aloud, but his uncle's bragging was getting a bit tedious, so he let his mind wander. He wondered if Rose were safe and warm, sitting before a fire in Mr. Cartwright's home, easing into her reason for traveling to New York. She'd be nervous, and Rose tended to talk a bit quickly when she was nervous. How was Mr. Cartwright taking her proposal? Would he laugh? Just the thought made Charlie's blood burn hot. Or would he fall to his knees and thank God such a beautiful woman had deigned him worthy of her?

A noisy group of men pulled him away from his pathetic thoughts. Back home, the pair he was looking at would have been the type to lift a rich man's watch without his being any the wiser. They had that shifty look about them. The young man, his Adam's apple bobbing as he talked excitedly to his friend, dug into his pocket and displayed what appeared to be a handful of coins. And then he saw, resting on the pub's floor, the familiar sight of a carpetbag with cabbage roses embroidered on the material, thick leather handles, and shining brass hardware. He stared at the bag a long moment, his brow furrowed. What were the chances that the man would have the exact same bag that Rose had been carrying?

And then the man pulled out a necklace, its blue sapphire stones glinting in the lamplight.

Charlie didn't remember moving, but the next thing he knew, his large hand was wrapped around the man's throat, the fellow's Adam's apple jutting into Charlie's palm as he tried to swallow.

"Where the hell did you get that necklace?"

The man just stared at him, his eyes bugging out of his head.

"Answer me," Charlie roared.

"I don't think he can talk wid your hand on his windpipe there, chum." This from the second man, who watched with near amusement.

Charlie adjusted his grip because he had been choking the life out of the scrawny scoundrel.

"Where. Did. You. Get. That. Necklace."

The man panted, clutching one hand to his throat. "Some lady just off the boat. She dropped it. It were just layin' there like she was beggin' someone to take it. So I did."

The roar in Charlie's head made it difficult to understand what the guttersnipe was saying. He didn't care. All he knew was that Rose was in a foreign country, alone, with no money, and no clothing except that which was on her back. Charlie grabbed the hand that was holding the necklace and he squeezed until the man cried out, dropping the necklace to the floor.

"The lady wants her things back, you piece of shit. Now get the hell out of here. If I see you again, I may not be so nice."

The other man grinned. "You might as well do as he says, Nate. This chap looks like he could mop the floor with you. Just off the boat and already itching to kill an American." The man laughed at his own wit. "Come, Nate. Cut your losses, eh?"

Nate gave Charlie a scathing and completely ineffectual look before heading toward the door, straightening his jacket as if he'd been the injured party. "Fuckin' foreigners," he muttered, just before walking out the door.

Charlie picked up Rose's bag and the necklace off the floor. The bag was heavy, which meant most of her belongings were likely still within it.

George came up to him and slapped him on his back. "I think we're going to get along real well, Charlie. What the hell was that all about, anyway?"

"These are Lady Rose's things. And that means she has no money, nothing."

George let out a low whistle. "She was heading to Fifth Avenue? Those cab drivers wouldn't have brought her anywhere if she couldn't prove she could pay."

"You mean she's likely walking?" Something dark and painful settled in Charlie's gut.

"Don't know how else she'd be able to get where she was going, unless someone helped her out. It's a good four miles. Maybe more." George looked out the window at the snow still coming down, blustering in a wind that seemed relentless.

"I'm going to make sure she got to her destination all right," Charlie said, shoving Lady Rose's bag in his uncle's hands and pocketing the necklace. He knew when he found her, she'd only care about the jewelry her grandmother had given her. "Do you remember the address? Eight hundred and something. Damn, I can't remember."

"Eight hundred twelve," George said with certainty, looking at Charlie a bit curiously. "I've got a mind for numbers. That's the address, I'm sure of it."

"Eight hundred twelve," Charlie repeated, trying to stem the panic in his heart. Surely someone had taken pity on her, a woman just robbed, new to America, and wanting a ride. Surely she was warm and safe, maybe already sipping a nice cup of hot tea. He refused to allow himself to picture her walking in the snow, cold and sick. And she *had* been sick, no matter that she'd said she was not. Why had he allowed her to go by herself? He should have demanded that she allow him to accompany her. Bloody hell, if something had happened to her, he'd never forgive himself.

Chapter 11

If your friends are really desirous to have you pay them a visit, they will name a time when it will be convenient and agreeable to have you come, and you may accept the invitation with the certainty that you will not incommode them.

—From *The Ladies' Book of Etiquette, and Manual of Politeness.*

Daniel Cartwright was exhausted and in a foul mood. Having gone directly to Washington, D.C., from England, he was glad to be home but carried with him the disappointment of his work. Nothing had gone as he'd wanted and it looked as though a new trade deal with England would take far longer than his political allies wanted. And, of course, they blamed him and with some good reason.

Now he faced an empty home, a pile of unread correspondence, and rooms that were uncomfortably cold. His staff hadn't expected him so soon and hadn't bothered to light the fires. They were busy doing so now, thank goodness. He headed to his study, the first room to have a fire lit, and settled behind his desk to stare bleakly at the large pile of correspondence that he knew he would have to go through before tackling his next project.

"Sir." His butler, Mr. Brady, stood in the doorway of his study looking slightly put out. No doubt it had to do with Daniel's neglecting to inform Brady that he would be arriving two days earlier than planned.

"There is a man to see you. He says he's from England and is inquiring about a Lady Rose."

Daniel furrowed his brow. "Lady Rose?" he repeated, searching his mind, for the name sounded familiar. "Where is he now?"

"In the foyer, sir."

And that told Daniel at least some of what he needed to know. If the man had been of the aristocracy, Brady would have immediately placed him in a parlor, fire or not.

"I'll see him," Daniel said wearily.

He walked to the foyer to find a man, snow clinging to his coat, pacing and leaving a trail of water in his wake. The fellow looked up when he heard Daniel's approach, his blue eyes slightly wild. Daniel knew one thing immediately—he had never seen the man in his life.

"Is she here?" the man blurted, coming forward, and Daniel immediately stopped, tensing. He had no idea if this stranger meant him harm and felt slightly comforted knowing that Brady had followed behind him.

"Who, sir?"

"Lady Rose Dunford. She sent a telegram. She was on the *Adriatic* and arrived today. She was coming here, but she was robbed and . . ." The man swallowed, clearly distressed. He stepped forward again, his manner almost threatening. "My God, man, answer me. Is Lady Rose here?"

"She is not." Daniel, for the life of him, couldn't imagine why she *would* be. He remembered her now, vaguely, a pretty thing who was about to be married to some duke. They'd talked about a mutual acquaintance, Mrs. St. Pierre, but for the life of him that's all he could remember. "Why would she come here?"

"Because she had it in her head that you'd be agreeable to marrying her," the man growled.

"Good God," Daniel said.

"Mr. Cartwright, if Lady Rose is not here, it means she's out there," the man said, his voice cracking. "I have to find her. She wasn't well and she was walking."

"Walking! From the pier? In this weather?" Daniel turned to Brady. "Get my coat immediately, and have Robert and Phillip report here. What is your name, sir?" he asked.

"Charlie Avery. I worked at Hallstead Manor and escorted Lady Rose here. It's a long and complicated story and I have no time to explain," he said, backing toward the door. "I'm heading south, toward the pier."

"Very well. We'll cover the other directions. We'll find her, Mr. Avery. Have no fear."

Charlie had never felt so desperate in his entire life. Where could she be? It was dark and still snowing, though it was finally coming down slower. It had been four hours since he'd said good-bye to Rose at the pier. Four hours she'd been out in this weather. Perhaps she'd found an inn or hotel along the way with an owner who had taken pity on her. Yes, that had to be it. Because it would not take four hours for Rose to walk five miles, even in this weather.

Unless she was ill. Unless she had collapsed on the streets and lay there now, frozen and dying. Tears coursed down his face and he wiped at them impatiently with his shoulder. He could not give up hope. She had to be somewhere; he prayed she was somewhere safe.

The streets were relatively empty, most people home trying to stay warm. Only a few hardy souls were walking, mostly men, heads bent against the howling wind, hands clasping their hats to keep them on. Each time he saw the shadow of someone walking toward him, his steps quickened, only to slow, again and again. It was so damned cold. A body could only take this cold for so long, especially someone as small as Rose.

Why were there so many human-shaped shadows lining the walk? Everything looked like a prone body, stiff with cold. The gaslight streetlamps gave a weak light, illuminating only the snowy patch beneath them. Charlie stopped, his heart sick. He wasn't going to find her. How could he? She could be anywhere. She could have taken a wrong turn, fallen. It was a huge city, sprawling and completely unfamiliar to her. Her coat had not been thick and warm; she'd not had her warmest hat and fur muff as she should have had in such weather. Her shoes. What shoes was she wearing? Certainly nothing serviceable that could have withstood such wet and cold. No doubt she'd donned her best pair, knowing she would be meeting Mr. Cartwright that day.

He wanted to scream. How could he live if something happened to her? If only he'd insisted he accompany her. Why had she been so stubborn? He clutched the top of his head with his hands and looked around desperately, swallowing down another sob. That's when he saw it, a small dark form on a stoop not thirty feet away. It might be a dog or a statue or even some trash the owner had placed in a sack.

Charlie started walking toward the dark form, trying not to get his hopes too high, and failing. *Please, God, please let this be Rose.*

"Rose," he shouted, and the form moved, making his heart soar with hope. "Rose!"

"Charlie?"

Thank God thank God thank God.

He rushed to her side, afraid to touch her, afraid he was dreaming. "Yes, love, it's Charlie." She looked up at him with a face so pale, his heart stopped in his aching chest. Her lips were blue, her brown eyes glazed and unseeing. Her gloved hands clutched the wrought-iron bars as if they were the only thing preventing her from toppling into the road. Those silly fine kid gloves would do little against the frigid night.

"My God, you're so cold. Here, let me carry you. You're not far. You almost made it. Almost."

He lifted her effortlessly, as if she weighed nothing. He could have lifted her if she weighed a hundred stone, he was that relieved to have found her alive. She wrapped her arms around his neck and he settled her against him, one arm beneath her legs, the other around her back. She draped across him as if just the energy needed to hold on was too much, and he held her close, his chin resting against her shoulder, her head pressed to his neck.

"We'll have you warm and in front of a fire before you know it, Rose. You'll be fine. And Mr. Cartwright, he was so happy to know you'd be visiting. He's out looking for you, too. Are you still with me, love?"

She managed a sound, it could have been a word but he wasn't certain. All he knew was that he had to get her warm and away from the cold wind and snow. He walked more than a mile, his arms aching by the time he reached Cartwright's home. He'd talked to Rose the entire way, but she'd stopped responding and he realized there was something worse than knowing Rose would never love him.

When he reached the house, he climbed the stairs and kicked at the door. Almost instantly it opened, Cartwright's butler there to usher him in.

"Call a doctor," Charlie said, following the butler, who led him toward the second floor and to a bedroom not far from the landing. A fire burned brightly in the hearth, making the room feel overly warm to Charlie. He stood, Rose still in his arms, as the butler tore back the blankets so he could gently place her on the bed. She was soaked through, her cheeks unnaturally flushed, her hair wet and plastered against her forehead.

"Mrs. Fitz," the butler called, walking hurriedly to the door. "We need clean dry clothes for the lady immediately. And someone to assist."

A young maid arrived within minutes, her arms filled with soft, dry clothes, no doubt donated by the staff.

"Sir," the butler said, when Charlie hovered by the bed.

Charlie looked at Rose, not wanting to leave her side. She looked so helpless, so lost, so unlike the woman he knew. He wanted to undo everything that had happened that day, to make her well.

"Sir," the butler repeated, this time with more vigor, and Charlie forced himself to turn away and exit the room.

Downstairs there was the commotion of some of the footmen returning, and Charlie hurried down to let them know Lady Rose had been found.

"I found her," he called, and the men let out a collective cheer. Charlie went to the foyer and stopped directly in front of Mr. Cartwright. "Sir, if I might have a word with you."

"Of course, this way." Cartwright let him to a large study where thankfully another warm fire glowed. Charlie was soaked through, his hands starting to hurt from the tingle of his blood returning to them. When they were inside, Cartwright motioned for him to sit, which Charlie did gratefully. He was suddenly exhausted and more worried about Rose's welfare than he could admit to this man.

"If you could please explain to me what Lady Rose is doing here, I would be grateful," Cartwright said.

"She sent a telegram," Charlie said. "Did you not receive it?"

"I've just arrived myself," Cartwright said, shuffling through his correspondence and unearthing the telegram, which he quickly read. "This says only she is coming to New York to visit. I may have been imagining things, and I sincerely hope I was, but I believe you said something about her wanting to marry. Me."

"Yes," Charlie said. "She got it in her head that you would make the perfect husband for her and that you would be agreeable."

The man looked amused and baffled. "Why on earth would she think that?"

Charlie shrugged. "I couldn't say."

Letting out a sigh, he stood and headed for a sideboard where a decanter of some dark liquor sat. "Brandy, Mr. . . ."

"Avery," Charlie supplied. "And yes."

Cartwright poured, then walked over to where he sat, handing him the thick, crystal glass. It occurred to Charlie that a man of such stature had never waited on him before, nor had he ever held such an expensive glass in his hand. No doubt the brandy was fine as well. He took a sip and sighed. Damned fine.

"You must realize my confusion, Mr. Avery. I met Lady Rose on the night of her engagement. And here she is, in my home, hoping for a marriage proposal. I couldn't be more surprised than if you told me you had a live elephant in your pocket."

Charlie looked down at the carpet, decorated with swirls and finely rendered flowers, and weighed how much he should tell Cartwright. It was Lady Rose's story to tell, but Charlie felt he should at least hint at her desperation. He wanted, if nothing else, for her to be safe, and this man sitting across from him seemed kind and even-tempered. And he had immediately set out himself to help find Rose.

"She was desperate," Charlie said at last, keenly aware that Cartwright had remained silent while he thought. "She was to marry the Duke of Weston, but he . . ." Charlie stopped and looked up at Cartwright, who sat, staring evenly at him, waiting for him to continue. "He hurt her," he said finally, and saw Cartwright flinch slightly.

"Hurt her. How do you mean?" he asked, his voice low but forged with steel.

Charlie shook his head, not wanting to say anything more.

"Did he rape her?"

It was Charlie's turn to flinch. "He wouldn't be alive today if he had," he said, and was gratified to see Cartwright give him a nod. "But he . . ." Charlie could not say it. He couldn't.

"Did he force her to do something unpleasant?"

Charlie swallowed, feeling sick. His chest felt as if it were on fire, and all he could do was nod.

"That explains it then." Cartwright said the words without inflection, but it didn't explain anything to Charlie, so he was slightly baffled how it could explain anything to this man. Cartwright took a sip from his glass and stared at the amber liquid for a long time before chuckling slightly.

"I fail to see anything amusing."

"I'm glad you do not," he said mysteriously, then sighed. "Lady Rose is a smart girl, if a bit naive." He shook his head, smiling, and for the life of him, Charlie couldn't imagine what the man was thinking. It was as if he was having an entirely different conversation from the one Charlie was participating in.

Brady appeared at the door of the study and knocked, even though both men looked up at his entry. "Dr. Landsdowne is here, sir. Shall I bring him to the lady?"

Charlie immediately got to his feet. "Yes," he said, but the man maddeningly looked to Cartwright for an answer.

"Of course, Mr. Brady. Show him up immediately."

Charlie felt a small bit of panic building in his chest. "Is he a good doctor?"

Cartwright gave him a sharp look, then smiled slightly. "The best. He was trained in Germany. One of my interests is to raise the requirements of men who become physicians. I find many inadequate to the task and some blatantly dangerous. Be assured, Mr. Avery, Lady Rose is being seen by one of the best physicians now residing in this country."

Charlie nodded shakily. He hated that a strange man, no matter how qualified, was with her, touching her. She might be frightened. "If you don't mind, I'll go up. I . . ." Charlie looked to where the butler had been standing moments before. "I feel so damned helpless and I feel partially to blame. She was feeling ill on the boat, but I let her convince me she was well enough to find her own way to your home. And then she was robbed. She's not used to being in a city, never mind alone. I never should have let her go without me."

"You say she's ill? I had no idea. I do apologize, I thought you asked for a physician only as a precaution, not from any real concern."

Charlie nodded, his throat feeling queer and thick, as if he'd swallowed a large bit of bread and it was stuck. "There was a woman on board ship. She became friends with Lady Rose and they spent quite a bit of time together." He was finding it difficult to breathe, never mind speak. "She died, you see. And now Lady Rose is ill and . . ." He couldn't finish, could not move any more words past a throat gone so tight, he could hardly swallow.

"I see," Cartwright said softly. "Why don't you wait outside her room so you can speak with Dr. Landsdowne when he is done with his examination."

"Yes," Charlie said. "Yes, I will."

"Mr. Avery." Something in the way Cartwright said his name stopped Charlie. "You love her."

Charlie let out a small, self-deprecating laugh. "Of course I do," he said, then headed out the door and to the second floor.

"You'll wear out the carpet, you will," Mrs. Fitz said not unkindly as she left Lady Rose's room for the second time, shaking her head when Charlie lifted his head in question. Charlie got the distinct impression the staff was a bit excited to have a real English lady under their roof. Despite the fact Charlie's clothing clearly proclaimed him a working man, they were polite and deferential. He gave another begrudging point to Cartwright. A well-run staff that appeared happy could only have a kind master who paid well. He didn't want to like Cartwright, but he found it was impossible *not* to like the man. He was pleasant, polite, and measured. Lady Rose and he would get along quite well. Hell, just thinking of them together nearly drove him to his knees. But this home, that man, they were where Rose belonged, not in some two-bit rooming house, which was all Charlie could afford.

Finally, after an eternity of waiting, Dr. Landsdowne emerged. He was younger than Charlie expected, neatly dressed and sporting a well-groomed and rather impressive mustache and muttonchops.

"How is she?"

The doctor started, unaware that anyone had been waiting outside. "And you are?"

"A friend."

"Mr. Avery works for Lady Rose's family and I expect he'll want to report to them," Cartwright said easily as he approached the two men.

"Ah, Mr. Cartwright." The doctor seemed almost relieved to see the other man walking toward them.

Charlie felt his hands curling into fists. He didn't very much like being ignored, as if he were nothing—even though, to these two men, that's exactly what he was.

"How is she?" Cartwright asked, glancing over at Charlie as if he were well aware he was repeating Charlie's exact question.

"She has influenza," he said in a clipped British accent that bespoke his origins. "And being out in this storm weakened her to a point that I am not certain she will survive the night."

Charlie felt the blood leave his head and he staggered, held upright only by the wall. The doctor looked at him curiously, as if unaware how very devastating his words were.

"I've given her jaborandi and so she'll sweat quite a bit. Do try to have her drink. It won't do to allow her to get too dehydrated. Her fever is dangerously high, her breathing labored. I am sorry, Mr. Cartwright, but it is in God's hands."

Charlie listened to the physician's words, spoken without inflection. He might have been talking about a tree that had been damaged in the wind and would have to be cut down.

"No," Charlie roared. "You do something. She has not traveled all this way to die. You do something, you cold son of a bitch. You're talking about a young girl in there, a girl who left home frightened and desperate, and she is not going to die tonight, because you are not going to let her."

The smallest bit of emotion flickered in the young doctor's eyes, there and gone and perhaps just imagined. "I am not God. And I am not immune to her suffering," the doctor said calmly. "But I also know from experience that her chances of survival, given how gravely ill she is, are not good. Would you rather I lie and tell you she is well?" he asked, as if truly curious about Charlie's answer.

"No," Charlie ground out.

"I am sorry you do not like to hear the truth but, good sir, it is indeed the truth," Dr. Landsdowne said.

Charlie stared at him, his eyes hot, his nostrils flaring, breathing like an angry bull about to rush toward a red handkerchief. Then he shook his head, calming himself. "If I were to perform a miracle this night, what would I need to do?"

Dr. Landsdowne looked away briefly before answering. "Keep her calm, give her whatever liquid you can." He reached into his bag and brought out a small jar filled with a white powder. "This is aspirin with a special agent that makes it easier on the stomach. It's a little concoction I borrowed from my good friend Mr. Gerhardt." At the two men's blank stares, Dr. Landsdowne furrowed his brow. "He's quite a well-known chemist. At any rate, give her a half teaspoon every three hours."

Charlie took the bottle and shook it a bit. "What does it do?"

"It should ease her pain and lower her fever. I've just given her a dose, so"—he pulled out his pocket watch—"don't give her another until eleven this evening."

"Anything else?"

The doctor looked at Cartwright. "Pray. Good evening, gentlemen. I will try to stop by tomorrow."

"She *what*?"

"Wants to marry me." Daniel watched with some amusement as his lover's eyes nearly bulged from his head. "And now that I've gotten used to the idea, I have to say it's not an all bad one."

James looked at him as if he'd gone mad, and perhaps he had. Because the idea of marrying had always been slightly distasteful, and not for the obvious reasons. Daniel had always felt that to get married, he'd have to trick some poor unwitting girl into thinking he loved her in all ways a man should. He didn't have the stomach for that kind of deception. But he had thought about it, especially lately. The rumors, the sly jokes, the questions. He'd tried, God above knew he'd tried, to be normal. He'd prayed, he'd even been to a doctor who'd given him electrical shocks to set him straight. Finally, he'd just given up. Or rather, James had made him give up, because every time he tortured himself, it hurt James terribly.

"So, you think I'm an abomination, is that what you think? Because if you think you're an abomination, that must be what you think of me." Those had been James's words, spoken in anger and pain.

Daniel didn't think James was an abomination. He loved James. It was all so damned complicated. And here was this gift, this girl who had been hurt and who had traveled across an ocean to ask him to marry her. He had a very strong suspicion why Lady Rose had suddenly decided he would be a good husband. No doubt she'd heard the rumors, the same ones that had held back his career, the same ones that had men, some of them his good friends, looking at him askance.

But if he were married, all those rumors would stop.

"It wouldn't be a *real* marriage. I suspect she *knows*."

James snorted. "How could she possibly know?"

Daniel shrugged. "I haven't the slightest idea, but I suspect she heard something. This will end up ruining my career, you know, unless I do something about it."

"But marry? It seems a rather drastic measure and not at all fair to her. Can you trust her?"

Daniel gave this some thought, and nodded. "I can. I'm sure of it. Her servant didn't know, you see."

"Servant?"

"The man who brought her here. He was her head groom and on his way to America, and she tagged along. She didn't tell him. He thinks she just wanted to get far away from her fiancé and I seemed a good candidate for a husband."

James slumped on the chair, one leg dangling off, and pouted. "I don't like it."

"Nothing would change," Daniel said softly. "It might even be better. If I'm married, you become just a friend in the eyes of the world. They'll say, 'Oh, I guess I was wrong about that Cartwright fellow.' Don't you see? It could be grand."

James shook his head. "She might die, so don't get your hopes too high," he said sullenly.

"You know, James, sometimes you can be a real ass." Daniel stalked from the room, not even knowing why he was so angry at James's callous words. Or maybe he did. The poor girl had crossed an ocean thinking he would keep her safe. How could he say no to that?

Chapter 12

Some attention is absolutely necessary, in this country, to the training of servants, as they come here from the lowest ranks of English and Irish peasantry, with as much idea of politeness as the pig domesticated in the cabin of the latter.

—From *The Ladies' Book of Etiquette, and Manual of Politeness*

Rose, her long hair loose and still damp around her head, lay motionless in a bed covered with a thick layer of blankets. Her cheeks were flushed and small beads of perspiration formed near her hairline. Charlie walked toward her and around the bed, lowering the flame on the lamp by her bedside so that the room was nearly completely dark but for a small halo of light. Her hands lay atop the covers, unnaturally still.

"Rose," Charlie said, his voice low. Her eyes fluttered opened. "Hello," he said, grinning, happy beyond reason that she was able to open her eyes. Such a small accomplishment, but it gave him hope.

"Hello," she whispered. "I feel quite unwell. How did I get here?"

"I found you huddled on someone's steps and I carried you here."

She furrowed her brow. "I don't remember. The doctor says I'm in Mr. Cartwright's house?"

Charlie nodded.

"These covers. Too hot." She weakly pushed at the blankets, at least four, covering her, so Charlie took two and peeled them down.

"Better?"

"No. All, please."

Charlie hesitated, wondering if she would be too cold without any covers, even though the room was quite warm.

"So hot," she muttered. Indeed, her face was covered with a fine sheen of perspiration. When he'd first brought her in, she'd been shaking uncontrollably. If she grew too cool, he'd simply pull the covers back up, he reasoned, drawing down the blankets.

"Holy God." He immediately averted his eyes. She was wearing only a thin cotton gown and was quite drenched with sweat, which allowed him to see things he oughtn't. Things he'd dreamed about seeing, but things at the moment—at any moment, really—he had no business seeing. "Perhaps one cover," Charlie said in near desperation. Her nipples, brown and lovely, were completely visible; it was a sight Charlie never in his life would have dreamed he would see. Her full breasts, her flat stomach, the dark hair between her legs, all there for him to gaze upon if he chose to. He tried not to look down, tried not to be tempted to look, but not being a candidate for sainthood, he did look—right before he drew up one of the blankets.

"I don't want you to become too chilled," he said. "The doctor says you should drink as much water as you can. Here." He brought a glass to her lips, placing one hand behind her head to help her lift it so she could drink.

"Thank you, Charlie. What would I do without you?"

That was the last lucid sentence she said that night. After she fell into a gentle sleep, Charlie sat in a nearby chair and allowed exhaustion to overtake him. The chair was large and sinfully comfortable, with a winged back that was perfect for laying his head against. Within minutes, he was asleep.

Her scream woke him up.

He jerked awake, his heart slamming painfully against his chest, and got up so quickly, he nearly overturned the heavy chair. "Rose," he said, surprised to see her sitting up.

She looked at him, her eyes glassy and unseeing, her breathing labored. "Where's your head?" she asked, looking terrified. "Your head is gone. Charlie, your head is gone!"

Charlie rushed forward and she moved back, as if he was indeed an apparition without a head. "No, no, love. I'm fine. I still have my head."

She refused to look at him, apparently convinced he was headless. He gently put his hand on her upper arm, withdrawing, shocked at how hot she was.

Mrs. Fitz came into the room in her dressing gown, her graying hair in a long braid and topped with a ridiculous nightcap, a frilly thing that contrasted with the woman's serious countenance. "Oh, the poor dear is burning up," she said, hurrying to the bedside.

"Mother? What are you doing here?" Rose asked.

"She's out of her head," Charlie said unnecessarily, his voice shaking. "What time is it? I was supposed to give her medicine to keep her fever down. And I was supposed to make sure she drank water."

"It's just past midnight, Mr. Avery," Mrs. Fitz said soothingly, but she gave him a long, searching look. No doubt she'd never seen a servant nearly go into hysterics because his employer was ill. "You can give the lady her medicine now."

"Of course," Charlie said, knowing he was showing far too much emotion. It wouldn't do to allow the servants to know how much he cared for his mistress; it wasn't a natural thing and would embarrass Lady Rose if word got round to the house staff. Just being in this room with her was highly improper, given he was nothing but a head groom and she a lady. But he'd be damned if he let propriety dictate whether he watched over her or not. He felt fully to blame for her being so ill. "I fear I feel a bit responsible for her welfare, given she's so far from home."

Mrs. Fitz gave him an uncertain smile. "There's no predicting these things, Mr. Avery," she said sensibly. "No one is to blame for an illness."

Rose was agitated, worrying the blankets almost frantically. "Where am I? Where am I?"

"The Cartwright home," Mrs. Fitz said, straightening the blankets efficiently. "Now, you lie back down and we'll give you some medicine to make you feel better." Mrs. Fitz gently, but firmly, pushed Rose so she was prone, ignoring the younger woman's protests.

"Lady Rose, you must be calm," Charlie said, and his words seemed to have an instant effect. Mrs. Fitz helped him to administer the water and aspirin powder, and soon Rose was quiet, her eyes closed.

"Has Mr. Cartwright shown you where you may sleep for the night?" the housekeeper asked pointedly.

"He has not, Mrs. Fitz, and I feel it is my duty to remain with Lady

Rose until I am assured she is well. No doubt you would do the same should Mr. Cartwright fall ill."

Mrs. Fitz pursed her lips but didn't contradict him, though he suspected if Mr. Cartwright did fall ill, she would leave his care to one of the maids. She left soon after, with a palpable reluctance, probably thinking he would do something unsavory as soon as she departed the room. Old bat.

An hour later, Mr. Cartwright entered the room, inquiring about the patient. Rose lay still, too still; the only way Charlie knew she continued to breathe was the slow rise and fall of the covers. Charlie didn't like the way Cartwright's eyes lingered thoughtfully on Rose's face, almost as if he were seriously considering what it would be like to have her as a wife. Such a marriage was for the best. Charlie knew this in his mind, but his heart rebelled at the thought of another man touching Rose, never mind marrying her and all that entailed.

"Mr. Avery," Cartwright said before leaving. "May I offer you some advice?"

"Of course, sir."

"You might find it to your benefit if you could somehow control how very transparent your thoughts are. You are aware, I am sure, how improper your feelings for Lady Rose are. Some might find them abhorrent."

Charlie clenched his jaw. "And you, sir, do you find them abhorrent?"

Cartwright gave him an odd smile. "I'm perhaps the last person on earth to judge a man for his feelings for another. No, Mr. Avery. But I'm also a realist with a realist's view of society."

Even knowing he shouldn't, Charlie allowed himself to look at Rose, unable to disguise what his heart felt.

"Does the lady know how you feel?"

"No, sir," Charlie said, feeling a familiar humiliation wash over him. "And she never will."

His answer seemed to satisfy the man, who nodded grimly. "Please do have one of the servants fetch me if I'm needed here."

"Yes, sir." Charlie watched the man walk out of the room, hating him and admiring him in equal measure. He knew most men would not have allowed a servant to attend to his mistress. And he also knew another man might have found his love for Rose ridiculous, as ridiculous as Quasimodo's love for Esmeralda.

When Cartwright was gone, Charlie pulled the wingback chair close to the bed and rested his arms on the bedcovers, not touching Rose but close enough to feel her warmth. He lay like that for hours, listening to her breathing, and thinking, *If she lives through the night, then she will not die.*

The top cover was pretty, a delicate pattern with lilacs and dark green leaves. He traced his finger on one flower, feeling overwhelmed with fear. Rose was not getting better. In the last hour, her breathing had become more difficult, rattling in her chest, and her breaths less frequent. It was almost as if she were slowly winding down, until eventually, she would stop breathing altogether. And there was nothing he could do other than try to spoon water into her mouth. At first, she'd reflexively swallowed, but now even that had ceased.

She was dying. The reality of it hit him like a black force he could not stop. He picked up one of her hands, listless and small in his calloused one, and pressed it against his lips as if he could draw the sickness out of her and into himself. "Please, Rose." *Don't die.*

Outside, he could hear the first birds begin their songs. It was still dark, but the East hinted at the sunrise, a faint glow, hardly discernible, and the birds somehow knew another day was soon beginning. He looked at Rose; pale, dark circles marred the delicate skin beneath her eyes. The blanket was hardly moving anymore. "Please, God."

He began to cry, overwhelmed by the pain of watching her suffer. He hadn't cried since he was a boy, and these tears were wrenched from him, as the purest agony he had ever felt burned his chest. Holding her hand, he lowered his head to the blanket, completely overwhelmed by grief. This was the torment and anguish Roger Browne had felt, helplessly watching his wife die.

All through the night and into the next day, he stayed by her side. When he left, even for a few minutes, the fear that she would die alone nearly overwhelmed him. At some point, the doctor came, but his visit was brief and not at all satisfying.

"She still lives, but she is far weaker than she was last night. I cannot give you hope for there is no hope to give," Dr. Landsdowne said with his maddening calm. "It is unlikely she will survive another day."

The man never directed his comments to Charlie, rather waiting for Cartwright to appear before speaking. "Is there nothing we can do?" Cartwright asked. He'd been in and out of the room several times to check on Rose, never staying more than a few minutes.

"Do continue to try to get her to drink water." Dr. Landsdowne let out a sigh, then frowned, as if angry with himself for showing even that much emotion. "I cannot do more."

After the doctor left, Charlie kept up his vigil, refusing to leave even to eat. He knew he was causing comment below stairs, but if the doctor's prediction came true, nothing would be harmed by his staying with her. And he had to stay with her.

For long hours, Charlie listened to her breathing, watching her chest move up, move down, and prayed as he had never prayed in his life. This was all so wrong, so unfair. Rose should not die so far from home, with only her servant by her side. Cartwright had telegraphed her parents, telling them that Rose had arrived safely, but had fallen ill, and promising to telegraph again when there was news. He couldn't imagine their reaction upon learning Rose was across an ocean and ill. Would they come immediately? Even if they did, it would be too late. She was too far away. They would be coming to take her home in a casket.

As the sun went down, Charlie's hopes darkened with the sky. He held her hand again, as he had most of the day, and laid his head by her side. He wished he could hold her, but that was not possible. It was bad enough he was holding her hand; he'd seen the look of censure in Mrs. Fitz's eyes but he didn't care. Even though Rose seemed unaware he was there, perhaps she did feel his hand on hers and was comforted. God knew, her hand comforted him.

Exhausted, Charlie fell asleep, the top of his head pressing against her side.

"Charlie?"

At first he thought he'd imagined her voice, but then he felt her hand on his head, trailing her fingers through his hair as she had done so many times before. He lifted his head and saw that her brown eyes were open and studying him.

Rose couldn't remember ever feeling so weak. Just lifting her hand to touch Charlie's soft curls had been a major effort. A lamp was lit nearby, making his hair glow unnaturally bright in the dark room. Charlie was looking at her so oddly, as if he hadn't seen her in years.

"Where am I?" she asked, frowning when she heard how her voice sounded. She was hardly able to speak and felt purely awful.

"In one of Mr. Cartwright's guest rooms. Do you not remember anything?"

She furrowed her brow. "I remember getting off the ship and meeting your uncle. Oh! And that horrible person who stole all my things. The cabbie wouldn't take me. How did I end up here?"

"You tried to walk but were so ill. Why didn't you tell me? I found you in the snowstorm, huddled on a step, half dead, and I carried you here."

She smiled weakly. "So strong, Charlie. I'm glad."

Charlie stood up abruptly and dug his hand into his trouser pocket. "Look. I've recovered your things." He held up her grandmother's necklace, grinning.

"Good for you. I feared it was gone forever." Her voice trailed off. She was so very tired it was nearly impossible to keep her eyes open. "Sleepy."

"Before you sleep, drink some water, my lady."

Charlie held a glass to her lips and helped her lift her head. Weak as a kitten, she was.

"Now you may sleep. I think your fever is gone, or nearly so. I shall be extremely happy to tell Dr. Landsdowne you will recover."

"Landsdowne," she muttered. She had no idea what Charlie was speaking of.

Rose closed her eyes, but before she drifted back to sleep, she heard another man's voice. He sounded urgent. Rose tried to rouse herself, but felt herself sinking into sleep.

Daniel had never been one to enjoy confrontations, and he was about to be thrown in the midst of one. It was just eight o'clock in the morning and his butler had woken him from a wonderful and much needed sleep to tell him an angry gentleman was in his parlor waiting for him.

"A Viscount Granton is here to see you regarding the lady."

"Oh, good Lord," Daniel muttered, realizing Lady Rose's eldest brother was in his home. He realized the viscount must have left England shortly after Lady Rose and her head groom in order to have arrived just three days after them. "I suppose he won't wait for me to dress," Daniel said, grabbing his dressing gown and shoving his feet into a pair of leather slippers.

He strode to the sickroom, calling out for Charlie. Her head groom looked the worse for wear; the poor man had hardly slept for two days.

"Her brother is here," he said, whispering so as not to awaken Lady Rose, who had apparently fallen back to sleep. "Is she . . . ?"

"Better. How is it possible that one of her brothers is here?" The man looked visibly ill. "Which one?"

"Lord Granton."

"Oh, God." Mr. Avery looked like he might cast up his accounts. "I'm a dead man for sure."

"Let's get this over with. I'm certain he wants to murder someone and I'd rather have it be you than me," Daniel said, trying for a bit of levity.

Mr. Avery gave him a withering look before following him out the door.

When they arrived in the parlor, a masculine room with dark paneling and comfortable leather furniture, they found Viscount Granton pacing back and forth like a caged animal. Or like a man who was worried sick about his sister.

"Good evening, Granton. What a pleasant surprise," Daniel said smoothly, choosing to ignore the reason Lord Granton was in his home. He couldn't imagine what was going through the poor man's head, but he doubted it was related to the truth of the matter at all. He looked haunted and angry, and the dark circles beneath his eyes were quite telling. Daniel had talked with Granton a handful of times and found the man to be pleasant, if not overly jovial. He was, like so many members of the peerage, entirely dedicated to his duty.

When they entered, Granton stopped his pacing and looked from one man to the other, reserving his coldest stare for Mr. Avery. Daniel was glad that look had not been directed toward him as it was absolutely fearful. To give Mr. Avery credit, he stood there, even when Granton marched toward them, even when he drew back his fist and swung with considerable force at Avery's face. Avery went down like a load of bricks. Daniel was frankly impressed, for he took the blow as if it was some sort of penance. Avery hadn't been knocked out cold, but he had the sense to stay down, lying on his back and propping himself up with his elbows.

Granton stood over him, fists clenched. "You bloody cur. If you have married her, I will kill you and make her a widow this day."

"We are not married," Mr. Avery said, sitting up and wiping a bit of blood from the corner of his mouth.

This seemed to incense Granton even more. "How dare you take my sister with you without the benefit of a wedding! You have ruined her, do you realize that? Weston won't have her now. No one will have her now. You are not fit to look at her never mind . . ." Raw pain was etched on the older man's face as he glared down at the head groom, fists clenched, as if willing the man to stand again so that he might strike him once more.

"I understand that you're upset," Daniel said, stepping between the two men and handing Granton a glass of brandy. "But this man saved your sister's life. More than once, apparently."

That gave Granton pause. "What do you mean?"

"Lady Rose is recovering now, but when she arrived, after Mr. Avery found her freezing on the street, she was quite ill," Daniel said calmly.

"She wouldn't have needed saving if this piece of shit hadn't stolen her from her home and ruined her." He stopped as if Daniel's words were just reaching his brain. "Ill, you say?"

"She very nearly died, and may still."

Granton began pacing back and forth. "And why would she come here? To you? She only met you that once, at her ball. What the hell is going on here?" the man shouted.

Daniel saw that the younger man was about to stand, but he shook his head in warning. Granton was raring to strike again and Daniel didn't much care for violence or the sight of blood. "If you recall, I said Mr. Avery saved Rose twice. Apparently she was escaping Weston."

"We know. Rose sent a telegram saying only that she could not marry him, but we are all baffled as to why. My mother is beside herself with worry and my father . . . let's just say it's a good thing for Rose that I volunteered to fetch her home. As far as I know, Weston remains unaware she's disappeared." Granton turned to Mr. Avery, who still sat, his forearms resting on his bended knees. By the look of the man, he'd be able to hold his own against Granton, but Daniel had no wish for fisticuffs in his parlor; he had far too many valuable artifacts for that sort of activity.

"Tell me, Charlie, is there any reason Rose cannot still marry Weston?" The warning in his voice gave Daniel the chills.

"Weston hurt her," Avery said, staring directly ahead.

Granton had gone quite still. "What do you mean? How do you know?"

"I was working with Moonshine in the stable and Lady Rose had been out walking with Weston—"

"His Grace," Granton snapped.

Avery gave Granton a hard look but continued. "His Grace. When Lady Rose returned, she was clearly upset. I thought they'd had some sort of spat. But I didn't have a good feeling about it, so the next day, I followed them." Mr. Avery stood and looked Granton in the eye. "When I came upon them, Weston was unbuttoning his trousers."

Granton reared back as if Avery had thrown a blow. "Are you certain?"

"Yes, my lord."

"I'll kill him," Granton said in a tone that left no doubt that Weston's life was, indeed, in danger.

"She had bruises on her neck. He'd forced her . . ." Mr. Avery shook his head, unable to complete his thought.

"Fellatio, I believe," Daniel supplied. Granton whipped his head around, his eyes so filled with rage, Daniel took a step back.

"Lady Rose was upset. She knew I was coming to America and she begged me to help her. I know it was wrong, but I couldn't very well let her marry Weston. She was very frightened of him."

Granton bowed his head, his anger deflated. "My God, why did she not say something?"

"I cannot say, but I know she did try to tell your mother." He stood, looking at Granton a bit warily.

"You could have come to me, Charlie."

"Lady Rose was ashamed and she begged me not to say a word. And she didn't come out and tell me what happened; I guessed. And then there were the bruises around her neck and what I saw. I did what I thought was right at the time, my lord."

"I suppose America seemed like a safe place for her," Daniel said. "And she knew me, where I lived, knew you trusted me. I suppose it seemed like a safe alternative. She wants us to be married, and given that she's been under my roof without a chaperone for two nights, I think that is likely the best option."

From the corner of his eye, Daniel saw Mr. Avery flinch, but he kept his eyes on the other man. The viscount's brows furrowed over his unusual golden-brown eyes, which seemed to look into his soul. "Is that what you want?"

Daniel nodded. "It is. I think we will get on quite well. I find Lady Rose charming and I need a wife who can move well in society. New York and Washington will adore her."

"You know this from one conversation you had with her more than a month ago," Granton said with skepticism.

"Yes, my lord, I do."

Then Mr. Avery said something Daniel would never forget.

"Then she is safe."

Granton looked at the head groom, then held out his hand. "I'm sorry about that punch, Mr. Avery."

Mr. Avery took his hand and the two men shook, staring directly into one another's eyes.

"I appreciate that you've tried to keep my sister safe, Charlie, but I don't agree with the manner in which you accomplished the task. Even if she does marry Mr. Cartwright, her reputation will be ruined in England, though I can't say that it will matter much. Thank you, Charlie. You may leave and carry on with your life here. I wish you well."

Mr. Avery looked taken aback, as if he hadn't thought that one day he would have to leave Lady Rose behind. "I would like to say good-bye to Lady Rose if I might," Mr. Avery said, and Daniel had to give the man credit; he sounded as if he didn't care one way or the other, but Daniel suspected if he left without saying good-bye, a small bit of his heart just might die.

"Of course," Granton said. When Mr. Avery didn't immediately move, the viscount said, "Now, if you please."

So this was it. Charlie would say good-bye and never see her again. Never hold her hand, never hear her voice. Never hold her or kiss her or make love to her. It felt a bit like a death, he thought, walking up to where she lay sleeping. She would never know she held his heart. Harry had been right—if Rose knew how he felt about her, it would no doubt embarrass her. She would pity him.

The room was still dimly lit by the lamp, the heavy velvet curtain blocking nearly all the daylight. It was cold and damp outside, so there wasn't much light at any rate. He didn't want this vision of her to be his last. She was still so pale, still ill, though he knew she would recover when she opened her eyes at his approach and smiled.

"Your brother is here, Marcus," he said, and hurried to add, "He understands and is not angry. I'll let him explain himself."

"How did he find me so quickly?" Rose asked.

"I imagine when an earl demands information from a telegraph operator, that the information is given posthaste. I wondered the same thing, but then remembered you'd sent Mr. Cartwright a telegram right before we departed. I've no doubt your brother found this information out and knew precisely where you'd gone. Or at least had an idea of who you would be visiting."

Rose looked at his lips, now slightly swollen and still bleeding a bit. "I take it he was happy to see you?"

Charlie chuckled. "It's fine now. I let him know you are safe and I was doing what I could to help you."

"Did you tell him about Weston?"

"Only that he hurt you. I think he understands."

Rose held out her hand and Charlie took it, willing himself to remember what it felt like in his. "Thank you, Charlie. You saved me twice."

"I would do so again, if need be," Charlie said, realizing that was more than he should say, more than he needed to. But he wanted her to know, just a bit, how he felt. "But now, I am here to say good-bye, my lady."

She immediately frowned and tried to sit up, as if she, weak as a kitten still, could physically prevent him from leaving. "Can you not stay a bit longer? Until I am up and about? No doubt Marcus is here to bring me home, but it will be a few more days before I am well enough for such a trip."

"I'm sorry, my lady, but I must go. I have stayed here longer than I should have already. I am due to begin my job tomorrow and haven't even seen my uncle's home, nor found a place to live."

She looked downright crestfallen. "Then I shall never see you again?" she asked, her voice small, and damn it to hell, her eyes filled with tears. "What shall I do if I need someone to save me?" She tried for a tremulous smile.

Charlie swallowed, refusing to allow his own tears to show. It wasn't his place to tell Lady Rose she would not be returning home with her brother. She would find out soon enough. The truth was, he didn't want to see her again; it would hurt too damn much, knowing she was marrying another, better, man. She would insist he visit if she knew they would be living in the same city. It was better to cut it clean. "I daresay one of your brothers will readily volunteer to come to your aid."

"Write to me and give me your address. Promise me you will write, Charlie."

He looked at her, knowing it was a promise he could not make. What husband would allow his wife to receive correspondence from a single man who was not her relation? A man who had readily admitted he was in love with that man's future wife. "I'm not much of a letter writer, my lady."

She nodded, the motion causing a tear to slip down her cheek. "I shall miss you."

"The same." Charlie tried for a smile that didn't quite work. His throat hurt as if something hard and sharp were lodged there, and he knew if he didn't leave immediately, he might not be able to hold back his emotions any longer.

He stood, then bent and kissed her on her cheek, lingering far longer than he had a right to. Then he bowed and said, "Good-bye, my lady, and God speed."

Rose watched as Charlie left the room, fighting the urge to call him back, to beg him to . . . what? Return to England with her? *Marry* her? The daughter of an earl marrying a head groom? They would both be ridiculed by aristocrat and commoner alike. Besides, Charlie would never think of her as anything other than Lady Rose, and she couldn't bear it if he felt he was less than she. And he would, right or wrong.

He was at most a friend, and even that was unfitting of her station. Then why did her heart feel as though it was being wrenched from her body? Why didn't the tears stop?

"Rose, what's wrong? Why are you weeping?"

It was Marcus, looking worried and stern. He never had been able to take her tears, even when she was a little girl. He would do just about anything to stop them.

"Are you feeling so ill then?"

Rose managed to shake her head. She struggled to sit up and held out her arms, and her big brother readily embraced her. "Oh, sweetling, please don't cry." Rose couldn't remember the last time she'd given Marcus a hug, for the two of them had not been particularly close. He was ten years her senior and he'd always seemed like a giant to her, apart from the rest of them, because of his position as heir.

"Charlie just left," she said, attempting to explain her tears.

Marcus pulled back, his face etched with confusion. "You call our head groom by his given name, Rose?"

"Goodness, you sound like Mother. I've always called him Charlie, ever since I was a little girl."

Marcus, ever proper, pressed his lips together. "I think it is entirely too familiar to call a male servant by his given name, Rose. And why would a servant's departure produce tears at any rate?"

Rose ducked her head and fiddled with her covers, not wanting her brother to see the blush that stained her pale cheeks. It wouldn't do for Marcus to know how close she and Charlie had become these past few weeks. "I'm ill and upset and tired. I cry easily when all those factors combine," she said, lying back down and turning her head away from her brother.

"Very well," he said, but she could hear the hesitation in his voice. He was no doubt appalled that she would shed tears over a mere servant and she wondered what he would say if she admitted how deep her feelings actually were for Charlie. She suspected she might love him; why else would she feel so bereft at the thought of never seeing him again?

"I have some good news, Rose. I feared that once you ran away, you would be ruined should anyone discover your absence. Weston doesn't know you went missing, but he is no longer in the picture. You're to marry Cartwright."

Rose turned her head, too shocked to respond. Even though this was what she wanted, it still came as a surprise that Cartwright had already approached Marcus.

"He has asked and I, as the only male family member present, have granted him permission." Marcus looked at her, his eyes unwavering. "Is this what you want?"

Suddenly, it seemed all wrong. Marry Mr. Cartwright when she was in love . . .

Fresh tears fell from her eyes. "Yes, it is," she said.

"I cannot begin to know what you've been through, Rose. Weston will pay for hurting you." When Rose's eyes widened, Marcus hastened to say, "Mr. Avery told us why you ran away. Do not worry that he spoke out of turn. I requested that he report to me what he knew."

"Before or after you struck him?"

Marcus smiled grimly. "After. I did apologize, but at the time I needed to strike the person I believed was responsible for harming my little sister." He looked at her until she became uncomfortable under his scrutiny. "You don't have . . . feelings for Mr. Avery. Do you?"

"He is a good man and he has kept me safe. Other than that, I do not," Rose said, feeling the lie like a pressure on her chest. How could she admit to any feelings toward Charlie when it was clear Marcus disapproved?

"Good." He looked troubled, as if he wanted to say something but was debating whether he should or not. Finally, he said, "Mr. Cartwright." Just two words, filled with so much meaning.

"I do believe he is the perfect husband for me," Rose said. "I enjoy his company and I believe he enjoys mine. We shall get on nicely. You like him, don't you, Marcus?"

Marcus smiled. "I do. He's an intelligent man with fine principles. But . . . I was a bit surprised when he asked for your hand. I'd heard he was a dedicated bachelor."

"I suppose I have charmed him away from bachelorhood," Rose said. "Was Mother very upset?"

"She was in hysterics when she read your telegram," he said dryly. "I think she will be heartbroken not to have a duchess daughter, but I daresay she'll get over it. It's probably best that you stay here for a while after you marry Mr. Cartwright."

"I was thinking much the same," Rose said. "I'm glad you came and not Father. I dislike it when he's angry."

"As do I. I'll stay until your wedding. If you'll permit it, I can walk you down the aisle if Mother and Father decide not to make the trip. I'll wire them with the news as soon as I can." He shook his head. "Who would have thought it would be you who would create such a scandal. I always thought it would be Stephen."

Rose let out a small laugh. "I never thought I would do more than create a ripple of anger."

"I will let you rest, shall I?" He bent and kissed her forehead.

"Mr. Cartwright said the doctor did not expect you to live. I am very glad he was mistaken."

Rose smiled, but her heart wrenched. Charlie had not given up on her. As sick as she'd been, she was aware of his constant presence, his stubborn attempts to get her to drink water, the cool cloths he would put on her forehead as she slept. Her throat closed painfully once her brother had left the room, and she allowed herself to cry a bit more. The only thought that made her feel a bit better was the realization that she was living in the same city as Charlie. Surely she would see him again.

Chapter 13

To really merit the name of a polite, finished gentleman, you must be polite at all times and under all circumstances.

—From *The Gentlemen's Book of Etiquette, and Manual of Politeness*

Five years later

Charlie Avery adjusted his sleeve, brushing a bit of lint from the fine light worsted wool, then checked the time on his new pocket watch, a costly affair of eighteen-karat gold with diamonds in place of the numerals three and nine. It was the kind of timepiece that had a man checking if he was running late even when he knew he was not. From the top of his well-groomed head to the tips of his brilliantly shined custom-made shoes, he reeked of money. A lot of money. His carriage, manufactured by the Studebaker Brothers, was created of the finest materials—silk curtains, glove-soft leather, and springs that made it seem as though the carriage were gliding down the streets. Charlie was a man of discerning tastes, so when it had come time to select a home in New York, he wanted it situated where men of wealth and power lived—Fifth Avenue.

It hadn't been intentional, his buying the house next to his former employer, but when his agent contacted him about a home that had recently become available, he decided to take a look even though he recognized the address. His home had been constructed in the Italianate style, with a white marble front, gleaming tall windows, and an entryway that bespoke the wealth of the people who lived within. It wasn't gaudy, for Charlie was always careful not to appear too eager, but it was lovely and grand and everything a man who aspired to be respected wanted in a home.

For two months, workers had renovated the inside, installing all the latest innovations in plumbing and lighting and heat. His home would not be warmed by individual fires but rather by a central heating system that used a large boiler in the basement. When winter arrived, his house would be the warmest in the city, and when he wanted a warm bath all he need do was turn a faucet.

It was the home of a successful man, and Charlie felt a deep sense of satisfaction with all he had accomplished in the past five years.

It had all started with a can of beets. Delmonico's kitchen was well equipped, but its method of opening cans was frustratingly slow and difficult. And it had been Charlie's job to open them. The restaurant's clientele had come to expect peaches in December and peas in February. If their chef decided on peach cobbler for dessert that evening, it meant opening dozens of cans. Can after can, until Charlie's hands ached and he started longing for the days of shoveling horse manure.

He had one day off a week, and on that day he started fiddling with an idea for an easier and more efficient design, and had a blacksmith friend create the prototype. The chef, Charles Ranhofer, back from a brief retirement, watched a demonstration and then kissed Charlie on both cheeks. The opener was mounted on a counter and a series of gears moved the can around as a blade opened it.

Two years later, Charlie quit his job to work at the small manufacturing plant he'd built. He had four employees and was starting to accumulate more money than he had ever dreamed of having. And his brain kept working, kept creating, kept making money. He hired smart men who knew more about business than he did and he learned from them while they offered advice and dreamed bigger than he ever would have allowed himself to.

Now, five years after he'd stepped ashore, here he was, wearing a suit that cost more than he used to make in a year, living in a house that rivaled anything the aristocracy had in England. Charlie Avery was Mr. Charles Avery and people called him sir. It was heady stuff.

As the carriage moved along Broadway toward Fifth Avenue, Charlie allowed himself to think about his neighbor and the coincidence that the house next door to hers happened to go on sale when he was looking for a home. He wasn't blind to the reasons why that particular bit of real estate seemed more appealing than every other home he'd looked at. Of course he still thought about her and he knew no matter what happened, a part of him would always love her. He knew it wouldn't matter if he were the richest man in New York (which he was not). To her he was still Charlie Avery, head groom. And to him she would always be Lady Rose, unattainable and so far beyond his reach it was humiliating just remembering how he'd pined for her.

And God above only knew just how much he'd pined for her. When he'd left her that day, still ill, he'd left a big piece of his heart behind. He'd been miserable and driven. All that mattered was trying to forget that she was marrying another, that she had chosen another. He tortured himself with that thought. She could have chosen him, and as preposterous as such a notion was, he couldn't help but think they might have been happy. In all those years, he'd only seen her once, on her wedding day. The marriage had drawn quite a bit of attention, what with the bride being an English lady, the daughter of an earl, and the groom being uncommonly handsome, wealthy, and politically well connected. Charlie had simply been one of the crowd, a man whose eyes burned into her, who willed her to see him, to know how much he loved her. He'd told himself, if she saw him, she would realize how much she loved him and she would run down the steps of the church and throw herself into his arms. That didn't happen, of course. She'd gone up those steps, looking so damned beautiful it hurt to look at her, and disappeared into the church.

He hadn't waited for her to come out. He hadn't wanted to see her brilliant smile or hear the cheers from the crowd that had gathered outside. He hadn't wanted to picture her, naked, yearning, being touched by her new husband. The night of her wedding, Charlie got drunker than he'd ever been in his life and ended up outside their house, looking up at the second floor, tears streaming down his face. Sobbing and pathetic. Even as drunk as he'd been, he'd known what a fool he would look like should anyone see him. He'd stumbled home, a broken man.

Bitterness replaced his misery soon enough, molding him into the man he was now, the man who was glad she could hear him pleasuring other women. It wasn't the most honorable thought he'd ever had in his head, but there it was. He wanted to hope that some part of her regretted her decision. But it was far more likely she hadn't given him another thought. He was a servant. He was nothing to her.

Why couldn't he get that through his thick skull? If she'd been kind, if she'd kissed him, it had only been a lark. It meant nothing because he'd meant nothing to her. And so he knew he'd relish the moment when she realized he was no longer anyone's servant.

As his carriage stopped in front of his house, he smiled, remembering her note to him. Opera, indeed. He wondered what she'd thought about the French actress he'd entertained. Picking up his top hat, he placed it on his head as he heard his driver drop the step, then eased out of the carriage, his eyes on his home, brimming with pride.

"Charlie?"

He recognized her voice immediately and schooled his features to remain impassive, even though his damned heart practically leapt from his chest. There she was, grinning at him.

"Charlie!" She walked over to him, her face lit up, clearly happy to see him. My God, she was beautiful. She had been a girl when he'd left her and now she had blossomed into a woman. Her dark hair was swept back and bundled together at her nape, and her brown eyes sparkled. He'd forgotten how dark they were, and how they came to life whenever she smiled.

"My goodness, Charlie, you're a sight for sore eyes. How *are* you? And how fine you look," she said, holding out her gloved hands for him to take. Charlie hesitated, not wanting to touch her, not trusting himself if he did. He braced himself even though her hands were gloved. He did the next best thing to not touching her, and that was to keep the contact as brief as possible. He did his best not to smile, not to let her know that his heart was hammering madly in his chest. Then he remembered she was recently widowed, and he was slightly ashamed of his physical reaction to her nearness.

"Mrs. Cartwright. I was sorry to hear about your husband's death. He was a good man," he said.

"Thank you. I miss him every day." It looked like she might cry, and Charlie felt a wave of jealousy. Over a dead man. He glanced at his home and had an awful moment of regret over its purchase. She followed his eyes with the oddest look on her face. "What are you doing here?" she asked. "Do you work here? I've yet to meet my new neighbor. He's quite a mystery." Rose looked him over, her face showing her confusion at his expensive clothing. Of course she never, not in a million years, would have thought him the owner, and part of him rejoiced at what he was about to tell her.

"I don't work here, Mrs. Cartwright," Charlie said.

"Oh?"

"I live here."

Oh, the look on her lovely face was priceless. It was clear that at first, she thought he was having fun with her. That's how unlikely it was that he was telling the truth. She even let out a small laugh, almost immediately stifling it when she realized he was not laughing with her. He watched the emotions come and go—amusement, confusion, and then the idea forming that perhaps he was telling the truth.

And then, it really was the loveliest sight he'd seen in some time, the awful dawning that he was her neighbor, the author of the note he'd sent, the man who had been disrupting her evenings with his performances.

"You live here? Do you mean to say you *own* this house?" Her brows were furrowed and her expression was downright adorable. She still couldn't quite believe that her former head groom lived in a house grander than her own.

"I do."

"You're C. A. Kitchen Tools?"

"I am."

"And you . . ." She couldn't complete the sentence, so he did it for her.

". . . enjoy the opera."

Her face turned the brightest red he'd ever seen on another human. She appeared both horrified and outraged, and he threw back his head and laughed.

"You are my new neighbor. My awful new neighbor," she said, quite unnecessarily.

Charlie gave her a mocking bow. "At your service, madam."

He had to give her credit. She held herself together quite nicely, keeping her composure in spite of what must have been a large shock to her delicate system. "I see. Well, Mr. Avery, welcome to the neighborhood."

"Thank you, Mrs. Cartwright. I enjoy it already," he said, feeling rather wicked for teasing her. The way she was blushing, one might think she hadn't been married for four years.

"It was lovely seeing you again. Good day." Her parting words were polite and spoken in a tone only a true English lady could use effectively.

He tipped his hat and watched as she pivoted and walked briskly back to her gate and entered it without turning around for a final look. Whistling a jaunty tune, Charlie strode up his front steps, feeling happier than he'd felt in a long time.

God above, he had missed that woman.

Charlie. Charlie Avery. It *couldn't* be. That man, that strikingly handsome, womanizing, richer-than-Croesus man was Charlie Avery. Sweet Charlie who had taught her how to kiss, who had been her friend, who had been so kind and caring and . . .

"It's impossible," Rose said, closing the door behind her. How could that arrogant, smirking, wickedly beautiful man be *Charlie*? She went immediately to her bedroom, not even pausing to remove her hat or gloves, and found that awful note he had sent on the back of her stationery. She had no idea why she'd kept it; the mere sight of it piqued her. She looked at his handwriting, bold and without flourish. It was not the fine hand of a gentleman; she'd known this immediately. But there was a certain amount of confidence that bespoke a man of accomplishment.

> *Dear Mrs. Cartwright:*
> *Please accept my sincerest apologies for disturbing your evening. I was unaware sound traveled so well between our homes. I will attempt to curtail the noise, but as some aspects of the performance are beyond my control, I cannot make any promises.*
> *A*

"I cannot make any promises," she said in a man's deep tone. Then it occurred to her that the entire time he *knew* who she was, that she was the one who had written that note. How he must have laughed at her. How could he? *Why* would he? He was not the man she'd thought he was. She remembered her mother telling her, "Servants are not your friends, Rose. This is their job and the only reason they seem to want to please you is to keep their job. Don't mistake that for affection."

At the time, her mother had been speaking of her lady's maid. After coming across the two of them giggling like old friends, her mother had admonished Rose for her familiarity. It turned out that her maid had been stealing from her. Rose had been stunned and hurt, but it had been a lesson well learned. Still, she had never put Charlie in such a category. Though perhaps she should have.

She cringed, thinking about that ridiculous note she'd sent over to him. And those ridiculous kisses they had shared—the only time she'd ever been kissed. Throughout the years, she often had thought about those kisses, brief though they had been. Had Charlie simply been playing with her, having a bit of fun with the lady of the family? Good God, she'd even fancied herself in love with him.

And now he was her neighbor. The very same one who liked to entertain women. Quite well, apparently.

Rose crumpled the note up and threw it in her fireplace. It was too warm for a fire, but eventually it would go up in smoke. Without conscious thought, Rose walked over to her window and looked out across the alley. His curtains, as well as the window, were closed. She'd often admired the home; it reminded her of the houses back in England. Perhaps that's why Charlie had been drawn to it. That thought made her snort aloud. She knew full well why Charlie had been drawn to that home—it was to thumb his nose at her, his former employer. Did he think owning such a house would make him her social equal? Rose stared at the white stone, feeling out of sorts and a little bit betrayed. It was almost as if this new Charlie had stolen all her fond memories of the old Charlie. She liked *him*. This new man, with his expensive clothing, neatly shaved face, and dapper top hat, was not the Charlie she had adored as a girl.

No, he was a man who knew how to please a lady and seemed to revel in that fact. Imagine telling her he was "enjoying" his home already, using that tone that men used to flirt with women. Charlie hadn't been a flirt. But Charles Avery was a skirt-chasing man-about-town, and Rose decided then and there that she would have absolutely nothing to do with him.

Chapter 14

Need I say that the knife is to cut your food with, and must never be used while eating? To put it in your mouth is a distinctive mark of low-breeding.

—From *The Ladies' Book of Etiquette, and Manual of Politeness*

For nearly five years, Rose had had dinner with the Campbells every Thursday night, taking turns at each other's homes and allowing their cooks to have a friendly competition. It was a tradition they'd kept up even after Daniel's death. While he was alive, the two couples were quite close, though she believed neither Genevieve nor Mitch ever suspected their neighbors' marriage was anything but perfect. And it had been, to a certain extent. She loved Daniel and he loved her, and they shared a common goal and affection for one another that was far deeper than she could have imagined. But as much as she adored Daniel, she did sometimes regret her decision to agree to a marriage without physical relations. Without children.

After Daniel's death, ironically from influenza that skipped by her that year, Rose allowed herself to think that perhaps she could marry again, have children. She was only twenty-three years old, an age at which some women hadn't even been married at all. Genevieve had mentioned it recently. Daniel had been dead more than a year and her mourning period was over. Perhaps she could begin to think about a true marriage now.

Rose looked in her mirror and tidied her hair. She hadn't bothered with fashionable clothes or intricate hairstyles in years and now realized it might be time to visit a dressmaker. She looked, she decided, downright frumpy and far older than her years. She frowned, wondering what Charlie had thought when he'd met her. Did he see her as frumpy and old?

"Stacy, do I have anything else in my wardrobe that would be suitable for my visit with the Campbells?"

Stacy, who had been repairing a small tear in one of her chemises, stood and walked to her wardrobe to study what was inside. Half of the dresses were black, brown, or gray, the other half so old she might as well throw them away. Fashion seemed to be changing rapidly, and Rose would rather not wear a dress from two or three years prior, the last time she'd had dresses made. All of those dresses were created for rather large bustles, and the more current designs conformed more closely to a woman's form.

"You do have the blue," Stacy said a bit skeptically. She pulled it from the wardrobe and examined it. The blue gown was one of the first she'd purchased when she'd officially put aside mourning, but it was a winter dress and overwarm for a late spring day. Still, it was the only one she had that was even remotely au courant, so she supposed it would have to do.

"It's a bit chilly this evening," Rose said with forced cheerfulness. "I do believe we need to take a trip to Madame Brunelle's."

Stacy beamed. "Oh, yes, ma'am, that would be a fine idea."

Once Rose was dressed, she pulled her hair back into her traditional serviceable bun, much to the disappointment of Stacy, who adored working with her thick, dark hair. "This will have to do," Rose said, looking at her reflection and trying to pretend that the wool dress she was wearing wasn't suffocatingly warm. "I'm already late as it is."

Thursday nights with the Campbells had truly been the only thing she'd looked forward to of late. She was living as if she were an elderly widow, not a vibrant young woman. Perhaps it was time to step out and attend more social gatherings. The problem was, she was no longer invited to the events she had been when she was married to Daniel. As a high-ranking member of the State Department, he had kept up with a social calendar that had been quite full. When he died, the invitations, understandably, came to an abrupt halt. Without family nearby, Rose had leaned heavily on the Campbells for whatever social excitement there was—and there wasn't very much of it. She certainly couldn't invite herself to a dinner or the theater. James had taken her out to the theater a few times, but he was so bereft at the loss of Daniel, he'd been poor company, and after a time, he'd stopped coming by at all.

Rose shook her morose thoughts away as she made the short journey from her front door to her neighbors'. Mr. Spark opened the door before she had a chance to knock, and he motioned her in and bade her follow him to the Campbells' parlor. She heard Genevieve's laughter and smiled, thinking how lucky she was to have such a lively friend.

Genevieve jumped to her feet when she entered, and her husband immediately stood. Mitch Campbell was a handsome man with piercing blue eyes and a headful of dark hair. At the moment he sported a Vandyke beard and mustache, which Rose thought made him look rather mysterious but that Genevieve disliked heartily. She kept threatening to shave her husband in his sleep.

"I'm sorry I am late," Rose said, walking toward Genevieve and taking her hands. The two friends were a study in contrasts: Rose with her dark, almost exotic looks and Genevieve, blond, pale, and green-eyed. "I realize I'm in desperate need of a new wardrobe. Would you like to go shopping tomorrow?"

Genevieve smiled. "Madame Brunelle's?"

"Of course. It's been so long, I daresay she will faint when she sees me cross the threshold. And I can't let her see me in this as it's not one of her creations. I fear she would be quite vexed with me."

When Rose heard footsteps behind her, she assumed it was Spark coming to offer her refreshment. She turned without a thought, ready to take the glass of wine he was no doubt offering, only to stop dead at the sight of Charlie Avery, his dark blue eyes assessing her as if she was someone he'd never before met.

"Mrs. Cartwright," Genevieve said, her voice overly bright, "this is your new neighbor, Mr. Charles Avery."

Rose whirled around to look at Genevieve, or rather to give her friend an angry flash of disbelief, which Genevieve of course ignored.

"We met briefly earlier today," Rose said, trying to recover. "In fact, Mr. Avery is quite well known to me—"

"We met some years back on the *Adriatic* when we were both traveling to America," Charlie put in quickly.

Rose narrowed her eyes at his blatant lie. So, he did not want anyone to know he'd once been her groom? He gave her a steady look, almost challenging her to expose him, and for a moment Rose was tempted.

"It is such a pleasant surprise to see a familiar face," Rose said, and noticed a slight ease in Charlie's tension. He had been afraid—likely far more than he was putting on—that she would contradict his story. It made her angry for a moment, that he should be ashamed of what he'd been, but she understood why he felt the need to lie. Or at least not tell the entire truth.

"Why that's wonderful," Genevieve said. "What a surprising coincidence!"

"It's almost hard to believe," Mitch said dryly, and both she and Charlie gave him a quick look. Rose had found over the years that Mitch's calm reserve hid a highly intelligent man. She often wondered if he had discovered the truth about her marriage to Daniel and had simply kept the information to himself.

"Yes. A pleasant surprise," Charlie said, taking a sip of his brandy, his eyes unwavering on hers. If she was not mistaken, there was gratitude in his gaze and Rose looked away, her cheeks suddenly pink.

"That dress must be quite warm, Rose, your cheeks are flushed."

If Rose and Genevieve had been alone, Rose might have given her friend a face, but instead she smiled, a spectacularly false smile that Genevieve apparently found extremely amusing. Rose knew what Genevieve was up to; she was attempting to matchmake. Rose wondered if her friend would have tried to pair them up had she known Charlie had been under her family's employ. Knowing Genevieve, and she did know her quite well, it wouldn't have mattered at all. Though Genevieve was the granddaughter of the Duke and Duchess of Glastonbury, she had grown up in a cabin with her father out West. Despite her cultured, aristocratic accent, Genevieve was the least snobbish person she knew. After all, her husband, though a brilliant portrait photographer, was hardly from the highest echelons of society (his mother was an actress, of all things!). No doubt Genevieve would be thrilled to know she was trying to match the daughter of an earl to that same earl's former head groom.

Genevieve lifted her head, acknowledging her mute butler, and said, "Dinner is ready. Shall we dine?"

That's when a terrible thought occurred to Rose. Her mother had always said that the true mark of breeding was the manner in which one comported oneself at dinner. Rose had been drilled on polite dining habits, something that Charlie's education had been sorely lacking. She remembered on the ship being surrounded by passengers who had not been as severely schooled as she had in proper dining. At first, she'd been rather appalled at the lack of manners many of the passengers had displayed—Charlie among them. Genevieve and Mitch were not sticklers, but they did comport themselves well and would no doubt look askance at Charlie if he did not.

As they sat, she watched Charlie, wishing she could school him quickly in how to act. She noted immediately that he removed his gloves and placed them on his left leg, then covered his gloves with his napkin. Rose was ridiculously proud of him.

The footmen filled their wineglasses, and Mitch held his up to make a toast. "Welcome to the neighborhood, Mr. Avery," he said.

"Thank you, Mr. Campbell," Charlie said, placing the glass down without taking a taste. "I fear I have misled you." Charlie glanced at Rose before continuing. "I have, in fact, known Mrs. Cartwright almost from the day she was born. You see, I was first her father's stable boy and later his head groom. I've never lied about my background and who I am and I cannot say in truth why I just did."

For some silly reason, Rose felt her throat burn and knew if she didn't get hold of herself immediately, her eyes would begin to glitter suspiciously. How brave Charlie was to admit such a thing. Everyone at the table was silent for a long beat, until Genevieve said, "How marvelous! You, sir, are a success story. Rags to riches. Quite exciting. I have my own rags to riches story to share, perhaps after dinner. Everyone has your gadgets in their kitchen, you know. The mark of a good kitchen is the number of C. A. Kitchen Tools one has. And quite pretty with that little flower on each one. Your kitchen has them, doesn't it, Rose?"

Rose gave her friend a smile of thanks; never would she meet anyone as charming and kind as Genevieve. "Yes, that is right. My cook nearly swooned when she found out who had moved in next door."

"You must tell me what Rose was like as a child," Genevieve said. "Not that she's so old now. Imagine your moving in next door. What a coincidence that..." Her voice trailed off because though Genevieve might be a bit naive at times, she was not stupid. "At any rate. Yes. How lucky for us all."

Everyone knew that Charlie's moving into the house next door to Rose could not have been happenstance, and an awkward silence fell over the table.

"It wasn't an accident, my moving in next to Mrs. Cartwright," Charlie said, his eyes on Genevieve, and Rose got the distinct feeling he was purposely avoiding her gaze. "Having Mrs. Cartwright as a neighbor was one of the home's most important assets to me." Rose could feel her entire body heat, though she wasn't entirely certain why . . . until Charlie looked at her. He was *affecting* her, as no man had since, well, since Charlie. How exceedingly upsetting. It was those women he'd entertained, their cries of passion and obvious pleasure. Would she never be able to look at Charlie without thinking such things? It was purely awful.

"I don't understand," Genevieve said.

"I don't want to be crass, but I haven't been wealthy all that long and I know only a few men who run in the circles that I must enter in order to make business connections. In fact, I was hoping that Mrs. Cartwright might be able to introduce me to New York society. Moving in next door was a calculated business move."

Rose told herself not to be disappointed in his revelation, but she was. She'd imagined he'd moved in next door for spite, to show her how far he'd come. She'd even considered that he'd chosen to be her neighbor to rekindle the small romance they'd had on board ship. No, that was the wrong word, for they hadn't truly had a romance. Friendship, perhaps? Still, to learn Charlie had no motive for buying the house other than making his own pockets more full was slightly upsetting. He had planned all along to use her? Suddenly, the evening felt far less joyous. Why she'd thought using her for business connections was far worse than moving there for spite, she could not say.

"I haven't been out in society of late," Rose said, making her voice cold. "I've been in mourning." She found small gratification in the fact that Charlie's cheeks reddened.

"We can help a bit," Mitch said quickly, obviously noting the sudden tension in the room. "Though we don't move in the same circles Mrs. Cartwright did, we can make some introductions." Mitch gave Rose a look of censure, which she decided to ignore. She was not in the mood to capitulate.

"Oh, yes," Genevieve said. "We certainly don't call the Astors our friends—can't really say that anyone does—but we are often invited to entertainments where you might rub elbows with the people you need to meet."

Rose watched as Charlie nodded. Something was so reserved about him, so tense. While he talked with Mitch about the connections he needed to make for his business, Rose took some time to look at him. He was uncommonly handsome, but she noticed telltale circles beneath his eyes (she knew for certain he wasn't getting a full night's rest), and brackets at either corner of his mouth that hadn't been there when he'd been a younger man. It was almost as if he'd been spending far too much time frowning. His hair, his beautiful dandelion hair, was cut short and tamed with a small bit of pomade.

Genevieve glanced at Rose before saying, "Will you also be searching for a bride?"

Rose snapped out of her reverie. As they waited for Charlie to answer, Genevieve pointedly did not look at Rose. Rose knew this, of course, because she knew Genevieve, and she also knew how difficult it was for Genevieve *not* to look at her.

"I'm rather enjoying the life of a bachelor at the moment," Charlie said, a small smile forming on his lips, and Rose suspected he was thinking about all his lady friends. "I suppose I may marry eventually." He hardly sounded enthusiastic about the prospect.

"What sort of women do you prefer?" Genevieve asked. It wasn't the question but the way she asked it that made Rose want to throttle her.

"Opera singers," Rose said without missing a beat.

Charlie took a bite of fine filet mignon and chewed slowly, looking very much as if he was trying not to smile. He even looked attractive chewing. How could that be possible?

"Actually," he said, dragging his eyes away from Rose to look at his hostess, "I'd prefer someone respectable. That is all."

"You don't care if she's pretty or intelligent or kind?" Genevieve asked.

"Of course, all of those things are important," Charlie said, looking as if he'd taken a bite of something he wished he hadn't.

Mitch chuckled, shaking his head. "You, sir, have opened a Pandora's box that I'm betting is best left shut tight. You do realize you've just given these two women permission to be matchmakers. Good God, man, I do pity you. You were going to tell us about what Mrs. Cartwright was like when she was a child."

Charlie gave Mitch a grateful smile. The very last thing he wanted Rose to do was come up with some list of eligible women he should court. He had no idea why he had said such a thing, because he already knew precisely whom he wanted to marry. His brain got all muddled when he was near Rose, it seemed. The minute he'd seen her, his heart had begun pounding madly and his brain had shut down entirely. And of course his body had reacted, as it always did. He had no doubt why he had moved in next to her and it sure as hell had nothing to do with business. If Daniel had still been alive, he never would have considered buying the home next to them. *Moving in next door was a calculated business move.* One of the most absurd things to come out of his mouth yet. Yes, he had moved in next door to the woman he'd loved for years, the woman he'd never forgotten and never truly gotten over, for *business* reasons. Good Lord, the fact that anyone accepted that load of donkey dung was beyond him. Then again, no one in the room, including Rose, knew he was madly in love with her.

"Lady Rose—that is what I called her then, even when she was very small—was exceedingly curious. I first saw her when I was about ten years old and she was four. She was . . . spectacularly talkative," he said, earning a laugh from Rose.

"I would hang about the stables and batter him with questions and questions. What was he doing? Why? Why couldn't I feed Moonrise oats? My brothers and I spent hours in the stables, much to my mother's horror."

"Why couldn't you feed Moonrise oats? And who is Moonrise?" Genevieve asked.

"Moonrise was my mare, such a sweet and courageous horse. I miss her dearly. And she was allergic to oats, so I wasn't allowed to feed them to her. Charlie was quite adamant. I do believe he loved her as much as I did." She smiled fondly at him and he felt his face turn red. Again. "She had a foal right before I left. My father sold her, the foal, not Moonrise, thank goodness."

Charlie could picture Rose perfectly, her big brown eyes, her dark hair often braided into pigtails and pinned atop her head. Those braids never did stay put and she'd end up with the two dark ropes of hair whirling about her. Even then, she'd held a special place in his heart.

By the time the two couples left the table to move to the parlor for dessert, Charlie knew one thing: he couldn't imagine himself married to anyone but Rose, but he was probably the last man on her list of potential suitors. Just out of mourning, she might not even be considering marriage yet. And even if she were, he doubted he would even appear on the list. If he possessed all the money in the world, it wouldn't stop her from considering him a commoner, a working man who had no business thinking about her, never mind marrying her. He understood this, as well as he understood he would go to his grave loving her.

Chapter 15

Learn to restrain anger. A man in a passion ceases to be a gentleman, and if you do not control your passions, rely upon it, they will one day control you.

—From *The Gentlemen's Book of Etiquette, and Manual of Politeness*

Rose had never been the type of woman to spy on her neighbors. She reminded herself of this fact as she watched another strange woman standing on Charlie's front steps to be admitted into the house. Watching this was no easy feat. In order to see his front entryway, Rose had to stand in her own foyer, get up on her tippy-toes, lean over a small table, and crane her neck just so.

After the woman had gone inside, Rose relaxed and sighed. Who *were* they all? The past three nights since her Thursday evening dinner with the Campbells, it had been silent next door. But during each of those days that had passed, she'd spied no fewer than two different women on three separate days enter his home. Alone.

She shouldn't care and she told herself it was none of her business what her neighbor did, as immoral as he apparently was. But she did care. Obviously. Her strained neck was proof of the fact. Unfortunately, the women were standing too far away for her to see their features, but Rose imagined they were young and pretty. And she had to admit, based on their clothing, they were respectable ladies. Were they contenders for the title Mrs. Charles Avery? What young woman wouldn't want to marry a rich, handsome man?

A woman, she told herself, who was completely aware of just how many women Charlie was interviewing for the position of his wife, that's who. Rose crossed her arms, curiosity burning inside her.

What were they doing? They weren't playing chess, that was for certain.

It would be completely unconscionable to actually go over to her property line and try to peer into his house. And she told herself she probably wouldn't like what she saw in any case. Just that thought made her cheeks burn—and other parts of her body were also strangely hot. Rose pressed her fingertips against her temples, not because her head hurt, but more to expunge the images in her head. Other than statues, Rose had never seen a fully naked man. Her only experience had been with Weston, which had been disgusting. Clearly, the women who visited Charlie were not disgusted, quite the opposite. Stacy nearly swooned every time she caught sight of him, and she'd heard her maids giggling more than once after he'd walked by.

"I won't be able to see anything anyway," she whispered to herself. It was highly unlikely they'd be doing whatever they were doing within sight of a window. Rose chewed on her lower lip, debating with herself and wondering why she was debating at all. *Because I want to know. Because if he is with a woman, I will be able to stop thinking about him. I will know and that will be that.*

Mumbling to herself about how wrong what she was about to do was, Rose walked to the back of her home and slipped outside, looking behind her as if she were a thief. As she walked around the house and entered her narrow side yard, she frowned. Facing her was a hedge that was just too high for her to easily see over. She walked along the hedge, casually, to see if she could find a thin spot where she might be able to peer through to the other side, but her gardener was far too good to allow a thin spot. Putting her hands on her hips, she looked about, as if a space would magically open up for her.

Then she spied the gate at the end of her property that separated her yard from his. It had never been locked, as Rose had allowed her old neighbors' lively brood to play in her garden. She'd enjoyed watching them and had often set up a game of croquet. Rose strolled to the gate, and again looked behind her to make certain none of her staff was looking out into the garden, then she slipped through, holding her breath, and closed the gate behind her.

"Oh, Lord." What would she do if she were caught in his yard? She had to have some sort of explanation other than the truth, which was too awful to even consider saying aloud. *Why, I thought I'd watch you and your lady friend cavorting. Surely there is nothing wrong with that!*

Oh, so, so wrong. But Rose started walking stealthily in the twilight darkness of Charlie's garden toward the first lit window she saw. She knew it was far more difficult for anyone inside the house to see her, but she was filled with fear at any rate and tried to walk as quietly as possible. The first window with light shining through was the kitchen, and Rose ducked down upon seeing members of Charlie's staff cleaning up after dinner. Lifting her skirts, she walked, bent over so she'd be below the window, along the house until she reached the next lit window.

She wished she knew more curse words, because they would come in quite handy at the moment and all directed at herself. What was she *doing*?

Rose slowly straightened, poised to run just in case Charlie or someone else was peering out the window directly at her, and looked inside. What she saw, well, it wasn't what she'd expected.

A man, whom she recognized as one of Charlie's footmen, was sitting at a piano, and Charlie and a woman were standing in the center of the room. The woman was talking to him as the footman looked on, hands poised above the piano keys. The woman was much older than he; her hair, which had been covered with a bonnet when she'd stood outside his door, was sprinkled with gray. She had to be at least fifty years of age. Then, as Rose watched, she instructed Charlie to place his right hand upon her waist and his left in hers, and raised their joined hands to shoulder level. Clearly, she was instructing him how to dance the waltz.

Something in Rose's heart shifted at that moment. Of course Charlie wouldn't know how to dance. How could he? And his manners at dinner, so impeccable; had he had a lady give him lessons in proper table manners as well? He certainly had to have learned it somewhere. It occurred to her that Charlie was learning to be a gentleman, learning all those things that had been drilled into her brothers from the day they were born. Drilled until everything was second nature—dining, conversing, dancing—all those little habits that separated the classes. They were not inborn, they were learned. Rose, of course, already knew this on a certain level, but watching Charlie's stumbling attempts at the waltz, his clear frustration, was almost heartbreaking.

Rose stood there, transfixed, as Charlie and his tutor stopped and started, again and again, until Charlie started to get it. He was so determined, his face set and solemn, finding absolutely no joy in the dance. It was like everything else, Rose realized: he needed to learn it and so he did. It was very nearly heroic, this simple waltz.

After some time, they moved onto a schottische, which Charlie clearly knew better than the waltz. Rose realized it was more likely that Charlie had already known the schottische. His tutor said something, and Charlie gave her a grim smile, so Rose assumed it was some sort of compliment. Charlie was an athletic dancer, not particularly graceful, but confident and strong. It would be thrilling to dance with him, Rose thought, her eyes on his hand, which rested lightly on the lady's slim waist. For a sharp instant, she wished that strong hand was on her.

Blushing hotly, Rose turned away and rested her back on the cool stone of the house. What was she doing, spying on him? Was her life so empty that the only entertainment she could find was watching her neighbor be tutored in dance? She looked up at the moon, barely visible through a thin layer of clouds, feeling lonelier than she ever had before. She stood there for several long minutes, watching the moon's glow brighten and wane, depending on the thickness of the clouds, allowing herself to slip into a bout of self-pity. When was the last time someone had held her? In truth, she couldn't remember. Perhaps her brother Marcus when she'd been ill? She wrapped her arms around herself in a rather pathetic attempt to comfort herself.

Angry that she'd slipped into self-pity, Rose turned back to the window and looked inside, only to see an empty room.

"What are you doing in my garden?"

It was Charlie and he was clearly angry. He looked from her to his window, quickly surmising what she'd been doing. Rose closed her eyes, knowing she had no excuse for looking into his window. She took a bracing breath and decided to act as if peering into someone's house at night was a common occurrence and nothing at all to be upset about.

"I was watching you dance. I adore dancing and it's been some time—"

"You have no right," he bit out, walking toward her. "You are trespassing, Mrs. Cartwright."

Rose felt her entire body heat with embarrassment and a little bit of fear. Charlie did seem so very angry. "I know, Charlie, and I am sorry."

"Mr. Avery," he spat. "I have not given you leave to call me by my given name."

Rose very nearly reared back. "I am sorry, Mr. Avery," she managed to say through a throat that was becoming tight. Of course, Rose knew she was completely in the wrong, but she hadn't thought about how much she was violating Charlie's privacy; she had only thought to assuage her curiosity. "I . . . It's just that I saw all these women coming and going and I'm afraid my curiosity got the best of me."

He took another step toward her and she took a step back, her heel hitting the stone foundation wall of his home. "Why do you care if I entertain a hundred women in my own home? *My* home, Mrs. Cartwright. A home I worked for, seven days a week, long hours, endless days. I earned this house *and* my privacy."

Oh, he was so very, very angry. Hot tears pricked at her eyes. She couldn't argue; she had no excuse. Rose had never been one to use tears to get her way, and the fact that she was crying was extremely annoying. She wiped at them impatiently, trying to think of something to say that would make the situation better.

"Why do you watch my lessons?" he demanded.

"I don't." He let out an angry sound. "I mean to say, I didn't know you were receiving a lesson."

"Then why were you outside my window . . . ?"

Rose felt as if she might combust from shame and embarrassment.

"You wanted to spy on me while I entertained my lady friends, is that it, Rose?" He stepped closer until he was mere inches away from her.

Rose turned her head away, unable to face him. This was perhaps the most mortifying thing to have ever happened to her.

"You wanted to watch me," he said silkily, moving his head next to hers so that his mouth was just inches from her left ear. "You wanted to watch me kiss their breasts, taste them. You wanted to see us naked, is that right, Mrs. Cartwright?"

She shook her head, just slightly, just so he'd know she was rejecting his words even though they were far too close to the truth. She could feel the heat of his body despite the fact that he was not touching her, and she had the awful urge to tilt her neck, an invitation for him to press his lips there. The thought came from nowhere, but his voice, soft and taunting, was making her feel things she didn't want to feel. A flood of desire made her weak, and she swallowed in an attempt to restore her senses.

"And you want me to do the same to you, don't you? You want me to kiss you, to bare your breasts and suckle you. To touch you between your legs. You always did like playing with the commoners, didn't you?" This last was tinged with anger.

"That's not true," Rose said vehemently, knowing he was referring to their time on the ship together. "It wasn't like that."

He pulled his head back to look at her, as if he were surprised by her words. It was still just light enough so that she could see his eyes glittering in the dark, but his expression was lost to her.

He tilted his head, a mocking gesture filled with anger. "Then, tell me, what was it like?"

She looked up at him, her dear old friend, and surprised them both by leaning closer, by pressing her lips against his, by letting him know that, yes, she did want him to touch her. She needed him to touch her. Rose moved her lips against his, trying to recall the proper way to kiss, letting out a sound of pleasure and frustration and terrible need.

He pulled back as if studying her, then, letting out a deep, guttural sound, he kissed her, slanting his head and thrusting his tongue into her mouth, moving his lips teasingly as if he wanted to devour her. It surprised Rose, but she always had been a quick learner, and she played with his tongue, a sensuous, wonderful new experience that was far more pleasant that she'd thought it would be.

Rose knew Charlie was treating her like a woman who'd been married, not the virginal innocent she was. He pressed his erection against her, and it was shocking and somehow wonderful. She brought her hands up to his hair and smiled, loving the softness of it, even though he'd cut it short. When he touched her breast, his hand was large and warm and welcome. And when he moved one thumb over her nipple, she cried out at the pure pleasure of it, sweet shards of sensation that seemed connected directly to the apex of her thighs. He let out a sound, purely male, when her nipple became erect beneath the pad of his thumb, and he pressed himself even harder against her.

Suddenly, it was too much, too fast, her senses were reeling, her body on fire, and she pushed him away, just slightly, just enough to let him know she couldn't take another second of his touch without losing herself completely.

They were both breathing heavily, Rose perhaps more than Charlie, who dropped his hands from her and stepped back.

"I apologize," he said, his voice sounding strained.

"No, please do not."

He took another step back, as if he didn't trust himself to be so close. "I'll bid you good night, Mrs. Cartwright."

Rose still stood with her back pressed against the cold stone of his house. "Good night, Mr. Avery."

He turned and walked toward the front of his house, then stopped. "If you want to watch my lessons, Mrs. Cartwright, you need only ask. Perhaps you could be of assistance."

She had kissed *him*.

That was all he could think of as he walked back into his home, feeling like a man who had just been stunned by a tremendous blow, one that hadn't hurt so much as left him reeling. The anger that had coursed through him when he'd realized she'd been watching him was like nothing he'd ever experienced. Now *that* had hurt. He'd imagined her peeking into his window, night after night, as he'd danced around like some awkward baboon. If he believed her—and he did—it hadn't been about spying on his lessons at all. It had been curiosity about what he'd been doing with the women who came to his door.

A week ago, she might have gotten an eyeful, but a week ago, he hadn't spoken to her, seen her. Realized he still had feelings for her and probably still loved her. A week ago, the only thing he'd cared about assuaging was his lust. Now it was different. She was back in his life. That was why the thought of her seeing him at his awkward worst was beyond humiliating.

Charlie had realized about six months earlier that if he was going to rub elbows with the upper levels of society, he was going to have to get some polish. His awakening occurred when he'd been invited into the Union Club for the first time and hadn't removed his hat immediately upon entering. He hadn't seen a place to put the thing, and no servant was there to take it, so he'd kept it on. Until a member of the staff quietly walked up to him and asked him to remove it. That was when he noticed several men staring at him as if he had a baby elephant on his head, not a damned top hat. He realized he didn't know and couldn't understand the rules by which he would have to live if he were to succeed in this new world. That was when he'd enlisted Mrs. Gendron, a wealthy woman approaching sixty years of age, whose husband had committed suicide upon losing everything during the Panic of '73. She'd been left with nothing and for years worked as a governess, a humiliating and devastating turn of events for a woman used to a very different life. Mrs. Gendron had opened a school and now taught etiquette and comportment to people like him, those who needed more than just a bit of polish. She called him her greatest challenge, not unkindly, and promised to sculpt him into a gentleman within a year.

Six months later, he could hold his own at a business meeting, had been admitted to the Union Club, and had been approached by J. P. Morgan about the possibility of joining the Knickerbocker Club. America was a wonderful place. This type of acceptance by men at the highest levels of society was heady stuff, yet he knew if he went home to England, his money and his manners wouldn't get him into the front door of any private men's club there simply because he did not have a *Lord* in front of his name. In England, he'd still be working in a stable.

In America, he could marry someone like Rose.

She had kissed *him*.

"You have a visitor, Mrs. Cartwright."

It wasn't the words her butler had spoken that made her look up but the slight inflection he'd used. Her butler, Mr. Brady, was not the taciturn ideal of a butler and never had been, but he was loyal to a fault and had been quite kind to her over the years.

"A gentleman, ma'am. Mr. Avery. He is waiting in the blue parlor."

Rose raised a brow at that, for the blue parlor had been Daniel's favorite room, a masculine and comfortable place filled with heavy, leather furniture, rich navy-blue velvet curtains, and a well-used card table. Daniel had loved whist and they had made excellent partners.

"Thank you, Brady," Rose said, rising from her spot by a window overlooking her garden. She placed her book, a mystery novel, on a side table and walked to a small mirror situated next to the door. She looked . . . terrified. Schooling her features, Rose smoothed already smooth skirts and walked down the main staircase to the blue parlor.

He was standing when she entered, studying a small statue of a shepherdess, a whimsical piece that was one of her favorites. She didn't know if she'd ever get used to the sight of this new Charlie. In her mind, she pictured the carefree young man wearing rough workman's clothing, with his dandelion curls and easy smile. The man standing in her parlor was dressed impeccably, wearing a close-fitting light brown jacket, tailored to perfection, his hair neatly groomed and smooth, with only the smallest hint of curl. He was, in one word, stunning.

This was the man she'd practically thrown herself at, and he was now standing in her parlor as if nothing untoward had occurred. "Hello, Mr. Avery, to what do I owe this pleasure?"

He looked up, and the look in his blue eyes nearly took her breath away. Placing the small statue back in its place, he held up a hand as if stopping her. "I was angry last night. You may call me Charlie, of course."

Rose smiled. "You had every right to be angry. I want to apologize again for my behavior. All of my behavior." She was so completely mortified over everything she'd done the previous evening, from watching the woman enter his home, to spying, to kissing him. It was almost as if another woman entirely had possessed her body.

"I've given that some thought," he said, surprising her and filling her with trepidation. She truly wished he would immediately forget the entire incident, though she did realize that was unlikely to happen. Goodness knew she would never forget it. "I wondered why you were so curious. Curious enough to go against everything you believe, every bit of politeness that is so ingrained in you. To be honest, it was difficult for me to picture you skulking about my yard just so you could peek into one of my windows. For curiosity."

Rose swallowed heavily but remained silent. Was he going to torture her by recounting the evening? For what purpose?

"And then there was that kiss."

Her cheeks flamed instantly. "Really, Charlie, we don't need to revisit the entire evening, do we? I have apologized and I am frankly mortified by my behavior. As I have said repeatedly."

"I am not recounting the events for any purpose other than to examine them further."

Rose lifted her chin, trying to regain some composure. "To what end?"

"You do remember, do you not, that I have kissed you before."

He could not be bringing up their time aboard ship; it didn't bear thinking about. "I think you should go."

"I remember that kiss, Rose. It meant something to me, even if it meant nothing to you. At that time, at any rate. I was a bit taken with you, but of course you couldn't have known that. My proposal, which was met with no small amount of horror, was quite sincere." He gave her a tight smile.

"You proposed?" Rose blurted out.

He tilted his head and stared at her, the expression on his handsome face one of faint disbelief. Then he nodded and let out a humorless laugh as he looked up at the ceiling. "My God," he said.

"It was five years ago," she said, frantically thinking back on that time. She'd been so young and so very afraid. Charlie had proposed? Surely she would have remembered . . .

And then she did, his offer to marry her. "But you weren't *serious*, Charlie. You said it jokingly if I recall." And then, in a small voice, "Didn't you?"

"No, it was not a joke, Rose," he said softly.

"Oh."

"But I took your rejection philosophically enough. I was, after all, only an employee and you were Lady Rose Dunford. I could have expected nothing less. I remember many things, including those small kisses in the ship. You were hardly experienced."

Suddenly, Rose wanted to flee. She'd been no more experienced the previous night than she'd been on that ship. He knew. And he was going to ask her why a woman who had been married for four years could possibly not know how to kiss, could have gasped in surprise at the lovely sensation of a man's hand on her breast. "Please leave," she said, not as a lady would, but like a woman who desperately wanted a conversation to end. She couldn't bear it if he learned the truth about her marriage. It would hurt him, that she had chosen a man like Daniel over himself. She couldn't pretend it hadn't been a choice; it had.

"I don't pretend to know about you, about your marriage. About how it's possible that you still kiss like a young, untried girl. Did he never kiss you, Rose?"

The pity she heard in his voice was humiliating. "I want you to leave, Charlie."

He stepped closer to her, not more than an arm's length away. "Why were you so curious, Rose? Why?"

Rose shook her head, unable to look at him. She had no answer. She didn't know herself why she'd so wanted to see what was happening, though she knew a large part of it was that if she had seen him with another woman, she might be able to dismiss him from her mind. She couldn't say that aloud, for it would be much too telling.

"I don't know," she said finally. "I don't know why I spied on you. I don't know." She turned away and took several steps, putting more distance between them.

"I don't believe you," he said calmly. "But it doesn't matter. Not really." He let out a gusty sigh. "I didn't come over here to discuss your trespassing at any rate, and I apologize if I've made you uncomfortable. As I am here to ask a favor, it was probably bad strategy on my part, but I believe it's always good to clear the air."

Rose nodded. "Then why are you here?"

Charlie's confidence seemed to waver, and he sat, then immediately stood, realizing his faux pas. Rose graciously sat in the nearest chair and Charlie, his cheeks turning a bit ruddy, sat again. "I have been invited to a charity ball and I was wondering if you would accompany me. I won't know many people in attendance and I thought you could help me navigate this bloody New York society."

Charlie had stunned her again. "A charity ball? At this time of year?"

"Is there a charity ball season?" Charlie asked, somewhat bemused.

"Indeed there is. November through February. A ball in April is quite unusual. Who is the host?"

"I'm not certain, but J. P. Morgan will be there. He's recently implied that I might be considered to join the Knickerbockers, and I can hardly say no to the invitation. Morgan would be a good friend to have. It would be best if I had someone along who could guide me. As you know," he said with a telling pause, "I have been taking the appropriate lessons so that I won't make a fool of myself entirely, but it would be good to have someone such as yourself by my side. I'm afraid I don't have acquaintance with other ladies of your ilk. Spying excepted, of course."

Despite herself, Rose laughed, glad the conversation had veered away from her inexperience in kissing and toward a much tamer and much safer topic. "I would be happy to accompany you, Mr. Avery," she said pertly. "When is it?"

"Tonight."

Rose's mouth dropped in a very unladylike manner. "A ball. Tonight. Charlie, I haven't been to a ball in more than a year. I haven't anything to wear. Do you?"

"I have a formal suit, if that's what you mean. Long tails, white tie, spats. I'm told I look rather dashing."

"I'm certain you do, but I don't see how it would be possible for me, unless . . . I was planning to see Madame Brunelle. Perhaps she has something that would require only small alterations. She is not going to be pleased, that is for certain."

"You will go?"

"If I find a dress, then yes, I will."

When Rose walked into Madame Brunelle's with Genevieve later that day, all heads turned in their direction. The two women might not have been part of the highest New York social circles, but they were well known and their presence in the shop would most certainly be noted, particularly Rose, who had been out of society since her young husband's death. One of the employees immediately disappeared, only to reappear moments later with Madame herself.

"Mrs. Campbell, Mrs. Cartwright, a pleasure," she said, smiling— a smile that quickly turned sour when she saw what Rose was wearing.

"You can see why I am here," Rose said, looking down at her dark gray dress. "Nearly everything I have that is in the current style is mourning or half mourning."

Madame Brunelle clapped her hands sharply and two young seamstresses immediately appeared. "Mrs. Cartwright needs an entire wardrobe. Get my fashion plates and some fabrics to show her." She looked back at Rose and added, "Quickly now, girls. *Rapidement!*"

Genevieve whispered into Rose's ear, "When she learns what you are truly here for, I'm afraid she may collapse."

Rose stifled a laugh before going up to Madame, who was still issuing rapid instructions to her harried employees. "Madame Brunelle, while I do indeed require a new wardrobe, that is not why I am here today."

Madame looked from Rose to Genevieve, who was impeccably dressed as always in one of Madame Brunelle's own creations. She looked at the two women again, her puzzlement clear.

"You might as well tell her, Mrs. Cartwright," Genevieve said, unable to keep her amusement from her eyes.

"I need a ball gown," Rose said.

"Oui, I am certain you do."

"For this evening," Rose said, grimacing slightly.

"I am sorry, Mrs. Cartwright, but my English. You said you need it this evening? *C'est impossible.*" She threw up her hands, proclaiming defeat.

Genevieve stepped between the angry Madame Brunelle and the frightened Rose. "Madame, surely you must have something my friend could wear for her first ball since her husband's tragic death."

"I do not sell off the rack," Madame said, clearly affronted.

"Perhaps Letourneau will have something," Rose said softly, but apparently not softly enough. Which was exactly what she'd meant to do.

"*Non!* You cannot go to that man's boutique. Do you want to look like a cow? *Non.*" She called for one of her shopgirls, speaking in rapid French, so rapid Rose caught only a few words, but she understood enough to know Madame would, indeed, be able to outfit her for the ball.

Madame turned to the two women and smiled. "What is this ball? It is April." She paused, her eyes widening. "Do not tell me it is the Tattering ball. *Mon Dieu.* Only one hundred have been invited and you . . ."

"Tattering?" Rose repeated. She'd had no idea Charlie was moving in those sorts of circles. No wonder he was nervous; now *she* was nervous. Certainly, she'd attended entertainments where the likes of the Tatterings, Vanderbilts, Morgans, and Pierreponts were in attendance, but Daniel and she had never been on such an exclusive guest list. How had Charlie managed it? "I imagine it must be." Only someone like Anne Tattering could hold a ball so soon after Easter and before the summer season began in Newport and get away with it. Rose had met the lady once and had been terrified, for she'd heard she did not like the English and wore her family's humble beginnings like a badge of honor—even if those humble beginnings were two generations ago. It was at that moment Rose realized why Charlie had been invited. Mrs. Tattering no doubt adored him and his mercurial rise from head groom to wealth and power. The fact that Charlie had been *her* family's head groom did not bode well for Rose.

But she had said she would go and would stick to her word. Part of her prayed Madame Brunelle would be unable to produce an appropriate gown.

"Voilà!" she said, when a young shopgirl entered the room with a breathtaking dress draped across her arms. It was the color, serendipitously, of the palest rose, with intricate lace and beadwork that Rose had to admit would look lovely with her complexion and dark hair. "I had forgotten about this creation. I made it for a young woman whose delicate condition made it impossible for her to wear. She returned to England without the gown, so there is no danger of her seeing you in it, I assure you." Madame took the dress and held it up to Rose.

"C'est magnifique," she pronounced. "A bit too long, but that is better than too short, *non*? Into the fitting room, ladies." With the energy of a woman half her age, Madame Brunelle charged into the room and the shopgirls, fluttering around her like twittering birds, began helping Rose to undress while Genevieve looked on, unable to hide her smile.

"I do believe it is fate that has brought you and that dress together so quickly," Genevieve said. "Mr. Avery will be quite pleased you were successful."

"Genevieve, I am doing the man a favor only," Rose said. As soon as she'd told Genevieve that Charlie had asked her to a ball, Genevieve had been giddily anticipating their wedding. Saying the words aloud put a bit of a damper on her feelings, because they were only the truth. It had not been some romantic notion that had made Charlie ask for her to accompany him. He was a pragmatic man when it came to business, apparently, and he was intelligent enough to know that to navigate New York society successfully, he needed someone by his side to help. Who else was there? Should he have asked his matronly Mrs. Gendron to accompany him? Or one of his lady friends?

The girls tugged on the dress, which fit remarkably well considering it had been made for another woman entirely. It was a bit too long, and the waist was a tad too snug, but otherwise the gown flattered her figure rather nicely.

"It looks better on you than its original owner," Madame declared. "A little adjustment here"—she tugged at the waist—"and a bit here." She pulled some material on the shoulder, bringing it up so that the bodice better hugged her breasts. "And look at the back. So beautiful. I'd forgotten how lovely is this dress."

One of the girls pulled around a mirror so that Rose could get a view of the back of the gown. It was so lovely, she gasped. It was a work of art. The cascading material fell softly to a small bustle and a train of tiny florets and pleated material so intricate Rose actually felt for the poor seamstress who'd had to sew it. "It is beyond anything I could have imagined," Rose said feelingly. "You are surely an artist, Madame, and I am honored that you are willing to make alterations so quickly."

"Mon plaisir," Madame said, looking pleased. "But after this ball tonight, you must return so I can create your new wardrobe, *oui?*"

"Yes. In the meantime, you can take my measurements and create some day dresses for me, if you would. I truly have nothing to wear that isn't black, brown, or gray and I am dreadfully sick of those colors."

"Of course. Mabel, take the lady's measurements." Madame walked around Rose, looking at her critically. "Who is this Mr. Avery?"

"He is no one," Rose said, seeing the gleam in Madame Brunelle's eyes. Why must everyone want to matchmake?

"Other than Mr. Campbell, he is the most handsome man I've ever seen," Genevieve said. "And they've known each other since they were children, and I do believe Mr. Avery is already in love with Mrs. Cartwright."

"Genevieve, really," Rose said, laughing.

"Ah, she blushes," Madame Brunelle said knowingly.

"The same way you blushed when I spoke Monsieur Letourneau's name," Rose pointed out, knowing that mention of Madame Brunelle's rival would instantly stop any discussion of her marrying Charlie.

"It was rage, not love that made my cheeks flush. At any rate, I am far too old for all the romantic trappings. You are still a girl."

Rose looked at herself in the mirror, and for a quick moment that's what she felt like: a girl about to go to her very first ball.

"Mr. Avery will be transfixed," Genevieve said, coming up beside her and looking at her reflection.

"It doesn't matter if he is or not," Rose said, but her friend's comment made her smile anyway.

Chapter 16

Never stand up to dance unless you are perfect master of the step, figure, and time of that dance. If you make a mistake you not only render yourself ridiculous, but you annoy your partner and the others in the set.

—From *The Gentlemen's Book of Etiquette, and Manual of Politeness*

Charlie felt slightly ill, knowing his performance this evening might make or break his future. Men like J. P. Morgan and George Tattering liked dealing with men like themselves—highly intelligent, highly motivated men of fine morals and impeccable manners. He wasn't quite sure how he'd ended up as a guest of George Tattering, but he damned well was going to go and do his utmost to show he could stand with the best of them. He needed Morgan's financing, Carnegie's steel and railroads, and Tattering's influence if he wanted to bring his businesses to the next level. Most people knew about C. A. Kitchen Tools, some were aware of Avery Hand Tools, but very few knew about his plans to develop a better, more powerful locomotive engine. His brain never stopped, and he was constantly pulling out a piece of paper to quickly scribble some sort of design. When he'd been a groom, he'd developed new designs for the tools of his trade, but now, the world was open to him.

Morgan was one of the few people who knew, and that had been quite by accident. Charlie had been invited to a small dinner party that Morgan had attended, and had slipped away to add to a drawing he'd begun earlier that day. Morgan had found him in a small library, frantically trying to get down his thoughts before they were crowded out by another idea. The two men had talked, Morgan glancing over his drawings with growing interest, not knowing who he was talking to until he stopped in midsentence and asked.

"Charles Avery of C. A. Kitchen Tools and Avery Hand Tools?"

And that had been the beginning of an unusual friendship between Charlie and the older man. Morgan liked Charlie's youth and enthusiasm, but was keenly aware Charlie was inexperienced at business, despite his small successes.

"Vision without execution is hallucination," Morgan had said, quoting his friend Thomas Edison. "You know who said that? A young man named Thomas Edison. You remind me of him, Mr. Avery." He winked. "That's a good thing, son."

At the time, Charlie hadn't quite known just how powerful Morgan was, but he knew now. And he also knew he didn't want to do anything to embarrass the man, to disappoint him. He knew what was at stake at the Tattering ball, and he also knew that with Rose by his side, he just might be able to pull it off.

The ball, to benefit soldiers who fought in the Russo-Turkish War, would be held at the Westminster Hotel on Irving Place, a large, imposing building, six stories high, that boasted proudly that Charles Dickens had once stayed there. At such balls, one was expected to make a sizable donation to the cause, though Charlie didn't know what was considered "sizable" to men such as these. He didn't want to appear uninterested, but at the same time didn't want to seem like a show-off, and so decided upon one thousand dollars and had his checkbook ready.

Charlie left his house, nodded to the footman who waited for him outside his carriage, and headed to Rose's home, his nerves growing with each step. Not only was he hobnobbing with the wealthiest men in this country, he was going to have Rose on his arm. It seemed ridiculously absurd.

Her door opened nearly immediately after he gave the doorbell a neat twist, revealing Mr. Brady, Rose's butler. The butler gave Charlie an assessing look before stepping back and allowing admittance, and Charlie wondered if the older man would have closed the door if he'd remembered they'd met five years earlier when Charlie had been frantically looking for Rose. His valet assured him his evening formals were of the finest quality and latest fashion, but Charlie felt a bit as if he were a little boy playing dress-up. His cuff links were diamond, his shoes shined to resemble a mirror, his hair neatly cut and combed, his cheeks smooth. But Charlie knew just putting on the clothes of a gentleman did not make one so, particularly in the eyes of men who were born into important families.

Mr. Brady was about to escort him to the same, comfortable parlor he had been in earlier, when a movement at the top of the stair caught both men's attention. He'd heard men say they'd had the breath knocked out of them, but Charlie had never experienced the phenomenon when looking at a woman. For five seconds, he couldn't breathe, could not draw even the smallest bit of oxygen into his lungs. She was that damned lovely. How she had managed to find so stunning a dress so quickly was beyond him, though he was terribly glad she had. Her neck looked somehow longer and more delicate. Her pale shoulders drew his eyes, and then the sight of the creamy softness of her breasts was nearly his undoing. How the hell was he supposed to stand next to her, touch her, and still hide how much he desired her? Even as he had that thought, he felt his trousers tighten. Good God, he'd better get a grip or everyone at the ball would see just how affected he was by the beautiful Mrs. Cartwright. He'd almost forgotten one of the rules of being a gentleman, to walk up the stairs to meet a lady, not stand at the bottom staring at her like some fool. He hurried up three steps, ridiculously proud that he had passed this first test.

"You are stunning," Charlie said, unable to stop himself. He thought she might be miffed; after all, he had invited her for practical reasons, but she beamed him a smile that made his breath get stuck in his throat all over again.

"Charles Avery, you are quite handsome yourself this evening," Rose said, holding out her gloved hand for him to take. He leaned over, one hand behind his back, the other holding her fingers, brushed his lips against the soft kid, and smiled. It was heady stuff, indeed, to have Rose look at him as if he were a man and not a former employee.

Quite handsome? *He* was the stunning one. Every woman at the ball under the age of one hundred would have her eyes on him. Rose had thought him dashing in his everyday suit, but in this formal wear, with his blond hair swept back from his strong forehead, his striking blue eyes, his . . . well, his everything. He was the Adonis Genevieve had said he was. Rose allowed herself to look at his mouth before glancing quickly away, praying he would not notice. She was allowing Charlie to escort her because he needed her to advance his career, not for any romantic reason. It wouldn't do for him to know where her thoughts had immediately gone. Never before in her life had she looked at a man's mouth and wished it was upon hers.

"Shall we?" he asked, holding up his left arm for her to take.

"We shall. So far, you've been the perfect gentleman," she said, and he looked down and winked at her. Not very gentlemanly, but it did something wonderful to her insides. How was she going to get through this evening without swooning at his feet? Just before they walked out the door, Rose stopped him. "This is the Tattering charity ball, is it not?"

"It is."

"Oh, dear, then I believe I must be forthcoming and let you know that Mrs. Tattering doesn't much care for English aristocracy. And as you know, I am, or at least I was, English aristocracy. I don't think she cares for me at all, Charlie."

He simply laughed. "Don't worry, Rose, Mrs. Tattering likes me well enough to overlook my companion."

Rose furrowed her brow, not liking the way he'd said that, almost as if he and Mrs. Tattering had a special relationship, one that didn't involve the lady's husband's business affairs but rather a different kind of affair altogether. "Are you suggesting that you and Mrs. Tattering . . ."

Charlie just smiled enigmatically. "I think she likes commoners even more than you do."

Rose pulled a face. "I ought to slap you for saying that," she said good-naturedly, though to be honest, she was a bit bothered by his comment.

The Westminster Hotel was ideally located downtown just a short drive from their homes. The ball, which included a midnight dinner, was one of the most exclusive of its type and only the highest levels of society would be in attendance. Which made it even more baffling to Rose how Charlie had gotten on the invitation list. Unless it was only because Mrs. Tattering held a *tendre* for him. Why, the woman was in her forties! Had Charlie truly . . .

Rose didn't want to think about it, didn't want to imagine him kissing that prune-faced biddy. Rose pretended to be interested in the view out her window, but she was actually trying hard not to be jealous. Mrs. Tattering, after all, was not at all prune-faced; she was an attractive woman who in her day had turned many more heads than Rose had.

Charlie sat across from her, jiggling one leg up and down and beating a loose fist against his thigh. His jaw was tense, his mouth set.

"Is this evening so very important?" Rose asked, and he immediately stopped his fidgeting.

"I believe it is a test and I fear that, even with you by my side, I shall fail. It is so very easy to do the wrong thing with these people, and I know they will be watching me."

Could that be true? "Surely not."

"I am under consideration for the Knickerbocker Club. I cannot underestimate the importance such membership would have to a man like me, with few connections and absolutely no background to speak of. Men like Tattering and Morgan make and break people all the time. Where do you think Thomas Edison would be without Morgan championing him? Nowhere. He'd be like poor Underhill, trying to get people to understand his inventions."

"Underhill?"

"See? You don't even know who he is, but you know Edison, do you not?"

Rose had to agree she did. "And you think that's because of Mr. Morgan?"

Charlie nodded once, sharply, and started up his fidgeting again.

"You cannot impress such men if you fidget like that, Charlie."

He gave her a dark look and she laughed lightly. "You're taking me along to gently guide you, are you not?"

The dark look remained. "I am."

"Then you must listen to me," she said, looking pointedly at his leg.

"I need a distraction," he said, and Rose's entire body heated when his gaze moved lazily to her mouth before snapping back to her eyes.

"Am I a distraction?" Rose asked.

"You are. Perhaps too much of one in that gown of yours. How on earth were you able to find something so quickly?" His eyes lingered perhaps a bit too long on her breasts, and Rose could feel another blush heating her. If he continued to do this all evening, she might just combust.

"My dressmaker was so horrified by what I was wearing, I do believe she took pity on me."

"It is lovely," he said, his voice rough and low.

"Heavens, Charlie, will you stop?"

He looked at her innocently, the same expression her chocolate-stained brothers would give Cook when she accused them of pilfering cocoa.

"It is important that you refrain from lustful thoughts," she said primly, to which Charlie burst out laughing.

"Then you shouldn't have worn a gown that makes you look like that," he said, waving his hands to indicate her entire body.

Rose lifted her chin imperiously. "Think of me as your business partner. You wouldn't look at Mr. Morgan like that—" He was doing it again. On purpose. "Really, Charlie, don't be so ill bred."

Instantly, his expression changed, hardened. "But I am ill bred," he said silkily. "And vulgar and all those words swimming around your pretty little head right now." He cursed beneath his breath and clenched one fist, knocked it once, hard, against his thigh, then was still.

"I didn't say you were ill bred," Rose said softly. "I merely cautioned you not to act ill bred."

"Hardly any difference, is there." He didn't look at her for the rest of the short ride.

The two waited silently in the carriage for a short queue of vehicles to release their passengers. Rose couldn't imagine what was going through Charlie's mind. His mood was mercurial, one moment worried, the next teasing and fun, and now he had slipped into a dark place that was almost frightening.

When it was time to disembark, Charlie got out first, then turned to hold up a hand to assist Rose, his face expressionless.

"You should escort me to the dressing room, go to the men's dressing room, then return for me," Rose said, and Charlie nodded. "Then we will go find Mrs. Tattering and you will thank her for inviting you."

"You've met?"

"Yes. Briefly. So you could still say, 'You remember Mrs. Cartwright.' And she'll give me a sour look and say 'Of course. How wonderful you were able to attend.' And I will smile politely and make her think I'm ever so happy to see her. You must not hint, even in the smallest way, that you have anything other than a passing acquaintance."

Charlie looked at her from the corner of his eye and his mouth curved up slightly. The cad.

"I can't whisper in her ear or brush a hand against her waist?"

"Most certainly not."

"Or invite her for a night of opera after the ball?"

Rose stopped midstride, fighting a smile. "No, Charlie. And you know it. Stop teasing me."

"I'm sorry," he said, sounding nothing of the sort. "You should know that Mrs. Tattering and I are nothing but acquaintances."

"I don't see how that concerns me."

She could feel more than hear Charlie's chuckle, and had to use all her restraint not to let him know how very miffed she was at the moment.

When they entered the ballroom, the strangest thing occurred. Perhaps it was her imagination, perhaps it was simply her heightened awareness of how important this evening was to Charlie, but as soon as they passed the threshold into the glittering room, it seemed as if every set of female eyes looked at Charlie and stared. He was a stranger, no doubt, but it was not curiosity Rose saw in their gazes, it was admiration. And when they looked at her—if they looked at her at all—their expressions were either dismissive or hostile.

Once they were announced, she and Charlie made their way toward Mrs. Tattering, who watched their progress with interest.

"Mrs. Tattering, a pleasure."

"Yes, it is," she said, smiling like she held some sort of secret, and Rose wondered if, indeed, Mrs. Tattering and Charlie were more than acquaintances.

"You have met Mrs. Cartwright, I believe."

"I have. It is lovely to see you out of mourning so quickly, Mrs. Cartwright."

Rose nearly gasped at the insult. "It has been nearly a year and a half since Mr. Cartwright passed. Time does seem to shorten as one ages, I know." Mrs. Tattering's eyes narrowed and turned instantly cold. *Oh, what have I done?* Rose thought desperately. *How could I insult the one woman Charlie needs to impress most of all?*

"You're not that old, Mrs. Cartwright," Charlie said with a good-natured laugh, and when Mrs. Tattering joined in, Rose relaxed a bit.

And that set the tone for the rest of the evening. Charlie was charming, Rose realized. Both men and women sought his company, and he might have been born into elite society, so effortlessly did he navigate the ballroom. He danced only twice, once with Rose and once with Mrs. Tattering, and held his own both times. Rarely, she would whisper something in his ear to remind him of polite behavior, but for the most part he did well on his own. When he disappeared with some of the gentlemen for a time, she did worry, but when he returned, he was smiling, so she imagined all had gone well.

The evening could not have gone better. The only thing that could make this the perfect night was having Rose in his bed, and he knew that could never happen. All evening, even when he was not by her side, he was aware of her. She had that indefinable quality that so many women wished for that set her apart from the ordinary. It wasn't just that she was beautiful, it was the way she was so attentive to everyone she spoke with, whether it was a young debutante or a doddering old man. The doddering old men seemed particularly captivated by her, Charlie noted, hoping they were as doddering as they appeared.

He could not remember being so happy that an evening was over, yet he still felt on edge, as if he should run a mile or go to his gym and pound a bag until he was exhausted. He knew it was partly because he was suffering, being so close to Rose, loving her and wanting her, and not being able to do a thing about it. He wished they were a married couple, that they were headed, happy and tired, to bed to make love before falling asleep together in his large, comfortable bed. Instead, he would bid her good night at her door, perhaps kiss her hand if he were very bold, and walk away, aching from unsated desire.

By the time they arrived home, a fine mist had begun to fall, creating a soft light on their avenue. Everything glistened in the gaslight and it was such an unexpectedly pretty sight, Charlie smiled as he lifted his hand to assist Rose out of his carriage.

"Why are you smiling, Charlie?" Rose asked, taking his hand. He'd removed his gloves in the carriage and he wished she had done the same. Just imagining touching her flesh made him hard.

"This mist reminds me of home," he said. "I think I don't miss it, and then I see a glimpse of something and I feel it. I wonder sometimes if I'll return for good." He walked her to her gate and lifted the latch to escort her in. "Why did you not return when Mr. Cartwright died?"

Rose looked up at her home and shook her head. "I don't know. I did think about it; my mother wrote and invited me. She was quite adamant, said she couldn't understand why I would stay here. But that's not my home anymore, and yet this doesn't quite seem like home either. I'm afraid I'm a bit adrift at the moment. I could go anywhere, do anything, but I just don't know what to do and so I stay. Sometimes I picture myself an old lady still trying to decide." She let out a sad little laugh. They stood at her front door, hidden from the street by the thick hedges, and it seemed as if they were the only two people in New York still awake. The silence was interrupted only by a slow drip from a nearby gutter.

Charlie looked down at Rose, and not for the first time he wished it was in his power to make her happy. The gaslight from the street lit the entry just enough so that Charlie could make out her features. "I should like to kiss you good night," he said softly, touching the bottom of her chin with his forefinger. He surprised himself with his boldness, but Rose seemed to accept this request easily. She lifted her head, a small smile on her lips, which he took as acceptance. "There is something you never answered, Rose." He kissed her, softly, briefly, just a touch. "Did Mr. Cartwright never kiss you?"

Rose grew still and looked at him, seeming to hold her breath, and Charlie was afraid his question angered her or would cause her to flee into the house. "No." So softly, he wasn't even certain he heard the word.

He kissed her again, this time longer, deeper, and when she let out a small sound of pleasure, he pressed his tongue against the seam of her lips and she opened willingly, meeting his tongue with her own. Oh, God, she tasted so good. He felt her hands on his shoulders, kneading, frantic in a way, and he put two hands at her waist and drew her to him, letting out a low moan when she came willingly.

Her soft breasts pressed against his chest, and Charlie couldn't stop himself from bringing one hand up and cupping a breast, moving his thumb unerringly across her nipple. She gasped, so completely responsive, and he brought up his index finger to apply more pressure, squeezing gently.

"Oh," she said, pressing her head against his collarbone, almost as if the pleasure of him touching her nipple through the layers of her dress and underthings was more than she could bear.

"Did Mr. Cartwright never touch your nipple, Rose?" he breathed, softly squeezing her nipple, then rolling it between his thumb and forefinger.

"No," she gasped, pressing her forehead harder against him. He kissed the top of her head, closing his eyes at the softness of her hair against his lips. In one swift move, he tugged her bodice down, exposing the breast he'd been torturing with his touch.

"Charlie." She sounded shocked, yes, but she also sounded like a woman who was highly aroused. He touched that same nipple, now hardened from his caresses, and let out a deep sound of male satisfaction. She arched against him, unwittingly pressing her body against his erection, and this time it was Charlie's turn to let out a gasp. As if driven by some force he had no control over, he dipped his head and took her nipple in his mouth, drawing it in, relishing the pure sound of female pleasure that came from her throat. He licked and suckled until she literally melted in his arms, unable to hold herself up any longer. He pushed down the other side of her dress and lavished the same attention on the other nipple, listening to her sounds, knowing she was so close to coming from these simple caresses, he need only touch her a few more minutes and she would shatter.

He stopped, lifted his head, and kissed her mouth again, ignoring her soft sound of protest that he had stopped his ministrations to her breasts.

"Charlie, now I know why those women seemed so . . . happy."

Charlie laughed, then kissed her deeply, pulling her against his erection, moving in an ancient rhythm, torturing himself. His hands were at her hips, drawing her close, as his mouth ravaged hers. They were unaware of anything but their mouths and hands and the pleasure they were giving one another. A carriage drove by the house, invisible behind the hedge, and Charlie had only the vaguest comprehension that it passed by.

"Rose," he said, breathing heavily. He placed one hand at the juncture of her legs, and she stiffened slightly. He pressed the heel of his hand where he knew it would give her the most pleasure. "Did Mr. Cartwright ever touch you here?"

* * *

Rose's breath caught in her throat and she swallowed. Charlie was making her feel things she'd never felt, sensations she hadn't even known she *could* feel, making her thick and drowsy with sexual need. He kept his hand hard against her, moving only slightly, allowing her to get used to the feel of a man's hand there. He knew. He must know that no one had ever touched her as he was touching her. She shook her head, at first unable to move the word past her throat, and he let out a deep groan and pressed a bit harder and it felt so good. Nothing had ever felt as good as Charlie's hand between her legs. "No." Now he would know and she didn't care, not with his large, warm hand making her want to press against him to relieve some of the exquisite pressure that was building there.

"I'm not going to ask you why. I'm not, Rose. That's for another time, another night. But right now, I'm going to touch you." His voice was low and filled with need. Did he mean to make love to her now? Out here on her front stoop? She wasn't worried anyone could see, for her hedges gave them complete privacy, but it did seem rather indecent of her to allow such a thing. She felt the cool night air on her legs as he lifted her skirt, and knew she should stop him just as she knew she would not. She ached for him. It was the strangest thing; no man had ever touched her body the way Charlie was touching her, but it seemed right somehow. Or perhaps he had drugged her with desire.

His hand moved up her thigh, and he kept saying things in her ear, how soft she was, how beautiful, how he would die if he didn't touch her. . . . And then he did, and Rose tried not to cry out.

"My God, Rose," he said when he felt how slick she was. She knew what that meant; she wasn't a child, after all. He found her most sensitive spot unerringly, and he let out another guttural sound that she now knew meant he was pleased. Charlie kissed her deeply as he began moving his hand against her, expertly teasing her. making her body sing, as if every nerve in her body were centered there, in that one spot. Her breasts ached, her knees were weak, her mouth swollen from his kisses. Her hips began to move and he made an encouraging sound as she clung to him, wrapping her arms around his neck.

"Yes, love," he said, just as she began to pulse, just as a bit of lightning went through her body, making her stiffen and jerk and nearly die from the feelings that coursed through her. She clung to him, fighting for breath, as her body came down from heaven.

And then, as reality returned, she realized, with no small amount of horror, that she was standing on her front steps, her breasts exposed, a man's hands up her skirts.

"Oh," she said, alarmed as she tried to right her clothes.

"It's all right, love, let me," Charlie said gently, pushing her shaking hands away. "I'm a cad. I never should have allowed myself to get so carried away. I'm so sorry, Rose."

"It wasn't as if I was struggling to stop you," Rose said. "It wasn't like . . . It wasn't, Charlie. It was lovely. I'm rather surprised that I was so completely, utterly, taken with things that I forgot where we were. You are quite talented. As you well know." It sounded like an accusation, even to Rose's ears, and Charlie stiffened.

"I was not taking advantage of you, if that's what you are implying, Mrs. Cartwright." He stepped back, swiping a hand through his now mussed hair. When had that happened? Oh, yes, when he'd been *licking* her breasts as she'd held him there, pressed him against her, as if she were afraid he would stop.

"No, no, no, Charlie. That's not it. I don't know what I'm saying. I'm shocked, that's all. Here," she said, stepping up to him and kissing him softly. "Good night, Charlie. Would you mind calling on me tomorrow? Perhaps for tea?"

He let out a low chuckle. "Of course, my lady," he said with a little bow, making Rose giggle.

"I did sound rather prim and proper, didn't I?"

"You did. Good night, Rose."

"Good night, Charlie."

She slipped through her front door, then leaned against it, letting out a long breath. "I'm afraid you are in very big trouble, Mrs. Cartwright," she said, then slapped a hand over her mouth to stop herself from laughing. From *laughing*. My God, she hadn't been this happy in years.

Chapter 17

His position as a man in society obliges him to call upon any lady who has accepted his services as an escort, either for a journey or the return from a ball or evening party; this call must be made the day after he has thus escorted the lady.

—From *The Gentlemen's Book of Etiquette, and Manual of Politeness*

"Mrs. Campbell is here to see you, madam," Brady intoned. Rose looked up at him through her lashes, her eyes twinkling, for her butler rarely bothered to sound so formal, and when he did it was just a lark. He usually put on his butler air, as Rose liked to think of it, when someone important was already visiting.

"You may see her in, Brady," she said, just as Genevieve whisked by him.

"You must tell me everything about last night."

Of course, Rose blushed, which, of course, delighted her friend. "I knew there was something more between you." Genevieve clapped her hands like a child about to receive a much wanted present.

"It was a very pleasant evening," Rose said sedately, trying to keep the image of Charlie ravishing her nipple out of her mind. "Truly, it was lovely to see some friends I haven't seen since Daniel's death. Everyone was quite solicitous."

Genevieve rolled her eyes. Having been brought up in a cabin in the woods, her friend was lacking a certain refinement, which was one of the reasons Rose so adored her. It was good to have someone who could be completely honest without using politeness as an excuse to avoid the truth. "Do not prevaricate, darling. You know why

I am here. Our lovely neighbor, Mr. Avery. Was he good company?" She raised one delicate eyebrow.

"He was perfect company," Rose said cautiously, willing the heat in her cheeks to dissipate. Just hearing his name brought back the moments they'd shared on her front stoop. She still couldn't quite believe she'd allowed him such liberties and then invited him for tea. All day, her stomach had been filled with butterflies, the anticipation of his visit growing with each passing hour. It was now three, and as much as Rose adored Genevieve, she did not want her friend still in her parlor when Charlie arrived. Feeling as she did, she was not sure she would be able to hide her infatuation.

Infatuation? No, this was more and she knew it. She'd loved Charlie when she was a girl, at least she'd thought she might have, and it was likely she still loved him. Over the years, she'd wondered about him, thought to find out where he was, what he was doing, but as the years passed, Charlie slipped further and further away from her consciousness. Until the day he stepped from his carriage and all those feelings came flooding back.

"Is it because he was your servant? You can be such a snob, Rose."

Rose's mouth opened in shock. "Can I?"

Genevieve shrugged, something Rose noted, and her friend pointed an accusing finger at her. "See? The shrug. You noted it. You cannot help yourself."

"But I was not being critical. I was simply noticing that you shrugged." Rose sighed. "You have no idea what it is like to be the daughter of my mother. The only time I ever got to be myself was when I escaped to the stables to be with my horses."

"And Mr. Avery."

Rose gave her friend a level look. "Yes, and Mr. Avery. He was my friend. And if I note that you shrug, it is only that you know better but simply choose to ignore society's rules."

To which Genevieve shrugged a half a dozen times, making Rose laugh. "You are impossible," Rose said when she could speak. "And to answer your question, it's complicated. At least it was far more complicated in England than it is here. You cannot understand the relationship between master and servant and how very strong the dividing line is. For me even to have considered Charlie my friend was deeply frowned upon."

"He is no longer a servant, Rose."

"No, he is not. And I am no longer a young girl."

Genevieve smiled knowingly. "I knew it."

A bit of pique entered Rose's tone. "You know nothing, Genevieve." Despite her words, Rose looked at the mantel clock, noting that it was now half past three. Charlie would arrive for tea at any moment.

Most women would have heard her tone and immediately either apologized, left politely, or changed the subject, but Genevieve was not like most women. "I think you have feelings for him. Are you ashamed of them?"

Was she? No. She was not ashamed of her feelings, she was surprised by them, overwhelmed by them. Frightened even. For she hardly knew Charles Avery, the man who was now a wealthy businessman, the man who entertained women in his home. Was Rose simply another one of those women? Was Charlie a rake now? That thought stopped her still. He certainly acted like one. Did he not seduce her on her doorstep? Had he not entertained two different women in the space of three days? What kind of man would have done such a thing other than a rake?

"Have I hit a nerve?" Genevieve asked worriedly.

Slowly, Rose shook her head. "I do believe Mr. Avery is a bit of a rake, and instead of encouraging a relationship between us, I believe you should be warning me away from him." She thought back on the previous evening, about the women who had fawned over him and the easy way he'd had of charming them even as he dismissed them. Rose, who had so little experience with men, had fallen for his charms without even the slightest resistance. She let out a small laugh.

"What evidence do you have of such a thing?" Genevieve asked. "It's not a very flattering thing to say."

"No, it's not," Rose said, at first not offering an explanation. "Suffice it to say, Genevieve, that your home is separated from his by mine and as such, I am much more privy than you to the activities in Mr. Avery's home."

Genevieve's eyes widened. "A woman?"

"Women," Rose said, angry with herself for becoming—or very nearly—one of Charlie's women.

"Oh, my," Genevieve breathed. "Then we must not encourage him. I had no idea."

"I'm not saying he's a bad man," Rose said, quickly coming to his defense for God knew what reason. "It's simply something to be cautious about. If he is a rake."

Brows furrowed, Genevieve asked, "Was he anything other than a gentleman last night?"

Cursing her flaming cheeks, Rose looked Genevieve straight in the eye, and lied. "Of course not."

Genevieve stayed a few more minutes and Rose promised to stop by her home the next day. It was nearly four and time for tea, so Rose had only a few moments to consider her revelation about Charlie's state of rakeness. Rakidity? She shook her head, thinking that she was giving the matter far more attention than she should.

Rose took up a book and was pretending to read when her house-keeper entered and asked if she would like tea. It was four fifteen. She was fairly certain Charlie knew what time tea was; he was from England, after all. It would seem odd if she waited, so she nodded, and for the first time wondered if Charlie wasn't coming at all. She knew he worked long hours, but she had invited him and he had agreed.

She took a thoughtful bite of her buttery biscuit. For years, even before Daniel's death, she'd sat in this very spot and had her tea and never felt lonely. Today, she did. Lonely and foolish. Charlie was not coming. Was he embarrassed by his behavior? Disgusted by hers? Horrified that she'd married Daniel? Rose felt her throat burn slightly and shook her head to rid herself of her foolish thoughts. It didn't matter whether Charlie came for tea at all; why was she making such a fuss about it all? Last night had been a mistake, obviously. Last night they'd simply been two adults who'd gotten a bit carried away by the night, the intimacy of the mist, the success of the evening.

Taking a fortifying sip of tea, Rose resolved not to allow herself to become any more infatuated with Charlie. And it *was* infatuation, she decided. Goodness, what a ninny she was. Not a few moments before she'd actually thought she was falling in love with him.

Long after he'd left Rose, Charlie lay awake thinking of the real possibility that she was a virgin, that her husband had never touched her. It made no sense, unless the man had been a homosexual or some sort of religious fanatic. Though he'd known Daniel only briefly, neither scenario seemed possible. Clearly, something had prevented an otherwise healthy man from consummating his marriage.

It was likely, Charlie realized, that Rose had been aware there would be no physical aspect to her marriage. It made sense, given what she'd just been through, how young she had been, how desperate to escape. He felt a surge of protectiveness, of possessiveness. It wouldn't have mattered to him had Rose had a normal marriage: he still would have loved her, wanted her. But in some base and carnal way, the fact that Rose was a virgin was quite wonderful. When they made love—and they would someday, he prayed—he would be her first and, God willing, her last.

Charlie welcomed the work he had the next day, losing himself in his locomotive engine design and the factory's operations. For long stretches, he did not think about Rose, about how sensitive her nipples were, about how wet she'd been, about the sounds she made when she reached climax. He'd wanted her before, but now it was a constant ache.

Charlie worked long days, always had. With nothing else in his life but work, and the occasional pretty lady, he'd never minded the long days. For the first time since he'd opened his factory, he was going to leave early and didn't feel even the slightest twinge of guilt. At half past three, Charlie began cleaning his office, knowing that the next day would be a long one. With his foreman out with a broken arm, he had no choice but to do his own job as well as his foreman's. The workers, while a good bunch, would slack off a bit without any supervision, and he needed to make an important order by the end of the week. Thanks to his relationship with J. P. Morgan, he'd been able to get an important contract with George Pullman to outfit his rail cars with C. A. Kitchen Tools. It was a huge order and Charlie wanted to be certain that not only was it fulfilled on time, but the pieces were the best quality possible.

Odd how difficult it was to concentrate on his business of late. Especially this day, when he was still reeling from the prior night's events. He never would forget the beautiful sound of Rose as she found her release for the first time with him. First time. That implied there would be more times and he hoped to God that would be the case. He wasn't certain he'd be able to go the rest of his life without hearing that sound again.

Charlie had meant to send flowers, then thought better of it. Sending her a gift seemed to almost sully what had happened between them. A note, perhaps. No. The last time he'd sent her a note it had been about other women, and that could only dredge up thoughts he'd rather not have her thinking.

He was staring blindly at a drawing of his locomotive engine when one of his workers interrupted him, and he realized at that moment the factory was strangely quiet.

"Sir, there's been an accident. John Sullivan. It's bad, sir."

He dropped his pencil and immediately followed the man. "What's happened, Peter?"

"His arm. Cut nearly clean off just below his elbow. It's awful, sir."

They ran to where a crowd of workers had gathered over John Sullivan, one of his finest workers and one who had been with him almost from the start. He was on the ground, writhing in pain, blood splattered everywhere, his arm nearly severed and twisted oddly.

"Ah, Christ, John," Charlie said, running to his side. Another worker was squeezing his arm above the gruesome injury, but that was doing little to stem the flow of blood. John was pale, and looked like he was about to faint. "Someone give me your braces," Charlie shouted, and within seconds, the straps were in his hand and he began tying them around John's upper arm as tightly as he could. Almost immediately, the flow of blood lessened, but the amount he'd already lost was staggering.

One of his workers, a young man he'd hired not two weeks ago, was openly weeping. Charlie looked up at him, and bit out, "Get him out of here." John didn't need that kind of thing when he was no doubt already terrified.

"All right, let's get him to the hospital. I need a cart. Now." Charlie turned to John, who was still conscious, as Peter ran to find a cart, which would be easier on the man than trying to hoist him into a carriage.

"It's bad," John said weakly, his eyes filled with terror as he looked down at his arm.

"Don't look, John," Charlie said. "We're taking you to the hospital and they'll take care of you there. Everyone else, the day's work is over. I'll see you tomorrow morning, bright and early."

When they lifted John onto the cart, he screamed in pain. Charlie took one side, Peter the other, and the two pushed the cart toward West Fifteenth Street and New York Hospital. Every bump they went over produced more screams, but Charlie knew they had to reach the hospital quickly, or John could die. It was only three blocks, but by the time the two men entered the building, they were both drenched with sweat.

"We've an injured man here," Charlie shouted, as they pushed the cart into the hospital's lobby. Almost immediately, two orderlies appeared. Heaving to catch their breaths, Charlie and Peter watched as the men picked up a now unconscious John and placed him on a stretcher to bring him deeper into the hospital.

"Holy God," Charlie said, wiping his forehead on his sleeve, and only then noticing he was covered in blood. "What happened, Peter? Do you know?"

"I can't believe he did it. John is always so careful. He was reaching in to get a piece that had fallen and he knows to stop the machine. But he didn't. He took the chance and that's how it happened. It's so loud on the floor, we didn't even hear him scream right away. Then I saw the blood and ran to get you."

Charlie took a deep breath. "You performed well, Peter. I need one more thing from you." Charlie looked Peter over and noted the man had no blood on him. "I need for you to take my carriage and go to his wife. They live at four twenty-one Houston Street on the second floor. She needs to be here and I can't go," he said, looking down at his blood-smeared clothing. "I'll stay here and if there's bad news to tell, I'll be the one to tell it. Tell Mrs. Sullivan only that her husband's arm was injured. No details, got that, Peter?"

"Yes, sir."

Charlie shook the man's hand and smiled grimly. "Good man. I'll see you soon."

After Peter left, Charlie inquired where he could clean himself up, and a nurse directed him to a water closet with hot and cold running water. Charlie looked in the mirror over the basin and grimaced, seeing his face splattered with blood. He washed the best he could, but there was nothing he could do about his stained jacket and shirt.

Once he was more presentable, Charlie returned to the nurses' station and inquired after John.

"He's in surgery, sir," the nurse said. "We have an area where you can sit if you plan to stay. Down the hall and to the right."

"His wife is coming soon. Will you direct her there?"

"Of course."

Though Charlie had never met Mrs. Sullivan, he knew her the moment she entered the room, and he immediately stood. Peter trailed behind her, looking grim. Mrs. Sullivan was a tiny woman with reddish-brown hair that was escaping its bun. Her cheeks were flushed, her brown eyes determined, almost as if she could will her husband better.

"What happened, Mr. Avery? Peter here would tell me nothing," she said, her tone softened by her Irish burr. "How is my John?"

"Why don't we sit?" Charles said, and immediately saw that was a mistake, for she thought the worst. "He's in surgery, Mrs. Sullivan. That's all I know. He injured his arm grievously and chances are they won't be able to save it. He lost a lot of blood, but they're taking care of him now."

She nodded and swallowed, and Charlie could tell she was trying hard not to cry. With quick movements, she walked to a line of wooden chairs and sat down, her back straight, her face set. "And what's to happen to us now?" she asked, looking up at Charlie.

"You'll be taken care of," Charlie said, and the wiry little woman relaxed slightly. "I take care of my own, Mrs. Sullivan, and your husband is one of my best workers. You'll not starve."

"It's our children. We've five, you see," she said, and her face momentarily crumpled before she got control of herself.

"As I said, you will be taken care of. And when he's able, John will have a job, hand or no. I'll find something for him to do. Please do not worry on that account," Charlie said. He'd had workers get injured in the past—there was no escaping it entirely, though he tried to operate a safe factory—and he'd always paid their wages until they could return. But no one had ever been injured nearly as badly as John. A broken leg from a fall, a knock on the head that had been downright scary, but no permanent disability.

Charlie and Peter sat opposite Mrs. Sullivan, who clutched her reticule on her lap, probably filled with whatever money they had in their flat. "I'll pay for the hospital stay, Mrs. Sullivan," he said, and was satisfied when the grip on her reticule lessened.

Charlie sent Peter home, and he waited with Mrs. Sullivan for another hour before a priest walked through the door and Mrs. Sullivan, stoic until that moment, broke down. "I'm so sorry, Mrs. Sullivan, but the blood loss was just too much for him. He received his sacrament and is in God's hands now, at peace."

Never before had Charlie witnessed a grief so all consuming. She fell to her knees, sobbing, clinging to the Father's hand, shaking her head, and saying, "No, it canna be true. Not my John. Not my John."

Charlie turned away, working his throat, trying to remain strong in the face of such anguish. The priest let her cry, let her clutch his hand for several long minutes, before he got down on his knees next to her, not to pray, but to hold her. The priest looked up at Charlie. "You are a relative?"

"No, Father, I'm her husband's employer. I brought him here."

The priest nodded. Finally, Mrs. Sullivan calmed, her tears ending so abruptly, it was if she turned them off. She stood, still clutching her reticule, and looked at Charlie. "Did he have any words for me?" she asked, her voice shaking.

"He told me to tell you that he loved you. You and the children," Charlie said, figuring a small lie wouldn't be too large a sin, even if it was said in front of a priest.

She nodded and smiled the tiniest bit, and Charlie wasn't sure if it was a smile of thanks or one acknowledging his lie. After a time, the priest left, leaving Charlie alone with Mrs. Sullivan, a shell of the woman she'd been when she'd walked into the hospital.

"I can bring you home, Mrs. Sullivan. We should go."

"Do you think they'll let me see him?"

Charlie fetched a nurse, who brought Mrs. Sullivan to her husband, while Charlie waited for her to return. When she did, they walked solemnly out the door.

"Strange that he won't be home when I get there," she said, sounding almost puzzled, as if she were still wrapping her mind around the fact that her husband was gone forever.

"Mrs. Sullivan, how old is your oldest boy?"

She stopped and looked up at him, a small hope sparking in her eyes. "He's twelve, sir."

"When he turns sixteen, send him to me and he'll have a job."

"Oh, but he's a big boy, nearly as tall as John. He could work now, he could and—"

"I don't employ children, Mrs. Sullivan. It is far too dangerous work for a child. Your husband's wages will be paid for as long as you need me to or until your son comes to work for me."

She stared at him, narrowing her eyes. "I'll not accept charity, sir, no matter how well intended."

"You can and you will. Your husband died working for me, likely rushing because he knew how important it was that we make our quota. He should have shut off the machine but he didn't and he died for it. You will allow me to pay his wage."

He recognized the stubborn set of her jaw, and recognized also the moment she agreed to accept her husband's salary. No doubt she was thinking about the five mouths she would need to feed.

"Thank you, Mr. Avery. You are a good man."

He didn't feel much like a good man at the moment. He felt partly to blame for the accident. Hadn't he given everyone a rousing speech at the beginning of the day about the importance of meeting this contract, about how vital it was to the future success of C. A. Kitchen Tools? He wanted to do more, but he also knew Mrs. Sullivan would not accept more.

When Charlie finally returned home, it was nearly midnight and he was more exhausted than he could ever remember being. As he alit from the carriage, his eyes automatically went to Rose's darkened house.

"Shite," he said aloud, remembering he'd not made tea that day and hadn't thought to send word. He'd make it up to her some other time. Surely she would understand.

Moving slowly up the stairs, Charlie thought about Mrs. Sullivan, about how difficult it would be for her to tell her children that their strapping father was dead. He felt like his shoes were made from lead.

His house was dark; he never expected his servants to wait up for him. All he wanted to do was wash up, rip off his fouled clothing, and get into bed.

"Bonsoir," came a cheerful woman's voice as he entered his bedchamber.

Oh, good God.

"Louise, what the hell are you doing in my room? Who let you in here?"

"I let myself in. And, of course, I think you must know why I am here, *non*?" She came up to him wearing only the thinnest of nightgowns. Charlie was man enough to recognize she was beautiful, but he was in no mood to make love tonight, particularly not with her. Especially not with any woman other than the one who had been torturing him for so many nights and who was no doubt a bit miffed that he'd missed tea.

"I want you to leave, Louise. Now."

"You say *non*?" Louise, whom he had always found particularly charming, put on a full pout.

"No."

"Charlie," she said, giving him a small smile. "You cannot say *non*. I need you in the bed. Here, let me help you out of this clothings." She furrowed her brow. "This clothings are stained. Is this blood? Is it yours?"

"No. An employee was injured today," Charlie said impatiently, having no wish to give Louise any details.

She reached for him but he gently grabbed her wrists and pushed her away. "I said no, Louise."

"And I say *oui*," she said loudly, her mood changing mercurially. *"Oui, oui, oui, oui, oui!"*

And that's when he heard the window slam from across the alley. Charlie let out a curse, and abruptly Louise's demeanor changed. No doubt he looked as if he wanted to murder her, which in fact he did.

"I shall leave you, Charlie, and see you again when you are in a better mood." Louise took up her cloak, put it on, and within moments she was hurrying down the stairs. Charlie would have laughed at her quick departure if he wasn't so painfully aware of what the sound of that window slamming meant.

Splashing his face with water and making certain every bit of blood was off his hands, he hastily changed his clothes and headed over to explain to Rose that what she thought she had heard was not at all what had happened.

Rose wasn't quite certain why she'd felt as devastated as she had when Charlie did not arrive for his visit. He was not *courting* her. But he could have sent round a note. Or flowers. Or given some indication that he was sorry to have left her waiting like some pathetic old maid hoping for her imaginary beau to arrive.

She hated that she'd tensed at the sound of every carriage that passed by, thinking it might be him, thinking he would soon be rushing to her door, full of good cheer and uttering apologies before taking her in his arms and kissing her.

As the hours had passed, she'd grown more philosophical about his absence. It was probably for the best. It wouldn't do to become too attached to a man who very well might be a rake. Who most assuredly *was* a rake. Thank goodness she had come to her senses before she allowed her heart to become too engaged.

She had fallen asleep early, congratulating herself on how well she was handling Charlie's rejection. She was awakened around midnight and drowsily sat up, uncertain what had woken her. Her one weakness was that she had kept her window open, just in case she heard Charlie return home. Perhaps she could peek out just to see if he were alone.

Foolish, she knew, but there it was.

She sat there and looked at her window, her entire body heating with anger when she clearly recognized the voice of a woman coming from across the alley. How dare he! Oh, the cad. The . . . the . . . rake! Yes, that's precisely what he was. She'd been right all along. And to think how she had allowed herself to suffer for that man. If he so much as smiled at her for the rest of her life she would turn her back. And then she heard, *"Oui, oui, oui, oui,"* and she slammed the window shut to block out the rest.

Hot tears pressed on her eyes, but she squeezed them shut, refusing to give in to her ridiculously misplaced emotion. "I hate him," she said fervently. Rose sat on her bed, glaring at the window, banging her heel against the bed's wooden slats almost painfully. She was still banging when she heard another banging, and stopped midswing. Someone was at her front door.

Grabbing her wrap, she hurried down the stairs and peered out the window beside the door, peeking through the sheer curtain. Charlie stood there, pacing back and forth like some sort of caged lion.

She opened the door immediately, forgetting her vow never to speak to him again. "Good evening, Charlie. Done entertaining?"

"I do realize that's what it sounded like, but it was not what you think."

"Really, Charlie, I don't care if you have a harem in your home as long as you are quiet about it," Rose said, wondering if Charlie thought she was completely naive simply because she was a virgin.

"Rose, I've had one hell of a day. I'm sorry I missed tea. I'm sorry I came home to find a woman in my room," he said, and with every sentence uttered he sounded more angry. "And I'm extremely sorry you jumped to the wrong conclusion. I was so sorry, in fact, that I felt the need to come to your door in the middle of the night to apologize for doing nothing. I'm tired and I'm going to bed. Good evening, Mrs. Cartwright."

Something about his voice, something raw and almost broken beneath the anger, drew her outside, and as Charlie turned away she grabbed his arm. "Charlie, what's wrong? What's happened?"

He stood on the landing, half facing toward the street, for a long moment before speaking. "One of my workers died today from an injury at work. I was at the hospital with his wife."

Rose heard the raw emotion in his voice, and his eyes glittered briefly before he impatiently rubbed them with the heels of his hands. "He has five children, Rose. Five."

"Oh, Charlie, I'm sorry. I feel simply awful now, getting upset about your missing a silly tea when you were dealing with that. And really, about the woman, it doesn't matter. I was just a bit angry to have been woken up, that's all."

"That's all?"

"Yes," Rose said firmly, trying to make her lie sound sincere. "I would hardly deny the ladies of New York your special skills." She'd meant it as a joke, but Charlie didn't laugh, not really. The sound that came out, a sharp burst of air, was not a joyful sound.

He held his hands out by his sides, palms up. "Then please do allow me to apologize for awakening you. In the future, we shall use the guest room on the opposite side of the house. Mrs. Jefferson is quite deaf and she hasn't complained once. Good evening, Rose."

Stunned by his words, Rose was silent as Charlie stormed down her steps and out the gate. Guest room! He'd been using a guest room on the days of silence? And here she'd thought that perhaps there'd been no one since the day they'd met in front of her house. She'd even thought perhaps that silence was because of her. Goodness, he had women waiting for him when he returned home?

Rose entered her home, her mind whirling. It made sense. Look what he'd done to her with just his hand. Of course women would want that, would wait for him to come home. Despite herself, a sharp blade of arousal hit her and she wrapped her arms around her waist in an attempt to stem it. How could she live next to him, knowing that each evening he was giving other women the same pleasure he'd given her? Except, he hadn't really. She was still a virgin. Would likely still be a virgin if she ever got married again.

That thought stopped her still. She could not be a virgin when she got married. How on earth could she possibly explain herself? She would never reveal Daniel's secret, not to anyone. The only people who knew of Daniel's homosexuality were her and James. And now Charlie probably. She could not allow her husband's memory to be sullied, but what choice did she have?

Chapter 18

Listen courteously to those whose opinions do not agree with yours, and *keep your temper*. A man in a passion ceases to be a gentleman.

—From *The Gentlemen's Book of Etiquette, and Manual of Politeness*

Two weeks after John Sullivan's death, Charlie left his office whistling, leaving behind gawking workers who had never seen Mr. Avery looking quite so happy. He'd received a note from Rose asking him for tea. The two hadn't spoken, even in passing, since the night he'd stood on her stoop at midnight, trying to explain how it was possible that he had a woman in his bedroom.

At precisely four, he knocked on Rose's door and was met by her smiling butler, Mr. Brady.

"Hello, Brady," Charlie said, handing off his hat and gloves. "Mrs. Cartwright invited me for tea."

"Indeed, Mr. Avery. She is waiting for you in the parlor."

"I can find my way, Brady, thank you." Charlie had a decided bounce to his step as he entered the femininely appointed room. Clearly, this was Rose's domain, an airy and light room painted a pale green. The lady was sitting on a small settee, reading a book. Though she was wearing a drab brown dress, she made a pretty picture sitting there with the sun shining upon her through the sheer curtains. The window was open, for it was a warm spring day, and the curtains blew softly, curling inward on the breeze. When he entered, she looked up and Charlie's heart skipped a beat when she smiled. He'd been a bit fearful that she would still be angry with him, but he detected no nervousness or anger on her face. He regretted his own words and hoped to use this meeting to apologize for them.

Rose stood and placed her book to the side, then walked to a near wall and pulled a cord, no doubt for tea. "Cook was delighted to hear you were coming for tea. She's made raspberry tarts, which are quite famous on the avenue. They are my personal favorite." When she sat back down, Charlie followed suit, sitting in a chair opposite.

"So," she said, and let out a nervous little laugh, clutching her hands in her lap. Ah, the lady was a bit uneasy after all. "I've given what occurred on the night of the ball a great deal of thought and realize you must have questions."

"I do not," Charlie said, and he could tell he'd surprised her. "You clearly held affection for your husband and I do not need to know the intimate details of your marriage. And to be honest, Rose, I do believe I've solved the mystery of your innocence."

Her cheeks reddened and she looked down, unable to meet his unwavering gaze. "I quite enjoyed that evening," she blurted, then closed her eyes briefly.

"I'm glad."

"I have a proposal to make." She looked up, her eyes steady. "I believe I will marry again someday and I don't care to explain to my new husband my untried state. I hadn't realized how evident my inexperience is, but I realized how odd it would be to marry a widow and realize that she is a virgin." She spoke the last as a whisper, then stopped and passed a hand over her forehead as if she were feeling weak. "I loved Daniel. My marriage wasn't conventional but I was happy, and I would hate to sully his memory in any way. People, if they knew, would be so hateful, and I don't think I could bear that. Especially not from a husband, who would guess the truth, just as you have."

Charlie tried not to let her words wound him. That she still didn't consider she could marry him told him more than he wanted to know. She planned to marry and was telling him her plans—for what reason, he couldn't begin to know. "I will not say a word, Rose," Charlie said.

"I know, Charlie. But I believe the truth about my marriage would be difficult for some to accept, that my reasons for marrying Daniel would not be understood. Which is why I'm going to ask you something. A favor. And because you seem to have some talent in the area, given what I have overheard and"—she coughed—"experienced myself."

Charlie felt the blood drain from his head. She couldn't be saying what he thought she was saying. My God, did she have no feelings for him at all?

Rose looked up to the ceiling, probably asking her dead husband for assistance. "I cannot be a virgin when I marry. I'm asking you to take care of that detail for me."

"Take care of it," Charlie said, trying to keep the hurt from his voice. And it did hurt, like the very devil.

"You must know how difficult this is for me," Rose said.

"To ask me to fuck you, you mean?" His anger was palpable, but she hadn't recognized it until he used the coarsest language possible.

"I've insulted you." Rose's eyes immediately filled with tears. Hell, he hadn't meant to make her cry, but didn't she know how callous her own words were? *Make love to me, Charlie, but don't think for one moment there could be anything more between us.* "But yes, that's the general idea. I do seem to come up with plans without thinking about the consequences. Please forgive me and forget this conversation." She sniffed and dug into her sleeve, her hand coming away empty, and Charlie pulled out his handkerchief and handed it to her. "Thank you."

And then the image of Rose, naked and soft beneath him, her legs wrapped around his torso, came to him in a violent and unexpected way. How could he say no to her? How could he say no to the one thing he'd dreamt about for years? Perhaps he would never marry her, but at least he would have had the pleasure of making love to her.

"I will do as you ask," he said, feeling a terrible mix of disgust and joy. Could he respect himself for providing such a sordid service? Could he live with himself if he let another man be her first? It was an untenable situation.

Rose had not imagined the conversation taking such a turn. Indeed, she hadn't thought about where the conversation would go other than imagining Charlie would be flattered and rather pleased with the request. She would be one more woman in a sea of women. He'd seemed to enjoy what they'd done, to a certain extent at any rate. Rose had never thought Charlie would be insulted or angry. She realized she did not know the man sitting across from her, staring broodingly at the empty fireplace.

Yes, Rose wanted to protect Daniel, but if she were completely honest with herself, she also wanted to experience the feelings Charlie had evoked in her. She wanted to banish the fear she'd held for years about the physical side of marriage and she knew Charlie would be a gentle, caring lover. Goodness, taking a lover was so risqué and worldly of her.

"When shall we do it?" Rose asked pertly.

"Now is ideal. I left work early, you see, and wouldn't want my time to go entirely to waste."

Rose turned her head to the window, seeing bright sunshine. She'd imagined a completely dark room. "But it's daytime."

"All the better. Did you think men and women only made love—excuse me, fornicated—at night? I need only to go next door and retrieve something." Charlie stood and walked a few steps toward the door before stopping and turning. "I assume this is a one-time event?"

Rose's face burned hotly. "Yes."

His eyes flickered with some emotion Rose could not interpret, anger no doubt. "Very well. I'll return shortly."

As soon as Charlie left the room, Rose buried her hands in her face. What was she *doing*? This was pure insanity. But if not Charlie, then who? She already liked him well enough and she knew he could please her. No, she simply couldn't imagine even kissing another man other than Charlie, never mind doing what they planned to do.

It seemed only seconds before Mr. Brady was escorting Charlie back into the parlor. Her heart was in her throat as she stood shakily upon his entrance. "Where shall we go?"

"This is as good as anywhere," Charlie said, closing the parlor door behind him and jerking his head toward a larger settee that would easily accommodate two prone adults. He sounded so cold, and Rose wished she had never made such a suggestion. Rose walked slowly to the settee in question and sat down, nervously worrying her fingers together.

Charlie's hands went to the buttons of his trousers and he casually began undoing them, the movements so similar to Weston's, Rose had to look away and again felt tears pressing against her eyes. "Lift your skirts, Rose," he said, sounding entirely unlike the Charlie she knew. Rose hesitated, her hands shaking, before she reached down and began pulling up her skirt and petticoats, unable to look at Charlie and feeling a sharp ache in her heart. She had not thought it would be like this.

"Jesus, Rose, stop."

Rose looked at him, standing with his trousers completely buttoned, his eyes filled with some raw emotion. "Why?" she asked, bewildered.

"Because if I'm going to make love to you, it will not be like this. I was trying to hurt you."

"Oh," Rose said, quickly pushing down her skirts. He had accomplished what he'd set out to do then, for the hurt she had felt had been staggering.

"Come here," Charlie said, holding out his hands to her. She stood and went to him, grasping his hands, shocked by the feeling of his bare skin on hers. His hands were warm and large, with a ridge of callus on the pads of his palms, and she couldn't help but wonder what those hands would feel like on her body. He looked down at her and smiled gently, his blue eyes intent. "I'm sorry if I frightened you." He lifted one hand to her cheek and wiped away a tear she hadn't even realized had fallen. "I never want to be the reason you cry, Rose. Are you certain about this, about what you want to do?"

"I am."

"Then let's go up to your room and do this properly, shall we?"

Rose took a deep, bracing breath. "Yes."

Her room was like the woman Rose had become, elegant and restrained. There was nothing of the girl who used to run, skirts held too high, barreling into the stable to say good morning to Moonrise. And to him. Rose had given her maid a half day off, which Stacy had accepted without a single word, though she had given Charlie a thoughtful look before she went happily on her way.

Rose walked in front of him, clearly nervous, then turned and seemed to wait for him to take the lead. Charlie felt far more nervous than he was allowing her to see; he had never taken a virgin and wasn't entirely certain how to proceed. And this was *Rose*. He walked around the room, taking in the Chippendale furniture, the rich, velvet curtains, the large four-poster bed. In one corner was a small collection of rocks and seashells, ordinary enough, but Charlie knew they were somehow important to her. She'd let a small bit of herself into this room, after all. Undoing the buttons of his jacket, he turned to her and smiled, trying to put them both at ease. When he'd returned to his home to retrieve a rubber sheath, he'd been livid. How dare she? How could she possibly use him for stud services, to prepare her for the man she would eventually marry?

He was not a man to be controlled by anger, but by God, he'd wanted to hurt her the way she had hurt him. Then he'd found he had no stomach for it. One tear, one shaking hand, and it was all he could do not to gather her into his arms and beg her to let him love her.

"This will be better if we are both unclothed. Would you like me to assist you?" he asked solemnly.

He saw her swallow and attempt a smile. "If you would. I dismissed Stacy and I can hardly call her back now with you here."

Charlie walked up to her and moved to her back to begin working on the small buttons that fastened her dress. It was a practical piece of clothing, thank God, and something he could easily tackle, despite the faint tremor in his hands. He was as nervous as he had been when he'd been a lad about to make love to a woman for the first time.

Little by little, he exposed her smooth, perfect skin as she stood, stock-still, hardly breathing, her hands clasped tightly in front of her. He pressed his lips against her back, right between the delicate curves of her shoulder blades, and smiled when he heard her breath quicken. In no time, the dress was dispensed with and Rose made short work of a small mound of petticoats before she began untying her corset cover, revealing to his heated gaze the most glorious sight of her standing before him in her corset, stockings, and bloomers. Charlie, unable to resist touching her again, reached around and cupped her breasts briefly and kissed her neck before untying the laces to her corset. Despite the passion they had shared the night of the ball, he wasn't certain how aggressive he should be. He wanted to shove down her corset and push his cock against her derriere, but he knew if he did that, it would frighten her, and he no longer had any wish to do that.

Once her corset was cast aside, he pulled down her bloomers, ignoring her small sound of protest, then slowly pulled down her silk stockings. She had, he thought, the most charming derriere he'd ever seen, round and plump and perfect for a man's hands.

"Turn around, Rose."

He heard her release a shaking breath, and then she turned, completely naked, her hands fluttering upward briefly, as if she wanted to cover her breasts, then resisted the urge. He let his eyes drift down her body, unable to quite believe he was standing before the woman he'd adored for years. "You are perfect, love," he said. His hands shook with the need to touch her and his arousal would have been clearly evident should Rose have had the courage to look down. He held out his arms, scarecrow fashion. "If you would, madam, I do not have a valet at the moment."

She let out a nervous giggle. "I'm completely naked," she said unnecessarily.

"Indeed you are. And soon I shall be, too. Start with the cravat, if you please."

And there she stood, her perfect uptilted breasts just inches from him as she began untying his cravat, her brow furrowed in concentration. His tie, his braces, his shirt, his undershirt, all removed and discarded unceremoniously on a nearby chair. She paused to look at him standing in only his boots and trousers, allowing her eyes to go no farther than his chest. Her cheeks flushed. "You are quite masculine," she said.

"A good thing for a man."

"Would you do the rest, please?" she asked, her eyes briefly touching upon his obvious erection. Brave girl.

"I will. Why don't you go lie on your bed and I'll join you momentarily." His politeness made him nearly laugh aloud. He was never polite in the bedroom and found it quite amusing that he was being so now. What he wanted to do was lift her up in his arms and throw her down onto the bed and thrust inside her to finally relieve the ache that had plagued him since the day he'd seen her outside his home.

Rose hurried to the bed, drew back the covers to the very end, and climbed in to lie there uncovered like a statue staring up at the ceiling. Smiling, Charlie walked over to the bed and took in her clenched fists, her flat stomach, the dark patch of curling hair at the crest of her thighs, as she stared upward. "A lovely sight," he said. "I could stare at you all day."

She let out a squeak, then quickly turned over.

"I think I like this view even better, Rose," he said, teasing her. She took a pillow and put it over her head, letting out another sound of embarrassment. My God, he could look at her backside for hours.

When Charlie was completely nude, he sat on the bed and placed one hand at the small of her back. "Rose." He waited for a moment. "Rose, I know you can hear me even with that pillow over your head."

She thrust the pillow away and looked at him, rebellion in her eyes.

"You asked me to do this for you. Do you still want to?"

She stared at him, her brown eyes wide, then nodded.

Thank God. "Very well. I shall make this as pleasant for you as possible. I want you to find your release, love, as you did the night of the ball." Then he pulled on the rubber sheath, explaining, "This will prevent pregnancy."

She watched in fascination. "That was very thoughtful of you, Charlie," she said.

She closed her eyes and he caressed her back, calming her. His hand drifted from the smooth indentation just above her derriere, up to her shoulders and back, until she let out a sound of pure contentment. Then he caressed each smooth leg, from her ankle up to the tops of her thighs, over and over, moving slightly higher each time, until he noticed she was moving a bit restlessly.

"Turn over, Rose."

She did, languidly, and he bent and kissed her mouth, deepening the kiss when she let out a sound of pure pleasure. He could listen to her sounds all day, each one slightly different depending upon what he was doing to her, where he was touching. As they kissed, he moved one finger slowly from her neck, across her clavicle, and then to the swell of her breast, ending at one turgid nipple, pink and hard and so tempting. He moved his finger across the tip, and she arched her back and let out a sound that went right to his cock. Breaking off the kiss, he looked down at her and smiled. "You are made for this, Rose. Your body sings to me. Would you like me to kiss you here?" he asked, lightly squeezing the nipple.

"Oh, yes."

Charlie knew not all women felt intense pleasure when their nipples were caressed, but clearly Rose did. He kissed the top of one breast, then licked the pink tip, looking up at her to see her reaction. Their eyes met and the look she gave him was enough to make him lose control. When he took her nipple in his mouth and sucked lightly, she closed her eyes and arched her back, one hand going behind his head. He loved her breasts for long minutes before touching her between her legs, where she was hot and wet. And ready. His erection was nearly painful, but it was too soon to complete the deed. He wanted her to still be pulsing when he pushed inside her, hoping it would lessen any pain she felt.

And so he moved his hand against the hard little nub at the crest of the thighs, back and forth, until her hips began moving, until her breath came out in ragged pants, until he felt her convulse beneath him as she let out a cry of pure joy.

"I'm putting myself inside you, Rose," he said, getting to his knees and pressing her legs apart. She was spent, looking up at him sleepily.

"All right, Charlie."

For some reason that made him laugh, or perhaps it was that he hadn't felt so purely happy in so long. He pressed his cock against her entrance, wishing he wasn't wearing the sheath. He wanted to feel her heat, her wetness, that glorious sensation of a woman's sex. Slowly he entered her, closing his eyes and gritting his teeth, both against the intense pleasure and the fear of hurting her. He was not a small man, and he knew he was larger than most.

"Relax, love," he said, then pushed all the way. She stiffened and let out a small sound of pain, and he stilled.

"Is that it?" she asked, her voice small.

"No, love. No." It could have been, he realized, as he waited for her to relax around him, for she was no longer a virgin. But he would be damned if he pulled out of her now, not when he was so very close to finding his own release. He began moving in and out, the sensation, even with the sheath, so incredibly arousing, he could hardly hold himself in check. "You feel so good, love. You've no idea. Are you all right?"

"Much better now, thank you."

He chuckled and kissed her deeply, all the time thrusting, gaining rhythm, until his body could take no more and he found his release in one long, pulsing bit of heaven.

* * *

Rose lay there, eyes wide, as Charlie came back from that won-derful place people go when they find release. He was magnificent, she thought, and perhaps the kindest man she'd ever known. It was that thought that started the first tear, and then all her thoughts tum-bled on top of one another—thoughts of her youth, of Charlie then and now, of years lost, of how truly wonderful physical love could be with the right man. Within minutes, she was sobbing and poor Char-lie was holding her, helpless to stop her tears. She realized that the last time she'd cried like that was in the stable back home against Charlie's shirt.

"I'm sorry, love, I'm sorry," Charlie said over and over, touching her face gently, kissing her jaw, trying to soothe her even though Rose was quite certain he had no idea what hurt he was trying to ease.

"You don't understand, Charlie. It was lovely."

"Then why are you crying?"

She looked up at him, trying to put into words what she was try-ing to say. "Because it was lovely and I never thought it would be."

He grinned down at her and something swelled in her heart. "I told you it could be wonderful with the right man."

"Are you the right man?"

He gave her a long look, his eyes unreadable; then he smiled. "I am today."

Rose lay beside Charlie, and decided she liked the feel of a naked man beside her. Maybe she liked this man beside her especially, she thought sleepily as she snuggled against him. He reached down and drew up the covers, enveloping them both in a warm, soft cocoon, and Rose closed her eyes. She hadn't slept well the previous night and was terribly tired.

She'd thought just to rest her eyes for a moment, but when she opened them again it was clearly dusk, the muted light coming from her window telling her it was nearly dinnertime. Charlie lay on his back, one arm flung over his head, the other still around her; he was sound asleep. Feeling a bit mischievous and more than curious, Rose looked at his body, so strong and solid, and taking up a great deal of her bed. She had been too nervous to look at him earlier. His chest had a light coating of soft, dark blond hair that ended at his rib cage, but for a thin line that went directly down to his male part. Curious, she lifted her head a bit to get a better look. It was far different now, a droopy appendage with no real shape. She cautiously reached down and laid one index finger on him, smiling at the velvety softness. She moved her finger from the base to the tip, pulling back quickly when it moved.

"Fascinating," she whispered, as it grew larger and shifted, almost as if it were a separate entity from the rest of him. She glanced at Charlie, and seeing that he was still asleep, she ventured another touch and was rewarded when it grew even larger. She very nearly giggled.

"Rose."

Pulling her hand back quickly, Rose blushed from head to toe.

"You may continue if you like," he said, his voice sounding rather strained. "In fact, please do."

"Please do?"

"Yes."

Rose tentatively placed her hand on his penis, and Charlie put his own hand over hers and squeezed. He grew immediately hard beneath her hand.

"It's lovely, Charlie," she said, making him laugh. "It is. Not two minutes ago, it was this little caterpillar and now it's, well, just look at it."

"That's what happens when a woman touches it." Rose frowned, thinking about all the other women who had likely touched Charlie before her. "But with you, all you need to do is be in the same room with me. It's quite unmanning."

"Is that true?" Rose asked, feeling slightly mollified.

"I swear. At the ball that night, I had to keep thinking about my locomotive design as a distraction."

She laughed, feeling quite sophisticated, lying naked in her bed with a man. Touching his gooser—that's what her brothers used to call it. She squeezed and he breathed in sharply and swelled beneath her hand.

"If you keep doing that, love, I'm afraid I'll either have to leave or go back on my word that we'd only do it once."

Rose looked at him, then ducked her head into the crook of his arm, her hand still on his erection. "I think we could do it again, if you like."

Charlie uttered a curse. "I don't have another sheath, Rose."

"All right." But she still held him, still looked down the flat plane of his stomach at her hand holding him, fascinated by the small bead of moisture that formed at the very tip. "You're leaking." She moved her thumb, touching him there lightly, just in that spot where the moisture appeared, and he hissed in another breath.

"Are you trying to torture me?" he asked.

"Yes," she said, giggling and kissing his jaw.

"My lady, you can only push a man so far," he said, joining her laughter. "I can pull out. That should be safe enough."

Rose got up and leaned on one elbow to look down at him. "What do you mean?"

"I'll pull out before I come, so it won't go inside you, and you won't get pregnant. That would work," he said. Then he pulled her down for a kiss, thrusting his tongue into her mouth, making his hips rise against her hand. He grabbed one of her legs and pulled it over him so that she lay on top, her hand trapped between their bodies. He kneaded her bum and she let go of him to wrap her hands around his neck, joining in the rhythm he was creating, his arousal pressing between her legs and giving her the most delicious sensation.

"You're not too sore, are you, Rose? We can stop. It will kill me, but we can stop," he said, lifting his hips in a way that caused a shot of raw desire that made her cry out.

"I'm quite fine," she said, and bent her head to kiss him some more. She could kiss him for hours, lying like this, feeling his hard body beneath hers, the soft hair of his chest, his erection pressing between her legs.

"Sit up, then, love, and put me inside you." Rose lifted her head, and the expression on her face must have amused him quite a lot, for he burst out laughing. "It's lovely," he said, lifting one wicked brow, and Rose had a feeling it would be lovely indeed.

Feeling awkward and unsure, Rose lifted herself and took his erection in her hand.

"Slowly, Rose, there." He was breathing heavily. "Just there." He was at her entrance and he pushed her down until he was fully inside, his face taut, his body rigid. He looked up at her, his blue eyes filled with raw desire. Then he moved one hand to where they were joined and touched her at the apex of her legs, on that spot he seemed to know so well, and the feeling that shot through her was unimaginably exquisite. Rose could feel herself getting lost in the sensation again, feeling the urge to move.

"Rise up, love. Gently, and settle back."

She did, her eyes widening at the sensation of him inside her and his thumb moving against her nub. "This is quite lovely," she said, moving up and down again, concentrating on all the sensations the movement created. Charlie helped guide her with his left hand as he caressed her with his right, setting a rhythm that was so carnal, Rose cried out from the pure pleasure of it. She was close to finding her release, and Charlie must have sensed as much, clever devil, for he increased the rhythm of his thumb, and she matched his movements with her entire body, lost in a haze of sensations that made it impossible to think. And then, in one wonderful flood, she was lost, moving uncontrollably as her body was wracked with wave after wave. She was hardly aware of the sounds she was making, the way she screamed when her release came.

In one swift movement, while she was still coming down from that place of perfection, Charlie rolled them over, still joined, and thrust again and again, his head pressing against the pillow, until he pulled away and let out a sound of pure male satisfaction.

The two lay side by side, spent and happy, both with smiles on their lips.

"By God, Rose, if you say we cannot do that again, I shall throttle you," Charlie said on a laugh.

"It would hardly be proper," Rose said, just to tease him. He growled, slinging one arm over her as if it took all the energy he had just to do that.

After a time, Charlie rolled over to his back and pulled Rose against his side "I have a horse farm, you know," he said. "Just outside the city. I wonder if you would like to see it."

"I should like that. I miss being around horses. I did wonder if you missed it, too."

"It was the first thing I bought when I had enough money. It's not a big farm, but I have six fine mares, two geldings, and a stallion that thinks he's king of everything. His name is Abbadon."

"For the devil? Is he that difficult?"

Charlie chuckled. "No, he's more angel than devil. But he very nearly died when he was born and it took the very devil to make him live, so that's what I called him. I have an excellent manager who cares for the property and the horses, but I wish I had more time to spend there. I'd planned to spend a month on the farm in the summer, but that hasn't happened. So you'll go?"

"I'd love to. When?"

"Tomorrow. We'll leave at two and be there in time for supper. We could spend the weekend if you'd like."

"Tomorrow is perfect, Charlie."

Chapter 19

You may set it down as a rule, that as you treat the world, so the world will treat you.

—From *The Gentlemen's Book of Etiquette, and Manual of Politeness*

Rose felt quite naughty, riding in a carriage with a man who was not her husband, ready to spend a weekend that was certain to include other naughty activities. In all her life, she had never felt like this. Everything was brighter, lovelier, sunnier. Had there ever been a more beautiful day? She was giddy and it was all due to Charlie.

He sat across from her looking stunningly handsome. He'd forgone the pomade and his hair was soft and curling, falling over his forehead and giving him an almost boyish look. They'd taken the train to Greenwich, Connecticut, where a driver met them to bring them to Charlie's fifty-acre farm along the edge of Long Island Sound. As they drove down the long drive to the home that overlooked the Sound, Rose gasped. She had not been expecting what lay before her, a lovely mansion with a well-groomed and expansive lawn that led to the water.

"Charlie, this isn't a farm, this is an estate," she said. Truthfully, she'd expected a small farmhouse dwarfed by a well-stocked barn.

He scratched his head. "I've made quite a bit of money, Rose. Not just with my businesses, but also my investments."

The home rivaled her own back in England, but the architecture was distinctly American, with its clapboard siding, mullioned windows, and covered porch. The air smelled of the sea and freshly cut grass. The barn was a large affair, whitewashed and immaculate.

Clearly whoever managed the property did an excellent job, as Charlie had said.

When their carriage pulled up to the home, three footmen immediately appeared to take their luggage, greeting Charlie smartly and deferentially. Rose gave Charlie a sidelong look and he looked down, appearing slightly embarrassed.

"Strange, isn't it? I still have to pinch myself sometimes," he said, looking up at the house.

"I must be honest, Charlie, I was expecting something a bit less expansive," she said on a laugh. "I was actually hoping for a cozy little cottage."

"And no servants about?" he asked, getting a look in his eyes that she was beginning to recognize as desire.

Her face heated. "Perhaps. Still, this is lovely, Charlie. When can we see your horses?"

"This way, milady," he said, holding out his arm for her to take. They walked along a gravel drive to the large barn. "There's a paddock behind the barn. That's where most of the horses will be this time of day. Poor Abbadon has his own paddock and those mares love to torture him."

As they walked around the barn, Rose noticed how well kept everything was. She heard a horse whinny and smiled. How she missed being around horses. Having a carriage pulled by a pair wasn't the same as seeing them prancing around a paddock or riding one, hell-bent, through an endless field. Charlie's estate would be the perfect place to let a horse stretch its legs.

Rose smiled, seeing five horses in the paddock, lazily nibbling on grass. A roan, a black, and a—

She turned to Charlie, her eyes filling with tears. "Oh, Charlie, I do love you," she said, placing her hands on each of his cheeks and kissing him soundly, quickly, before turning and running to the fence.

"Moonrise, you old girl, remember me?" she called, her voice cracking with emotion. "Charlie, I can't believe it. I can't." She shook her head, her eyes so tear-filled, all she saw was a gray blob running toward her. Moonrise trotted to the fence, immediately nuzzling Rose's head and letting out the dearest sound of welcome. Rose, heedless of her skirts and ignoring a gate that was a dozen yards away, climbed the paddock fence so she could greet her old friend properly. Throwing her arms around Moonrise's neck, Rose buried her head against the side of the mare and cried for a long moment before lifting her head in time to see Charlie quickly wiping away some of his own tears.

"You are the dearest, dearest man," she said, her voice watery from crying.

After a time, she returned to Charlie's side, this time using the gate, and grasped his hands. He smiled down at her, looking adorably uncertain, as if he wasn't quite sure whether she liked his surprise. "Thank you," she said. "Shall we ride tomorrow? I'd love to see the rest of your estate."

"Of course."

They began walking toward the house, the sun now beginning to set, leaving the sky a vivid pink behind the trees. Charlie was silent by her side, which allowed her to think about what he'd done. She and Charlie hadn't been in touch since the day he'd left her, still ill, all those years ago. He could have brought any horse he wanted from England; there was a gelding Charlie had been especially fond of, but she hadn't seen that horse in the paddock. Why Moonrise?

Hope surged in her breast, that this had not been an idle gesture. It would have taken weeks to secure Moonrise and ship her to the States.

"How long has she been here, Charlie?"

"About a year now. I sent an agent to England when I read about Mr. Cartwright. I thought having Moonrise would help, but then I just couldn't bring myself to write to you. I started thinking, my God, Charlie, the woman just lost her husband and you think a horse is going to make it all better? So, I kept her and waited for the right time." He gave her a sidelong glance. "Are you angry?"

"Angry? How could I possibly be angry, Charlie? That's the nicest, kindest, sweetest thing anyone has ever done for me. Now we must remain friends so I can visit her."

Every time Rose said something like that, she unwittingly wounded him. It wasn't her fault; she simply could not think of him as anything other than Charlie, her former head groom who happened to be rich now. He could buy every bit of property in Manhattan and when she looked at him all she would see was Charlie, never Mr. Charles Avery.

Rose stopped still. "Charlie, you don't let your other lady friends ride Moonrise, do you? I don't think I would like that."

He gave her a hard stare. Other women could ride him, but not her horse? "I do not bring women here," he said succinctly, and started walking more quickly to the house, forcing Rose to run by his side. Then he turned to her again. "I don't bring women into my house in New York, either. Not since the day I—" He stopped, clenching his jaw.

"You don't?" she asked in a small voice.

"No. I do not."

He began walking again and Rose jogged a bit to get in front of him. "Truly?"

"Truly," he said, stalking by her.

"I'm glad, Charlie," she called after him. "Very, very glad."

If he'd walked into a brick wall, he wouldn't have stopped any faster. Whirling around, he looked at her, her face pinkened by the setting sun, her hair seeming to glow in the ethereal light. "Are you," he said, letting his voice drop.

She nodded and smiled.

In two steps, he was pulling her against him, kissing her as he'd wanted to do all day. She fit so well against him, molding her soft body against his. "I should like to give you a tour of my home tomorrow. Tonight, I only want you to see my bedroom."

He grabbed her hand and she followed him, giggling happily as she struggled to keep up with his long strides.

By God, he didn't know a man could feel this happy. She was glad. Glad! And she had told him that she loved him. Yes, he knew it was only that she'd been so very delighted to see Moonrise, but he was allowing himself to hope that perhaps she really did love him, that perhaps it was the thought of all those supposed women he'd been entertaining that had been holding her back.

As they strode up the steps, a few panicking servants tried to properly greet them, but Charlie waved them away. "I'll make introductions tomorrow," he called, pulling Rose up the long, curving staircase. "Tell Mrs. Trumble to send something up to my rooms in one, no two, hours."

"Charlie," Rose hissed, ruining her outrage by laughing. "This is mortifying."

"Don't care," Charlie said as they reached the second-floor landing. He was kissing her before they even reached the room, holding her against him as he kicked the door closed and moved unerringly to his large bed. He picked her up and threw her in the middle, immediately following her down and pulling her atop him.

"They'll all know precisely what is happening," she said, burying her head against his neck.

He moved his hands to cup her bum and pull her against his erection. "Not precisely, Mrs. Cartwright." Her entire body was shaking, and for one horrible moment, he thought she was crying, thought he'd completely misread the situation.

But she was laughing, then kissing his neck, his jaw, his mouth, and then she wasn't laughing anymore, she was making those glorious sounds of pleasure that he knew he would never get tired of hearing.

Rose lay next to Charlie, the man she loved with all her heart, and trailed her hand through his soft dandelion hair as he nestled his head against one breast. She could not remember ever feeling so happy, so utterly content. So right. She thought back on her life, on how strict and demanding her mother had been, on all those lessons in language and deportment, on sitting straight and stifling laughter, and never being allowed to simply be herself. Unless she was in the stable, unless she was with Charlie.

How could she live without him? She couldn't. It was that simple. How was it that she'd ever thought she could?

Getting on her knees and playfully batting his hands away as he tried to fondle her breasts, she announced, "I have something very important to say to you, Charlie Avery."

He lifted one brow in question.

"I was lying there thinking about my life, about how nearly every happy moment I can recall has you in it. Every one. The only time I'm truly who I should be is when I'm with you, Charlie. And I was thinking how awful it would be to live my life not feeling like myself every day and being happy, and I've decided that I won't. I won't do it, Charlie. And so I'm asking you, sir, if you would be so kind, if you would do me the greatest favor on earth, and become my—"

His hand covered her mouth so quickly, she let out a muffled screech.

"Oh, no, Rose. No, you do not do that to me. You do not deny me the one thing I have been dreaming about since the day you came back from finishing school looking so completely beautiful I nearly died right then and there." He got up on his knees and faced her; they were both naked, both grinning like fools. "Rose, my love, my heart, I have loved you forever. And I should like to love you for the rest of my life. Would you do me the honor of becoming my wife?"

Rose looked up at him, her eyes sparkling with mischief. "How do you know what I was going to ask you?"

"Was I wrong?" He looked so utterly happy, Rose couldn't bear to tease him any longer.

She shook her head and smiled. "What is your answer then? Will you be my husband?"

"Yes, I will," he said, laughing, drawing her flush against him. "Can we stay like this forever?" He nuzzled her neck, tickling her.

"No. I should like to go to sleep in your arms and wake up at dawn and ride my horse, which my wonderful future husband bought for me just so that I might be happy." Her eyes filled with tears.

"What a watering pot you've become, Rose."

Rose lay back down and Charlie followed, so they were facing one another. "It's just that I'm so very, very happy, Charlie. And so very sad that I nearly lost you. I was so foolish."

"No, Rose," Charlie said fiercely. "I was always here."

"I did not realize. But we'll have a lifetime to make up for it."

"Your family is going to be outraged."

Rose pressed her lips against his. "Yes, they will," she said, closing her eyes, loving the way his mouth felt against hers. "I think that just might be the best part of all."

"Marcus might kill me."

"Marcus has enough things to worry about. Did you know his wife died? It was about the same time Daniel was so ill, so I wasn't able to return home to see him, though I wished I could have."

"Oh?"

"It was a horrible scandal, far worse than marrying you."

"My lady, you have wounded me," Charlie said.

Rose bussed him on his lips as an apology. "Sir, it was completely unintentional, I assure you." Charlie drew her to him and kissed her, leaving her breathless. "Let me continue my sordid story, please. Then you can kiss me all you like. Eleanor fell out of bed and cracked her head on the side table. It was a freak accident, but that's not the scandal, of course. She was in bed with another man and quite, quite drunk. Poor Marcus. He was devastated and now he's living in Whitby, of all places, at an estate none of us has visited since we were children. He walks the moors like some sort of Heathcliff."

"Heathcliff?"

"He's a character in a novel I read. Quite romantically tragic, it was. Mother is beside herself and Stephen says Marcus will see no one. He's become quite the recluse. So you see? Nothing I can do will shock my family."

"Not even marrying your former head groom?"

"Very well, they will be extremely displeased. But we have an entire ocean between us, so I hardly care."

"Is your story done?" he asked, kissing her softly.

"Indeed it is."

"Then I plan to kiss you all I please."

The next morning, they woke early, just as Rose wished, and went for a ride around the property. It was a lovely spot, with wooded trails and a large field where she let Moonrise gallop with abandon. Charlie loved watching her, the pure joy on her face, and felt his heart swell to near bursting. Never in his life had he felt this euphoria, a joy that came with knowing the woman he loved with all his being, loved him.

Rose brought Moonrise beside his gelding, a handsome boy he'd named Fleck due to the light spots across his nose. "I wish we could stop time and stay here forever," Rose said, as she looked out onto the Sound. "It's so lovely, Charlie."

"The minute I saw the farm, I knew I had to have it. At the time, it was very dear and I was hardly able to afford it. My banker thought it was a rather foolish investment, but I'm glad it's mine. Ours, soon, love."

Rose grinned. "Ours. That's a lovely word."

Charlie looked at Rose as she gazed out over the water. She was so damned lovely, and she was finally his. Their children would grow up on this land, would learn to ride and swim. By God, he couldn't wait for the future and all it promised.

As if reading his mind, Rose turned to him. "I just realized something, Charlie. We're going to have children."

"I do hope so."

"I didn't think I would. I . . ."

"You're not going to turn into a watering pot again, are you?" He never felt as helpless as when Rose was crying and he couldn't yet tell the difference between happy tears and sad tears.

"No," she said, smiling, but her eyes were tear-filled.

They spent the afternoon exploring his estate and the evening making love. At odd times, Charlie would blink hard, just to make certain he wasn't in some sort of wonderful dream. How could it be that Rose was beside him in his bed, as he'd dreamed so many lonely nights, as he'd pictured her with her husband. She would be his forever and that thought made his heart swell in his chest to the point of pain.

At around midnight that night, Rose sat up after briefly sleeping, her hair tumbling around her shoulders, looking so lovely it was all Charlie could do not to drag her back down and make love to her again. He was becoming aroused just looking at her, something she noticed with a smile.

"Oh, no, sir, I am famished. I'm going down to your kitchen for some food." She hopped out of bed, screaming a bit when he tried to draw her back.

"I'm too tired to follow you," he said, grinning at her as she wrapped herself up in his dressing gown. It was far too big for her and she looked absolutely adorable. He watched as she lit a small lamp, the light hitting her lovely face. He was daft over her, he realized, and grinned like a fool.

"I'll bring you back something," she said, then leaned over and kissed him, a kiss that lasted far longer than Rose intended, no doubt. Finally, she withdrew, giving him a sleepy smile.

"Food, sir."

Rose headed down to the kitchens, already familiar with Charlie's home, her bare feet making small slapping sounds on the smooth wood floors. Holding the small lamp to light her way, she moved quietly, not wanting to wake any of the staff, and headed directly to the pantry. His kitchen was large and airy, with an enormous preparation table in the center. It was well equipped and modern, and Rose had to smile when she thought about how her own cook, Mrs. Faring, would sell her soul for such a kitchen. Attached to the far end of the table was one of Charlie's famous can openers, which Rose had promised Mrs. Faring she would purchase for her after the cook mentioned that not having such a gadget put her at a disadvantage to other cooks in the neighborhood.

She went over to the opener, took the handle, and gave it a whirl, smiling at how smoothly the thing moved. Charlie was so very clever, she thought, watching the gears move effortlessly against one another. That's when she noticed the flower decorating the base, and her heart stilled. Poppies. Her favorite flowers were beautifully embossed on this utilitarian piece, making it almost lovely.

She stared at that decoration a long moment, her throat working, her eyes burning. Charlie had told her he loved her, had loved her for years, but she supposed she hadn't recognized the reality of those words until she saw those poppies. He'd loved her even after she'd married Daniel, even after he must have known she was lost to him forever. He'd decorated his kitchen tools with a poppy, her favorite flower, and the heartbreaking pain of that forced a sob from her throat.

"Oh, Charlie," she said, touching the decoration with her fingers.

"What is it, love?"

She looked up through watery eyes and laughed, embarrassed suddenly to be once again crying happy tears and terrifying the man she loved above all things. "They're poppies," she said.

"Yes."

"My favorite flower."

"Are they?" he said with a smile, walking toward her.

"You knew they were. And you decorated your tools with them. I feel horrid. And happy, but mostly horrid to know, oh, Charlie, to know how your heart must have broken when I married Daniel. I'm so sorry." She threw herself into his arms, once again wetting his shirt with her tears.

"Don't, love. You didn't know. You couldn't know."

"I should have," she said fiercely, grabbing a bit of his shirt in her hands.

"Please stop crying, Rose."

She sniffed and looked up at him. "Five years. I could have been with you all these five years."

"And by now you'd be quite sick of me. I do have some terrible habits, you know."

"Oh?"

"When no one's looking, I use my knife as a fork. And I belch when it pleases me. Once I scratched myself in a very private place on a public street. No one saw, but still it was not the thing. I'm not a gentleman, Rose, though I can pretend I am well enough to fool these American blokes."

"Everyone belches and gets itchy, Charlie." She swallowed some air the way her brothers had taught her years ago, much to her mother's horror, and let out a noisy belch.

"Ah, my perfect girl," he said, drawing her into his arms. "Not very ladylike."

"No. But it's me, Charlie."

"I love that me."

She laughed and kissed him, feeling as if her heart were free for the first time in her life. She scratched an itch and laughed again, knowing she'd never be anything but herself, knowing she'd always have Charlie to remind her who she truly was—a woman completely over-the-moon in love.

Epilogue

Rose went through the post as she did every morning, hoping for a letter from Stephen. She hadn't heard from him in weeks and was rather cross that he hadn't written. Perhaps he thought he needn't write as he was planning to visit shortly after the birth of their baby, but that wouldn't be for several weeks. She planned to write to her brother immediately if she didn't receive a letter soon.

And then she smiled.

"Good news?" Charlie asked, putting aside the newspaper. They sat in his breakfast room—now theirs—having decided his home was better for a couple planning to have a large family. They woke early each morning and breakfasted together before Charlie headed to his office. He'd completed his design for the locomotive and production was going to begin in a week. Rose had never seen Charlie so nervous. He'd worked endless hours, leaving early and coming home late, getting ready to manufacture his design. Already he'd garnered interest from some of the most important men in the country, and for Rose it was all rather thrilling.

"I've a letter from Stephen," she said, opening it quickly and scanning the contents for any momentous news. Her brother had a tendency to bury the most important bits at the end of his letters. Rose read, growing still as she read her brother's words.

"What's wrong?" Charlie asked, apparently noticing the blood leave her face.

"Weston's dead," she said, and then read, "'His Grace met his end at the hand of his sister-in-law.'" Rose looked up. "Oh, my goodness." She continued to read. "It says, 'The duchess claimed her sister was jealous of her marriage and murdered the duke out of spite. There is an investigation and many here doubt Her Grace's story, but her sister has disappeared and some think it's foul play.'" She looked up. "I can't believe Weston's dead."

"Good riddance," Charlie said, stabbing a piece of sausage.

"That poor girl. I've always felt sorry for her. She was only sixteen when she married him."

"Poor girl is right," Charlie said.

"I wonder what happened to the sister. Do you think she was murdered, too? It's all very exciting. And tragic, of course."

"I expect we'll find out in due time. Did you ever meet the girl?"

Rose shook her head. "She wasn't even out when she married the duke. I don't know what her parents must have been thinking."

"That they'd have a duke for a son-in-law," Charlie said pragmatically.

"I think having you as a son-in-law is much better."

Charlie gave her a skeptical look. She'd written her mother and father about her marriage and hadn't heard a single word, not in the nine months they'd been married. It did hurt a bit, but Rose tried not to let it bother her. If they believed marriage to a horrible man like Weston was better than marriage to a wonderful, kind man like Charlie, they were not worth even thinking about.

Rose went back to the beginning of the letter, her brows furrowed as Stephen recounted an attempt to visit Marcus. Apparently, the estate he was living on was quite old and in disrepair. The one servant that Stephen had seen pretended he didn't know who Marcus was.

Rose put aside the letter when she felt her baby moving about. "I think the baby enjoyed breakfast and is ready to romp," she said, holding her hand over her stomach.

Charlie, smiling broadly, reached over and laid his hand over hers. "He's a feisty little man this morning," he said, leaning over to kiss her. Rose looked down at his hand, a workman's hand, strong and broad, his wedding band somehow making it look even more appealing. Just like that, her eyes filled with tears, and she laughed at herself.

"Crying again, love?"

She nodded and swallowed. "Every time I think about how lucky I am to have you, I start to cry."

He chuckled and gave her a lingering kiss. "Cry all you want, just as long as they're always happy tears."

"They will be, Charlie. Always."

Jane Goodger's Lost Heiresses series continues with
LADY LOST,
coming from Lyrical in October.
Read on for an excerpt!

L ilian had never quite felt so out of sorts in her life. Her head still reeled when she stood, and she nearly fainted dead away after she'd used the chamber pot. What a lovely sight that would have been, to have someone come in and find her so discomposed. With bare feet, she carefully padded over to the window and drew back the thick, velvet curtains, revealing an overcast day and a stunning view of the Black Sea. Lilian had never seen anything quite so lovely as when a sharp needle of sunlight pierced through a rare opening in the clouds and lit a patch of the sea below.

"Good, you're up and about. You may leave now."

Lilian let out a small scream at the unexpected arrival of a man, no doubt Lord Granton. Not only because he startled her, but because she was standing wearing nothing but her shift and bloomers. Keeping her back to him and turning her head slightly, she said, "Sir, can you not see that I am unclothed?"

"I'm covering my eyes with my hands," he said blandly.

Lilian peeked behind her and gasped. "You are not," she said. He was not smiling, as one would expect from a man who was such a prankster. He simply stared at her, his expression unreadable, almost as if he were completely unaware of how improper he was acting. "Will you please turn around so that I may get back into bed, Lord Granton?"

He gave her a small bow, then turned. Lilian sidled to the bed, just in case his lordship decided to spin around, but he remained still, almost at attention, as she moved as quickly as she could to the bed and pulled the covers to her chin, her head spinning slightly from the movement.

"You may turn around now."

"May I?" he said, mockingly. "Thank you. I am glad to see you up and about. As I said, you may now leave."

He'd not moved farther into the room, but remained just inside the door, looking at her with a frown as she efficiently bundled her thick curls into a loose bun. He was a tall man and younger than she'd thought, with thick, dark hair and piercing eyes an unusual golden brown. Despite her nervousness, Lilian couldn't help but note he was uncommonly handsome, though he was in need of a shave.

"This is my room," he said as explanation.

"Oh, I'm so sorry, my lord. I didn't know. I do appreciate your hospitality and of course, saving me from the moors. I fear I don't remember what happened or even how I came to be here."

"I'm afraid you have me at a disadvantage, as you know my name, but I do not as yet know yours. Who are you?"

"Sadie did not tell you?"

"Obviously not, as I am asking you."

Lilian swallowed down a bit of fear. Lord Granton was known to be a hard man and she was certainly seeing proof of that now. What would he do if he knew who she was? Perhaps Sadie had not heard of the duke's murder, but Granton certainly would have. Feeling tears pressing against her eyes, she looked down to the coverlet and worried the soft material between her fingers before looking up again, straight into his stony expression. "I am Lady Lilian Martin."

She watched him carefully. She'd certainly surprised him, but that was all. "Your sister is Weston's wife. You were the older one, the one who escaped."

Oh, God. He knew. He knew and he would turn her in. Of course, he would. That's what any man confronted with an accused murderess would do. "Yes," she managed to say, though her throat was constricted with fear.

"I pitied your poor sister," Marcus said blandly. "My own sister escaped marriage to Weston. Do you know that story?"

Lilian was besieged with confusion. Why was he talking about his sister escaping ... He didn't know! He'd been talking about escaping marriage, not the authorities. She nodded quickly, trying very hard not to smile, for that would have been completely inappropriate given the topic of their conversation.

"What are you doing out here, my lady? I daresay it is not the usual place to find the daughter of a peer."

Lilian had a strong distaste for lying, and so gave the gentleman an honest answer. "I was living with my sister and we had a falling out," she said, swallowing down an unexpected and horrifying urge to laugh. "I was on my way to visit my stepfather in Scotland, but ran out of funds."

"And clothing."

She could feel herself blush. "I left rather hastily, my lord."

"Indeed."

Lilian tried not to fidget beneath his level gaze, but it was impossible not to. He had a way of looking at a person that somehow made one feel self-conscious.

"It appears you have recovered adequately," he said after a long moment. "You may leave immediately. I don't enjoy guests and am not set up to receive them. I have no other room for you." He moved his lips slightly upward and Lilian thought that perhaps he was attempting a smile politely to lessen the blow of his words.

"I would like nothing more than to be on my way," Lilian said. "But I have no clothes and no shoes. Certainly you would not send me out onto the moors in my shift."

Something dark flickered in his eyes. "No, I would not. I will talk to Sadie about procuring an appropriate dress." He looked as though he were about to leave, but stopped. "You fainted twice, my lady. Is there any chance you could be with child?"

Lilian's jaw dropped slightly. "There is none. Unless it is a second immaculate conception, my lord."

He gave her a long look before letting out a soft burst of air, almost a laugh but not quite. "If I don't see you again, my lady, I wish you well in your travels."

He stepped out of the door, a short journey indeed, for he hadn't gone into the room more than a few feet, leaving Lilian to stare at his departing back in shock. Had she ever in her life met a more disagreeable man? Actually, thinking of Weston, she most certainly had.

JANE GOODGER

Behind a Lady's Smile

Don't miss the first of Jane Goodger's Lost Heiresses series,
Behind a Lady's Smile,
available now!

THE LOST HEIRESSES

*It's one thing for a girl to lose her way, quite another to
lose her heart. . . .*

Genny Hayes could charm a bear away from a pot of honey. But
raised in the forests of Yosemite, she's met precious few men to
practice her smiles upon. Until a marvelously handsome photographer appears in her little corner of the wilderness and she convinces
him to take her clear across the country and over the seas to England,
where she has a titled grandmother and grandfather waiting to claim
her. On their whirlwind journey, she'll have the chance to bedazzle
and befuddle store clerks and train robbers, society matrons and big
city reporters, maids and madams, but the one man she most wants to
beguile seems determined to play the gentleman and leave her un-
touched. Until love steps in and knocks them both head over heels . . .

ABOUT THE AUTHOR

Jane Goodger lives in Rhode Island with her husband and three children. Jane, a former journalist, has written and published numerous historical romances. When she isn't writing, she's reading, walking, playing with her kids, or anything else completely unrelated to cleaning a house. You can visit her website at www.janegoodger.com.

www.ingramcontent.com/pod-product-compliance
Lightning Source LLC
Chambersburg PA
CBHW021242260626
47155CB00004BA/1268